Dame Fiona Kidman OBE is one of New Zealand's most highly acclaimed novelists. *New Zealand Books* said of Kidman, 'We cannot talk about writing in New Zealand without acknowledging her.' Born in Hawera, she has worked as a librarian, radio producer, critic and scriptwriter. Her first novel, *A Breed of Women*, was published in 1979 and became a bestseller. She has since written more than 25 books including novels, poetry, non-fiction and a play. Fiona Kidman lives in Wellington, New Zealand.

SONGS FROM THE VIOLET CAFÉ

FIONA KIDMAN

Aardvark Bureau
London

An Aardvark Bureau Book
An imprint of Gallic Books

First published in 2003 by Random House New Zealand
Copyright © Fiona Kidman 2003
Fiona Kidman has asserted her moral right to be identified as the author
of the work.

First published in Great Britain in 2017 by
Aardvark Bureau, 59 Ebury Street, London SW1W 0NZ

A CIP record for this book is available from the British Library
ISBN 978-1-910709-17-7

Typeset in Garamond Pro by Aardvark Bureau
Printed in the UK by CPI
(CR0 4YY)
2 4 6 8 10 9 7 5 3 1

For Reuben and Thomas and Raphael

Author's Note

Songs from the Violet Café is a work of fiction. With the exception of some events in Cambodia which reflect the history of that country, all other situations come from the author's imagination. Any resemblances to actual people, their names or circumstances, are unintentional, and should not be construed as real.

Contents

Index of Characters

2002

The Andersons, owners of the house by Lake Rotorua once lived in by the Messengers

1943

Hugo's Family

Hugo, a piano tuner who moved from Manchester to New Zealand after the First World War and married *Magda*, who died of cancer

Ming, his second wife, who moved from China to New Zealand to join her first husband, who died

Chun (also known as *Harry*) and *Tao* (also known as *Sam*), Ming's children from her first marriage, adopted by Hugo

Joe, Hugo and Ming's son

Wing Lee, the boy brought to Hugo and Ming by Violet

Violet Trench, daughter of a New Zealand tin canner who served alongside Hugo in the war, offered Hugo her help as a nineteen-year-old when Magda was dying and later moved to Europe, studying music at the conservatorium in Versailles before moving to England. Married with a daughter, *Caroline*, her husband is away at war

1963–4

The Sandle Family

Irene Pawson, a war widow, remarried

Jock Pawson, her second husband, a government clerk

Grant, *Belinda* and *Janice Pawson*, their children

Jessie Sandle, Irene's daughter from her first marriage

Aunt Agnes, Jock's sister

The Linley Family

Sybil Linley, a divorcee land agent

Marianne Linley, her younger daughter, waitress at the Violet Café and engaged to *Derek*, a banker and rugby player

The Messenger Family
Lou Messenger, sells sports goods and fishing tackle, a keen boater
Freda Messenger, his wife, a radio shopping reporter
Evelyn, their daughter, waitressing at the Violet Café before starting
  university

The Hunter Family
Hal Hunter, a pastor, founder of the Church of Twenty
Lorraine Hunter, his wife
Belle Hunter, their youngest daughter, a dishwasher at the Violet
  Café
Wallace, her fiancé, a preacher and follower of Billy Graham

The Hagley Family
Ruth Hagley, bookshop owner, a widow
Hester Hagley, her only child, a seamstress and a cook at the Violet
  Café
Owen, her fiancé, a farm labourer

At the Café
John, a cook at the Violet Café
Felix Adam, the doctor
Pauline Adam, his wife
Shorty (Nigel) Toft, the butcher
David Finke, a radio technician and pianist at the café, lives in the
  boarding house

1980
Annette Gerhardt, a Swiss doctor with the Red Cross
Donald, her assistant
Kiem, a driver
Bopha, a young Chinese Cambodian girl

Part One
Burning
2002

On a perfectly still night, that night of the year when the trees begin to wheel with light and the stars come tumbling, and backyard bonfires illuminate the children's faces, the Andersons push the boat out over the lake.

'Whose boat do you suppose it was?' Don asks his wife, when she first tells him of her plan.

'Who knows?' She is like a high-tailed pony, flicking her gathered hair from side to side, her face alight as she phones first one friend then another, telling each one on her list: this is the way we'll get rid of our old baggage, what a sight, it's something different don't you think. 'Look, does it matter?' she asks him, when he still seems irresolute. 'It's not as if you can do anything with that boat. It must have been sitting in the basement at least fifty years by the look of it. Haven't you seen the rot in it? One of the boys might try and use it, even if you tell them not to. You know what kids are like when they're in the mood.'

Of course, he can see that she's right. She is about most things — their finances, what schools to send the children to, whose parents they should be celebrating Christmas with this year, all those things that he never cares to consider. He doesn't know why he hesitates over the rowboat that's been sitting in the basement since they bought the house. Once a solid wooden craft, painted red that has faded to a dingy rust colour, a strip of yellow drawn around it, missing a rowlock, it might have been built by a boy in the backyard. He thinks it is this homely quality that makes him not want to part with it. When they bought the house on the edge of the lake he saw the list of people who held the title before him, but it was meaningless. The people who can afford to live by the lake these days are people like him, transient in their living arrangements, moving from one better house to the next, able to afford shiny new boats. Upwardly mobile, a term his own mother had lighted on in the eighties. She says it with pride. My boy. My son. He's doing well for himself.

'It's not as if we're breaking any law, are we?' his wife asks.

'Perhaps you should check,' he says absently, studying a window frame that he thinks he might like to shift. This house won't suit his family for ever but, while they are here, he restores and adds to it as previous owners have. In the evening, he walks down to the water's edge at the end of the garden, watching midges dance above the transparent water and trout rise. He will not own the derelict boat for ever, any more than the house. He won't change it and improve it and make it safe for his sons to use. Not that they would, not a boat they would care to be seen in, although there is something about its flowing bow that shows a kind of grace, despite its faults. This evening, before the fireworks are about to begin, he wonders fleetingly about a boy who might have stood under the leafy trees at the water's edge, hammering away on a night like this, getting his boat ready to launch in the summer holidays.

'Please,' his wife had said, when they were holding their territory on the far sides of their king-sized bed the night before. She has small compact breasts and fair skin with a pale moony whiteness that makes him think of treasure. 'I've told everyone, they think it's so neat.' Her voice was sorrowful in the wasteland of duvet between them.

'It's all right,' he'd said. 'Just do it.'

When dusk is settling, and his family and their friends, wrapped up against the breeze of late spring, have eaten the barbecued meats and salads, they cry, 'It's time, let's set off the fireworks.'

The boat is waiting where it has been dragged down to the beach, not quite floating but bouncing around among the reeds. The women and children have brought an assortment of items to put in the boat. Mostly it is the women, their shining made-up faces gleaming in the light of the fire behind them, who place inside the hull what he thinks of as offerings to the gods. One puts in a bundle of old letters; her sly smile and the nod of appreciation from the other women tell him that they are love letters. Another adds a calendar for what she says was a very bad year, someone else a stained quilt, another some yellowed school books. His wife's best friend whispers to her son that it's his last year's school reports and he need never see them again. Then there are things that would normally go in the white elephant sale, such as a paper lampshade decorated with hieroglyphics. (There is only one rule, that everything must be combustible. He's worried about the quilt and the metal rings in the lampshade but should he say anything? He doesn't.) One by one, then, the women toss in notes they have written, all the old bad karma they are discarding. He tries to see what his wife is putting in the boat, but he can't. It's something very small and she puts it in quickly among everything else. Alongside her, one of her friends wraps an offering in a wad of tissue and slides it in with the rest. She is a slim wily woman, dissatisfied and hungry. When his wife first introduced them, he was surprised by the friendship, she hadn't seemed like his wife's kind of person. But he knows her scent.

Suddenly, he's afraid. This whole idea has always been a mistake.

Finally, the boat is ready for its last voyage. He walks back up to where the bonfire is still smouldering and seizes the end of a flaming log, carrying it quickly through a crowd of spectators. As well as its freight of cast-offs and memories, the boat contains newspaper impregnated with kerosene. His wife's friend emerges from the shadows and runs to the bow of the boat, now riding the small waves that lap at the water's edge, fossicking for something, as if she's changed her mind. He holds his breath. Her skirt is wet at the hem. Without looking at him, she turns and walks back up the beach. He plunges his brand into the paper and a flame roars, ripping straight away through the length of the boat. The men help him to heave it away, sloshing through the water to push it as far as possible into the eddies of the lake.

And there it burns, this barge carrying its cargo of nightmares to the bottom of the lake. On the shore, the women and children cry out and clap. Some of them join hands and begin to sing.

Perhaps there *is* a law against it. If there isn't, shouldn't there be? What was the message his wife placed inside the boat? Will she really sleep better, released from the dreams that sometimes cause her to wake in panic?

The boat glows in the dark for an hour or more, the sides collapsing inwards, fragments and sparks scattering in all directions. The wind rises and the licks of fire and the choppy waves seem to become one. In the end, there is just a scum of flame, the quilt perhaps, and it too subsides into the depths of the lake.

Part Two

Hugo and Ming and Violet

1943

The lake was settled like skim milk, the afternoon Hugo saw the woman rowing across the water towards him, a small child seated beside her. As soon as he saw the figure in the boat he knew who it was. Something about the soft slope of the shoulders when she rested on the oars, the defiant tilt of the head. He had had her letter in his pockets for months, warning him of her arrival. I don't know when I will come, she wrote, because to get a ship from England, the way things are with this war … well, God knows, I may never get there. I'll simply turn up, if that's all right with you.

All right with him? The presumption of it. But she'd done this before. It wasn't as if she didn't know about the changes in his life. She knew exactly where to find him, sending the letter to the correct address, when most people from his past would have thought him untraceable. As for her, she had sent no return address. That was her way though, even when she was a child — a touch of imperiousness, a certainty that made opposition seem unthinkable.

A bank of dun-coloured cumulus cast sullen shadows between the horizon and the thin surface of the lake. It was one of those days when the smell of sulphur lay especially heavy over the garden, his own uneasy earth. This was dangerous country, water boiling away under a volcanic poultice, setting traps for the unwary. Even at the water's edge soft bubbles rose from underground springs. As he watched her rowing towards him, a drift of clouds separated above, allowing weak sunlight to filter through, illuminating the shape of her face, so that for a moment she seemed closer than she really was. Then the clouds closed in again and all he could see was her black shape and the outline of a smaller figure beside her. Only, now that he had glimpsed that luminous remembered quality, he saw the delicate grace and surprising strength of the woman, like that of a dancer with enormous reserves of power. A surge of anticipation swept through him unbidden, as if she were a lover coming towards him. He steadied himself against his hoe, a thin stooping man with a job to do, a row of cabbages to be weeded. His face was worn, an old avocado of a face, with tobacco-coloured eyes. His long fingers were thickened from planting in all weathers, the hands of a piano tuner and sometime musician gone to rack and ruin. Braces supported his pants around his skinny waist, a cigarette drooped from the corner of his mouth. But a good-looking man, you would have to say. He was handsome once, even if his nose is too big for his face, and a pity about his teeth, like scrambled tent poles.

'Husband. Come and take tea.' His wife, Ming, walked across the paddock, calling to him, although she knew he scarcely heard her. It had been years since he heard any sound distinctly, but he knew what she said; their understanding of each other was seemingly telepathic.

A beam across Ming's shoulder supported the tea billy on one side; on the other hung a bucket of pig manure to spread on the garden. A sack apron, pinned across her front, covered a long sombre-hued dress. Her hair, drawn back severely from her face, fell in a single plait all the way to her waist.

Hugo ground his cigarette out with his heel and looked past his wife towards the house. The corrugated iron roof was held fast with extra planks nailed horizontally along a shallow arch, the timber walls were unpainted and bare. He and his stepsons had built this house together. Only a symbol painted above the doorway relieved the drab exterior. The symbol is for lightness and peace within the soul, his wife said, and he believed her. Ming had a lightness of spirit that made all of this bearable. He had promised himself to her when she was alone in the world and so, for that matter, was he. After the girl, Violet, had gone away. He vowed to be her good husband and he believed that he was.

When Ming drew level with him, she stopped, following his gaze across the water.

'Who is she?'

She asked in English, as if the woman were already there and she must make herself understood. When Ming first came to New Zealand she had had to pass a literacy test of up to one hundred words, chosen randomly at the pleasure of the examining customs officer. She had learned five hundred words, which, as it turned out, was enough on the day. They included please, thank you, yes, forgive me, yellow, dog.

The memory of that day was scored in Ming's memory, as if drawn there by the pillar of stone at the peak of Meng Bi Sheng Hua, both terrible and beautiful, otherwise called Tip of the Magic Writing Brush.

'Her name is Violet,' he said.

Violet had come to him when she was nineteen, hardly more than a child in his eyes. His first wife, Magda, was dying of cancer. The Depression era was looming and he had no idea how he was going to carry on nursing her at home. The work was too hard and he had too little money. Sleep was a rare bonus in his life. The girl wrote to him, the sheltered daughter of a man who had become strange and possessive, and of a mother who had given up on life. I am so unhappy here, she told him then, everything is stifling me, the tennis parties Mother sends me to, just to get me out of the house so she can brood in peace, the mealtimes that go on forever in bitter silence, not to mention the beef stews — why couldn't my mother have learnt to cook decently? I've asked my brothers if I can go to them but they are like my father, obsessed with work, and their wives are tied up with children and complaints. Even though I could help them, they don't seem to see that. I could come and help you now. Why don't I do that? The nuns at school at least taught us to look after people. I've bathed sick people in the infirmary. I have been saving my allowance. My father may have lost his mind but he has not lost his business — remarkable these days, but there you are. Perhaps you could spare me for an evening or two and I could go to some concerts, if there are any shows left in town. *So go on, what do you think?*

Her father had been his friend in the past, when they shared the same battlefield during the war — Hugo an infantryman from Manchester, Violet's father a young colonel in a New Zealand regiment. It had been one of those odd juxtapositions, when a cup of water on a French battlefield saves a life, and roles are reversed. Later, when Hugo visited the man to whom he had offered his mug, in a shadowy, ill-lit English hospital, the colonel said, 'There'll be another war and England's sure to go down next time round. I'd get out of it now. You chaps will be in trouble then.' Meaning Hugo's race, the unmistakable Jewishness that set him apart in his youth, the fragile unexplainable quality in himself that he had never understood, because his family had set themselves outside the memory of their ancestors. The man's head was swathed in bandages.

'You'd be better off out in our part of the world,' the colonel said. 'Plenty of work out there. I'm a bottler.'

'Bottler?' Hugo said, puzzling over this.

'Tin canning. I preserve fruit for a living. I'll give you a job in my factory.'

'I tune pianos,' Hugo said.

'Pianos. Well, never mind, we've got plenty of them in New Zealand. Book yourself a passage. My treat.'

On receiving the daughter's letter, Hugo had written back: My dear, it simply wouldn't do — your father would not take kindly to me stealing you from him and using you in such a manner, and I must respect his wishes. He wrote the letter several times, crossing out the parts that said, indeed it would save my life but I cannot allow it, or, I have thought long and hard about it. *I cannot allow it,* he wrote firmly and without embellishment, in his final draft.

He remembered how much easier in himself he had felt when the letter was posted. As he walked briskly from the red letterbox at the corner of the street, he plunged his hands into his pocket, finding sixpence. He whistled some Schubert, that section from 'The Trout' where the water rushes over the rocks in the stream, and because the sound came from inside his head, he heard the music perfectly. He had no idea how he would see out this bad time. Soon his wife would have to go into hospital, although it was not what she wanted. But at least he had made a right decision. A correct one. He didn't need the complication of the girl. When he returned to the house a telegram was waiting for him. The girl had already left on the train. *Arriving tonight. Violet.*

For her embarkation in New Zealand, Ming was dressed in a long blue linen frock with a high collar, her black hair parted carefully down the centre and plaited braids gathered in loops around her ears. Her face was solemn with a composure she didn't feel, as she waited for the moment when she would see her husband again and all the years between them would fall away. When she passed through the gates onto the wharf, after completing the dreaded language test, nobody was there to meet her. Her two sons had come with her on the boat. Their father, her husband, had left China seven years before; she had struggled to raise her boys in the village near the mountain, waiting for the little money he sent home from New Zealand, and for the call to come and join him. When the call finally arrived, she left accompanied by the boys and a small trunk that contained their clothes, a bolt of red silk embroidered with black roses, a rolled-up painting of yellow reeds, Chienmen cigarettes and a smoking pipe for her husband, and some cooking pots. In her hands she carried a wickerwork basket and a silk umbrella. She thought she would die of grief leaving her mother and brothers and sisters.

At first, she stood on the street, in Auckland, looking up and down, thinking that it had been such a long time since she and her husband had seen each other that they had walked past each other, without recognition. Her sons stood huddled beside her like babies as they sensed her alarm. She saw others who had travelled with her being met. Chun Yee must surely be waiting for her.

'Where are the husbands?' she asked a woman who seemed at ease, as if she already lived there. 'There must be more husbands.'

The woman spoke to her in Mandarin. 'Are you the wife of Chun Yee?'

'Yes,' said Ming, her heart already full of dread.

'It's too late,' the woman said, shaking her head. 'My husband went to Chun Yee's funeral last week. Your husband is dead.'

'How can that be?' Ming said, thinking that it might be a trick. The boys clutched their boxes more firmly. The elder one, who was ten, stood up straight, trying to make his head level with his mother's.

'Come quickly,' the woman said, 'or they will send you back. Tomorrow we'll find the papers to show that he's dead. If they catch you on the street without a husband you'll be in trouble. They'll send you back for sure.'

That night Ming and her sons sheltered with the woman's family, in a house in Freeman's Bay, where her husband had an opium and pakapoo house. She felt as if she were dead too: afterwards, she told her second husband, it was as if I was dead, there is nothing anyone can do to someone who has been already dead. See, I have a strong spirit that was brought back so that I could be with you. I know what it is like to be already dead. I did not like it dead, but it is bearable. She talked to the men who came to visit the house, about the last days of Chun Yee, and how he had died of tuberculosis. Yes, he knew he was sick when he wrote to her, they said, but he thought that when she came he would get better. In the morning, she went to the Births, Deaths and Marriages office to get Chun Yee's death certificate.

'Does immigration know about this?' asked the man behind the counter.

Ming shook her head. She didn't know which of the five hundred words were the right ones with which to answer him. 'Sorry,' she said.

'You're in trouble,' said the man. 'Big trouble. You know trouble?'

'I know much trouble,' said Ming in a low voice.

Behind her in the queue stood a man who had also come about a death certificate, for his wife. His long thin face might have been humorous at another time, nice-looking, although his mouth was full of crooked teeth.

'Be kind to her,' he said to the official behind the desk. 'Can't you see, she's just had a shock?' He returned her gaze when she looked at him with her grave steadfast eyes that said *I have nowhere to go.*

'Wait for me,' he said.

Ming's body was not much thicker now than when he met her, a tiny blade of a woman. She harboured strength, in much the same way as he remembered in Violet. She makes two of him, whatever they do. Sometimes he blushed to remember the beginning of their time together, when he first lay down with her as his new wife. He had touched her as if she were a porcelain doll to whom he had no rights at all, and she responded as if she were a knife that had to strip away his own delicacy and pare him down to the truth of his own needs. As she unplaited her hair over her bare light sepia back, it was she who put her fingers to her lips, *Do not be afraid.* They have had a son of their own, as well as Ming's boys. Too old, he said at first with a self-deprecating pride, I'm too old. Later, he just said it to himself, with a small astonished murmur, because she didn't like him saying this. He did not say, what will they make of me, this old man from a shack at the edge of the lake with his rakes and hoes, but he knew, even before it happened, that his children would burn their report cards and letters from teachers, rather than have him turn up at the school.

The town where he took her was a bustling place in the summer where tourists came to visit, or at least they did before the war, to take in the thermal sights and enjoy spas in pretty gilded buildings. The visitors stayed in huge hotels with high ceilings and chandeliers, smoking rooms and dining rooms set with crystal and silver, glamorous flower arrangements and liveried waiters; they looked across the streets from their balconies, strolled on the streets, so that you could close your eyes for a moment and think that you were in some other place. At the dazzling blue-and-white-tiled swimming baths, there were tearooms and a band that played jazz. He took his children when they were small but Ming stayed at home. The local people lived in comfortable bungalows spilling this way and that from a railway line carved out of the makeshift changing landscape, or, if they were Maori, near the lakes where they caught fish. The lakes and streams and tributaries spilt out across the countryside, filled with rising trout. When it was dark, the Maori sang, their voices travelling across the surfaces of the water. It was a place where it was possible to live unnoticed if you kept quiet and looked straight ahead when you walked down the main street. But cold, it got cold in the winter.

When he first met Ming nobody could afford luxuries like piano tuning, but now that it was wartime, everyone wanted their pianos to sing for them. His hearing, though, was all but gone, the part of his listening skill that followed a scale like an animal after its prey, separating one interval from another. None of this worried Ming, the woman from Huang Shan, the Yellow Mountain. Slowly he learnt of her past, of the mountain shrouded with mist and pine trees and fantastic rocks, of her favourite peak, Shi Xin Feng, the Beginning to Believe Peak, of her work in the rice fields, the growing and preparation of food.

She said she liked it where they lived. It reminded her of home, especially the hot springs, for in her village there were clear springs that maintained a warm steady temperature and never ran dry, even in the worst droughts, of which there were many; times when poor people like her came close to starvation. She had seen the springs and the sapling pine trees that grew in plantations as a sign that this was where they should seek land for a market garden. It will be all right, she told him, if I stay with you I will find food and harmony enough for both of us. Music that came from a piano was music made by man, she believed, but the sun, the mountains and the earth itself vibrated with never-ending frequencies. The seventh dragon is the dragon that listens, she said. You must not let the dragon lie down just because you can't fix the black boxes that stand in the corner of ladies' parlours. Ming had never attended a concert, had no wish to. She was unmoved by Western music, but not, she insisted, by music itself. He thought of that, watching the oars dipping and rising as the other woman rowed towards him across the mirror-glass lake and supposed that, even at this minute, he was hearing a kind of music, coming closer and increasingly persistent. When she was a child, he had tuned the piano at her parents' house. It was an ordinary enough little instrument but when it was tuned the child, Violet, produced a sound radiant with possibility. I sound awful, she would complain when he turned up at her house on his travels through the country (for he was a known expert in those days and it was only his friendship with her father that took him to the out-of-the-way place where they lived). When he left Violet absorbed over the keyboard, he thought it was worth the visit, even though he wasn't paid. He never thought of not returning.

'Tell me,' Ming asked, 'who is coming? Who is this woman?'

'She's the person who wrote me a letter,' Hugo told her. 'The letter that came a while back. I think I mentioned it to you.' Not that he had read the letter to her, or discussed it. More like an implication that he'd had a letter from an old friend. Nothing much. I used to tune this person's piano, he might have said. A word of advice, a note of warning. Any of these ways he might have described the letter, but he had said nothing.

'What does she want?' Ming stood in front of him, making quite sure that he saw her lips making the question.

'I don't know exactly. She's in some kind of trouble.'

'That.' Ming turned away, her voice contemptuous, as if she perceived already that the woman's difficulties were different from her own. 'She is sometime wife?'

'Not wife.' Ming never complained about anything. This transparent note of anger, even jealousy, about a woman she had not met and of whom he had never spoken, was alien and alarming. He had learnt to love Ming, the woman from Yellow Mountain. How could he begin to explain the role this other one had played in his life? Or, in that of Ming herself?

The woman was now so close he could make out her features, but she rested more often on the oars, as if she had become tired. Or afraid.

As if reading his thoughts, Ming said, 'Maybe bad woman.'

'Not,' he said, straightening himself. 'Not bad.' The boat was within hailing distance. A fleet of shoreline ducks followed in its wake. The woman would see smoke rising from the chimney behind them. He had loved three women in his time and two of them were about to meet each other. Inwardly, he cursed himself for his evasion, the way he had put off telling Ming about Violet's letter.

'Over here,' he called. Turning to Ming, he said, 'She's asked that we look after a child.'

Ming gave a startled cry. 'A child? That child?' Her eyes darted towards the boat, then wildly around the smoking garden as if seeking a way of escape.

'A little boy,' he said, looking away. 'Her father was my friend.'

'You knew,' his wife said. 'You knew she bring a little boy.'

He walked towards the water's edge, the water slopping around the ankles of his rubber boots as he stepped out to catch the bow and bring the boat round, running his hand over the familiar timber. He knew this boat, wondered how she had come by it. The woman looked up at him with those astonishing, brilliant eyes of hers, her mouth, always too large for the oval of her face, parted with exertion. He was shocked to see how roughened and dark her skin had become. She was dressed in a light cotton shirt and trousers, like a man, the pale ash-brown hair, already threaded with grey, tied carelessly behind her head. The collar of her shirt was open and he saw that her throat at least was still the colour of an arum lily, remembering the small muscles that rippled there, never still even when she was not talking or laughing.

'Hugo,' she said, looking up with such pained recognition that he understood again how much he too had changed. She turned to pick up the drowsing child beside her. The boy was perhaps two years old, round-eyed and small-boned with a large head of dense hair supported on the slender thread of his neck, one hand curled over the edge of the blanket wrapped around him. Hugo thought he saw a resemblance between them, but perhaps it was his overheated imagination.

'Moses in the bulrushes,' she said, pulling a face.

'Violet, this is Ming,' he said, as his wife advanced on them. Ming had drawn herself up to her full five feet. She glared hard at the woman, almost causing her to turn away.

'You've told her?' Violet said, when Ming didn't respond to the introduction.

'You have to speak loud,' Ming said in a scornful voice.

'I haven't asked her,' he said, humbled.

'We have enough children here,' said Ming.

'What a hell of a place to live,' the woman said, offering up the child. Ming held her arms by her side. 'Why here?'

'Because of the war,' Ming said, before he could answer. 'They think I am Japanese woman.' She held the other woman's eye steadily. 'Japanese, phoo. They know nothing here, they think everyone looks the same.'

He was taken aback, hearing this blunt statement of the necessity of their lives. Ming had never spoken of her need to be invisible. Sometimes he wondered whether she was even aware of it. Already, he thought, things are changed.

'You will come into our house, please,' Ming said to their visitor.

'I don't want to stay,' said the woman. She spoke to Ming more loudly than was necessary, as if it was she who was hard of hearing, then flushed when she realised what she had done. She tried to speak more evenly. 'I've come to bring the boy. His name is Wing Lee.'

'Your baby?'

'My friend's child. I've told your husband, he knows about him.' Despite her determination, her voice had begun to rise in a shrill and frantic way. 'Take him quickly. I can't stay. I'm sorry it's taken me so long to get here but the ship was holed on the way out from England, it was terrible, it was taking water and we were going for the lifeboats but the captain told us to hold on harder, and we were rescued. We slept on the deck of a dirty little steamer that took weeks to get here. I can't tell you how bad it's been.'

'I think this is your child.' Ming's words were flat and unfriendly.

'As I said. My friend's child. I can't keep him in London, there are bombs falling all the time, and my daughter's gone to the country.'

'So. You have a child already?'

'A girl of my own. Yes.'

'But this child. He is a Chinese baby, like my youngest one, a little Chinese, a little not Chinese.'

'His mother is dead, she was killed by the bombs. Whoosh. Boom.'

'There's no need for that,' said Hugo sharply. 'She understands what a bomb is.'

31

The woman coloured again. 'I'm sorry, Hugo.'

'So,' Ming said, 'you can come many miles far, but you cannot keep your friend's child. You'd better come inside now.'

Hugo lifted Wing Lee out of the woman's arms, although for a moment the child fought him, clinging to Violet. When he had prised him away, Hugo cradled his head against his shoulder. 'I'm sorry,' he said to Violet, 'but you see how it is. There's a way it must be done. She won't just take him in.'

'Not even if you tell her to?'

He allowed himself a smile. 'Things are all very equal here.'

'A modern household. Well, it's not what I expected.'

They followed Ming into the house.

Don't go, he had said when Violet prepared to leave, the day after Magda's funeral. I need you here. When he thought about it now, he was ashamed of that weak moment of longing. Looking back, he thought how piteous he must have sounded. All the same, he had pleaded with her. I know it's not right with Magda just gone but, well, you know how it is, a fellow gets lonely on his own. When she was silent, he'd said, you feel it too, I can tell. They were sitting in the bay window of the small bungalow he rented in Ponsonby, looking out on a clutter of ramshackle cottages with wet washing flapping on the clotheslines.

Don't be silly, Hugo, she said then, I've got all my life worked out. I've had time to think.

What was it, he wanted to know. What sort of life?

A reckless life, she told him, and he remembered the rich way she laughed, as if she had grown up and grown away even then.

As she walked shoulder to shoulder with him from the shore of the lake towards the house, he thought that's how it will have been. Reckless. But not without regrets. I'd do anything for you, he told her when she left. Anything at all. Only, now he was to be put to the test, he didn't know whether he could deliver. He was married to a woman of such strong disposition that once she made up her mind it was almost impossible to change it.

He'd asked Ming, more than once, how she had survived all those years on her own, that period of her life when she was in China and she was a wife but not a wife.

Through meditation and discipline, she told him. I went to the mountain for inspiration. More than that. She had gone underground into the caves, with hundreds of people at a time, fasting in total darkness, only a ration of water and an apple to sustain them. Her spirit was purged, tempered, ready for what might befall her. She was not like the reed in her picture that hung in its shabby splendour above the smoking fireplace. She didn't bend this way and that.

Ming took her place at the wooden bench that ran down one side of the main room, picking up a knife with a long flashing blade to continue the task of food preparation, begun earlier in the day. She took a handful of green vegetables from a bin and chopped them on a board with long hard strokes. 'Always, there is a friend,' she said, tossing the remark over her shoulder.

'What do you mean?' asked Violet.

'I told her you were the daughter of my friend,' Hugo said.

Ming took two plucked ducks from a platter, their heads and beaks still attached to their bodies, and rinsed them in a bowl of bloodied water. 'Friends,' she said, derisively.

'That was all,' he said, finally provoked into reminding her that he was, after all, her husband. 'She wants us to take this baby and care for him, because her husband's at war and he's been injured. Soon he'll come back from the hospital and

Violet will have to be free to look after him. She'll give us some money now and send more each month.'

Ming cleared fat from the birds' body and neck cavities. She mixed chopped onion and celery with spices and a dash of rationed sugar, and soy sauce tipped out of a Mason jar. Violet opened a thin canvas purse slung over her shoulder and extracted a wad of notes. 'There's three hundred pounds here.' She laid the money out on the table in front of them.

Ming eyed the money, her eyes at once covetous and contemptuous. It was easy to see how much she wanted the money, how much easier it would make their lives. 'I think,' she said. 'After food, I tell you.'

'I can't eat,' the other woman said. She glanced round with evident distaste for her poor surroundings, a fretful child near the bench.

'That boy needs sleep,' Ming said to Hugo. 'Put him down.'

He laid Wing Lee on a blanket roll near the fire, tucking the covering around him. As soon as the child touched its soft fabric his eyes snapped into sleep. A silence settled over them. Violet sat down, her hands folded awkwardly in front of her, watching Wing Lee.

'Come into the garden,' said Hugo abruptly, after a time in which nobody had spoken. 'I'll show you round the place.'

Ming didn't look at them as they left the room. The atmosphere was alive with her reproach. Outside, a light wind had risen, so that the surface of the lake stirred.

'I really should get going,' the woman said, 'it'll be dark soon.'

'I'll get one of the boys to row back with you later.' He nodded to two young men carrying sickles and rakes and spades, as they finished their day's work in the garden. They were swarthy young men with handkerchiefs tied around their heads, wearing old mended clothes. They passed her with curious glances. One of them shrugged, and spat on the ground, but he could have just been clearing phlegm from the back of his throat. He pointed to the boat, saying something quick and sharp in Mandarin.

'My sons,' Hugo said. 'Chun and Tao.'

'Surely not. They're too old.'

'I adopted them. I'm their father. It's not that difficult.'

'Neither of them wanted to go back to China?'

'Well.' He hesitated, because this was something he had wondered about himself, but his sons had never told him, and he hadn't liked to ask. 'I think they're people of China, but there's no way back for them really. I wish they'd come here earlier because it hasn't been easy for them at school. The younger one could have gone to university, but it's too late now. His mother was disappointed, but I'm sure he'll be persuaded to leave here. He doesn't say much. And then we have one of our own, a late surprise, although I'm afraid Joe's life will be difficult. A problem at birth. Ming feels it's her fault, but it was a medical problem.'

'You've got your hands full with the spirit of China.'

'It's no joke,' he said sharply. 'I wish I could have gone there myself. I believe I would have fitted in.'

'Really?'

He gestured helplessly, unable to convey to her what his family meant to him.

'I do see,' she said, as she followed him into the vegetable patch. 'You might think I wouldn't, but I understand the way it draws you in, once you've started down that path towards Asia. It is so compelling.'

Thinking about the boy she had brought with her, he decided she would know, but like his sons and their secrets, she would be keeping that to herself. They stood among the cauliflower rows, Violet looking out over the water rather than at the garden. There wasn't much for him to show her. He thought of her inside her clothes, as he had imagined her that summer when Magda was dying. Her presence in the bathroom, the perfume of her body when he lay down in the bath where she had been, the sight of her clothes hung out to dry on his clothesline, the glimpse of her breast as she leaned over the sickbed. She was not a child then, even if she was used to being treated like one. Remembering that summer gave him a ghostly glow, a shiver of recognition, the distance between what was right and what was not. She had been there and he had wanted her, even on the nights when they turned Magda's rotting body together and comforted her as best they could. He thought the girl felt it too, the way their eyes met over the bed, or her hand brushed his. Magda had been a bird-like woman whose eyes were piercing in their directness, even more so in that last appalling illness. It's all right, she had said to him one night when they were alone, take care of yourself. Violet will take care of herself, don't grieve when she goes.

'You played Schubert in the afternoons,' he said. 'And sometimes, Delius. I thought you might have carried on with your music.'

'Well, I tried. I had a stint at the conservatorium in Versailles but I soon found I wasn't good enough. All very romantic, those cobble-stoned alleyways and the cathedrals, and music pouring through every window, even the children playing in the streets making polished music. I mean, look where I'd come from. The nuns were very encouraging when I was a child, but it was different over there. I was just a girl from down under.'

'Perhaps you didn't practise enough.'

'Oh, practice.' She sounded weary. 'I got sidetracked. There was so much jazz in the cafés at the time. And blues. I liked that stuff. Do you still play at all?'

'Well, as you know, my hearing's gone. It's got worse.' On what would I play, he might have added.

'I remember what you told me once when I asked how you knew the piano was tuned.' She spoke in a normal voice, as if refusing to acknowledge what he'd just said. 'You said, tuning is constant motion. It's knowing when to stop, you told me. I can see you lifting each hammer and putting it down on the next pin and settling it. And all the time you were striking the piano key with your other hand, pushing and pulling, pulling and striking. Then you'd stop and you'd know. And I said, *how*? Do you remember what you said?'

'Well, it was just the moment to stop,' he said, embarrassed.

'You said that you stopped when you heard perfection, not a sound at all. You said it was like silence would be, if we could hear it. Only of course we can't.'

'What do you hear now?' he asked quietly.

'Chaos. A piano in need of tuning.'

'I can't help. This isn't the way.'

'Don't worry about me,' she said, her eyes filling. She wiped her face with her sleeve, as if hoping he wouldn't see. 'If it doesn't work out, I'll find some work, do something.'

'Have you worked before?'

'Have I worked? Good God, yes, of course, what do you take me for? All over the place, all sorts of jobs. Lady's companion, nanny, I worked in a flower shop for a while, I've even washed dishes in Soho.'

'You?'

'And in Paris, of course, when I was in school. The men are beautiful there, but they give you a terrible time when you work for them. Don't look so shocked. I enjoyed it. One learns a thing or two in places like that. Then I got married.'

'Oh yes. Your husband?'

'Pleasant. What do you want to know? Is he rich? Above

average, but not fantastically so. It's not *noblesse oblige*, nothing like that. His parents farm. Country people. He has a brother and an uncle who work on the farm, more than enough men to do the work. My husband was a soldier before this war started, it was a career. My father would have approved. We met when he was on a weekend leave in Paris. We had marvellous times on his leaves. Our daughter was born six months after we got married. The wedding was in London — not his village as you'll understand, in the circumstances — but our daughter was christened there wearing a lace gown that my husband's great-great-grandmother had worn. It was yellow with age and I thought Caroline might get asthma from the dust in it, because it was so brittle, of course it couldn't be washed. It was a relief when the war came. She's staying with her grandparents now. It's not that bad, she could have been sent to strangers. Enough? You need some shelter belts round here, don't you, something to keep off the wind and frosts. I seem to remember the winters are very cold round here.'

He nodded. 'We're putting in a row of oaks.'

'Oaks. You're still English at heart, aren't you?' Violet said. 'Some people never get over it. I'd have thought closer ground cover would have been better. You should grow tomatoes by the way.'

'Too much trouble.'

'People will want more of them, believe me,' Violet observed. 'The Europeans depend on them. The next best thing to an onion.'

He smiled at this. 'Well, I have onions, as you'll see. People have never had much of a taste for tomatoes in this country. Except cowering among lettuce leaves, plastered in mayonnaise.'

'Tell me, do they still make it with condensed milk here? My father tried canning tomatoes. It's true, they were disgusting.'

Both her parents had died since she last saw him. This was something he already knew. His friendship with her father had collapsed after Violet's defection to him, and then her disappearance, for which, it seemed Hugo was to blame. I should send the police after you, her father had written, this is a clear case of abduction. Don't think you'll get a penny out of me. You Englishmen are all the same. Not that Hugo thought her father was sane. He had seen the way he walked through the house where Violet grew up, holding his war-damaged head in both hands and shouting curses. As for Violet, there had been a letter or two, and then silence for years. Until this.

'The food's quite different in Europe,' she was saying.

He sighed, bringing himself back to the present. 'It must be quarter of a century since I was in Europe. Several lifetimes ago.'

'Things'll change here. You'll see, Hugo, after the war, people will start wanting different things. You should be prepared.' She took a tin of cigarettes out of her shoulder bag and offered him one. They lit up, his lungs filling with strong Egyptian tobacco smoke. In repose, her face looked naked with grief, lit by the flare of the match he used to light their cigarettes. The dark was settling around them, and he thought that he was making the whole thing worse by the moment, standing outside here with the woman, smoking and talking and gazing at the lake.

'Hugo, I think I'm going to die,' she said, leaning against him so that he had no option but to put his arm around her. She reminded him of flowers, even her name, of cool earth and violet light at evening. Like now. He dropped his arm, removing himself from her.

'Was there nobody else who could look after Wing Lee?' he asked sharply, hoping to move things along, to come to some resolution. Because he couldn't promise her that the boy would be able to stay. He found himself thinking about the money on the table and tried to push these thoughts away. I'm human, he told himself and, in the next instant, that the amount she had left there would keep all of them, never mind the boy, for a year or so. He wondered how she had come by so much.

'Your wife was making dinner,' she said, straightening up. 'D'you think it'll be ready?' Nearly two hours had passed since her arrival.

Hugo nodded as they turned away from the garden. 'Just get it straight in your head,' he said, 'that if she lets him stay, he'll become her child. Ming's suffered a great deal, and I won't let you play fast and loose with her. I want you to understand what it is you're doing.' Their backs were to the chilly lake; the house looked more inviting, crouched in the dark, a light burning inside. Violet walked steadily towards it, without answering, but by the way she had drawn into herself, he knew he had been heard.

In the kitchen, the ducks were cooked, their steam rising from a huge serving platter Ming had placed on the table, along with bowls of rice. She held her fingers to her lips as they came in. Both little boys were now asleep, head to head in front of the fire. It was impossible to tell what Ming was thinking. There was no sign of the money Violet had left on the table.

All the family, except the two sleeping children, seated themselves on planks running down each side of the table, supported by saw-horses. The guest, now she was used to her surroundings, seemed unfazed by their appearance.

'All these boys,' she said, without looking at the children by the fire.

Ming motioned for the family to stand back and wait while

she served the woman a portion of the duck. Violet tried the food at once, because not to have eaten would have given offence. At once, her face lit up.

'It's very good,' Violet said. 'You're a terrific cook, Ming.'

Ming nodded, knowing perfectly well that the food was irresistible, the duck so crisp on the outside, the flesh beneath meltingly tender and full of subtle flavour.

'Perhaps you could tell me how you did it. A recipe, if you have one.'

'She just makes it up as she goes along,' Hugo said, thinking that Violet would know this, but wanting to humour both women.

All the same, Violet persuaded her to tell her what the sauce was made of, writing down the ingredients on a page torn from one of Tao's old exercise notebooks. Once it was written, Hugo thought she might not look at it again; perhaps it would float away on the lake even as she was leaving. But she'd remember what she'd been told, in the way she could once remember a musical score, as some people remember whole poems, or mathematical equations.

Ming said something in rapid Mandarin to her eldest son, Chun, who also went by the name of Harry, and they both laughed.

'What did she say?' Hugo asked the son, because Ming was still laughing and wouldn't tell him.

Chun hesitated, glancing at his mother. She nodded, allowing him to speak, her eyes suddenly cruel.

'She says, in China, the duck would be especially tasty because they would have made him dance on a red-hot stove before he died to get his blood racing.'

'I have to go,' Violet said, agitated again. She pushed herself violently away from the table, causing everyone seated on the same plank to be pitched backwards. Outside, through the uncurtained window, a crescent moon was rising, a curved slice of light.

'Tell her,' said Ming, through her son, 'that children are without price here. They are not for trade.' She took the money Violet had given her earlier, and laid it on the table beside the unwashed plates.

The woman's hand flew to her mouth. 'I can't take him back,' she said.

The two little boys had thrown their arms around each other, nuzzling with tender blind-eyed butting as they shifted in their sleep.

'The boy stays,' Ming said, 'but we do not buy.'

'What then,' asked Violet, 'what am I to do about it?' She glanced fleetingly at the children and turned away.

'We'll take some board and lodgings for him,' said Hugo, asserting himself at last. 'That's all. That's fair.' He rolled fifty pounds off the roll of notes. 'Here,' he said. 'That will be enough.' He looked at Ming so sternly that for once she dropped her eyes. Turning to Violet, he said, 'Chun will follow you with a flare.'

He expected her to make preparations for leaving, that at least she would say goodbye, bend over the sleeping child and touch his face, perhaps even wake him for a sleepy kiss.

Instead, she walked out of the house without a backward glance, beginning to run, sure-footed and fast, towards the edge of the water where the boat was pulled up on the sand. She shoved it out with one strong heave and jumped in. He followed her, his heart pounding and old. Already she was pushing the boat into the stream.

'I'll send you a present,' she said, 'after the war is over.'

'Bring yourself back,' he said, 'that'll be present enough.'

'Who knows?' Her oars dipped in the water. Chun, lighting a brand of brush and holding it aloft and flaming in one hand, pulled his boat clear of the shore with his free hand.

'Tell him not to come,' she called.

But Chun was following, his strokes longer and stronger than hers, so that he pulled alongside her and rowed with her. By the light of the brand, now wedged in front of Chun's boat, and the thin moonlight, he saw how her face grimaced with pain, arms stretched to the oars. He thought that her brief presence that night would resonate through the years ahead.

'Tomatoes, Hugo,' she called. 'Be sure to grow tomatoes.' He strained his ears for a long time until he could no longer hear the stroke of the oars, and then everything was silent, as it was before she came.

Part Three

The Mothers

1963

JESSIE'S MOTHER

The decision to leave home the day she turned eighteen was not one that Jessie Sandle could explain easily to herself, then or later. She knew that her mother would explain it away to people as her sensitivity, a perfectionist's fear of failure in her university examinations. But that was too easy an answer; Jessie had passed her first half year of law without difficulty.

The head of the china section in the department store where she worked part time in the late afternoons, and during the university holidays, would say it was because she had broken a valuable piece of china that afternoon. It was a very good piece of Royal Winton no less, so hard to come by, with the length of time it took for things to be shipped from England, and she wanted to get out of paying for it. The woman, whose name was Miss Early, told the women on the jewellery counter that Jessie Sandle was an awkward girl, not suited for the work, and a trifle above herself, which was rich in a place like this that provided a quality experience. For a start, she looked a fright, too bony and angular by far, and her hair all over the place, and her mother was a bit of a worry. You know, with those children who are such a handful in the restaurant. Miss Early was referring to the tearoom, where old women sat at tables covered with heavy white cloths and ate tiny bite-sized cucumber sandwiches made with thinly sliced brown bread, and lifted freshly baked cakes from three-tiered silver stands.

Miss Early spoke of Jessie's half-brother and two half-sisters as Mrs Pawson's children, because Jessie had a stepfather and didn't share the same surname as her mother and those objectionable children. Although, Miss Early had a long memory, short on specifics, the children were at school now. The days had gone when they sat and sucked orange sherbet through their straws and blew fizzy dust back over the nearest tearoom patron, or crawled around under the tables between their feet. Now their mother sat on her own in the tearoom and gazed into space, as if hoping she might conjure up an image of something or someone she barely remembered.

What did Mrs Pawson think about? She read a great many books and often forgot to return them to the library. She'd loved books all her life, she told Jessie. Her mother had been friendly with a girl at school who finished up writing books. She was quite famous. Irene had met the writer once or twice during her childhood when her mother ran into her, not that the friendship had survived. The conversation was polite and strained. But Irene remembers the woman, a vivid, spirited person, with a lame leg and a reputation that was spoken about in hushed whispers. Could it be true that she had had a baby when she wasn't married? Irene's mother wouldn't talk about that. Do you know what happened to her? Jessie asked. Oh, her mother would stretch and sigh at this point. She went to China and got caught up in the war and then she died. Or so I heard.

China? How did she die? Did she get killed there?

No, no, it was afterwards. And at that point, Irene Pawson would stop, as if she had gone too far. As if the dead war correspondent's death was something so unspeakable that it must be put to one side, and not thought about again. Nobody Jessie knew had killed themselves but, with a fascinated horror, she suspected that this was the secret. But surely this was not what her mother thought about as she

48

stared into space and let her tea grow cold. Her daughter wondered if she might be thinking about Jessie's own father, the thin-faced airman with the corporal's stripe, rather than about her stepfather, Jock Pawson.

In the late afternoon, the day before Jessie Sandle left home, she encountered a group of young women from university. She had just collected her satchel from the store cloakroom where she worked, and was heading out to catch the bus on Lambton Quay, her head held high as she marched past the china department. Jessie didn't mix with these girls much, for they seemed more free-spirited than she knew how to be. But she was embarrassed by Miss Early's stinging rebuke, and it suddenly seemed better to be leaving with friends. One of them, a girl she remembers as Alicia, linked her arm through hers and suggested they go to the movies. They were good-natured young women from country towns where they had earned scholarships, or their parents (or at least their fathers) were already in the professions and fancied the novelty of daughters who might shine before marriage. They lived in bedsits, and looked intense and serious, worn from lack of sleep. All of them recognised each other as clever. You had to be to have come as far as this. *Cleopatra* was showing at the Embassy, starring Elizabeth Taylor and Richard Burton, although the idea of Elizabeth Taylor in this role seemed slightly ridiculous. Her nose is too short, somebody remarked cleverly, and they all laughed.

'Antony shall be brought drunken forth,' Jessie cried, inspired by their wit, and for a few minutes everyone laughed so hard she felt as if she fitted in.

They agreed that they deserved a night off thinking about their legal studies. First they would drink coffee at Suzi's, and then see what came of the evening. And Jessie thought it sounded lovely, that she would like nothing better than to spend her birthday with these clever capable girls who were managing their lives so well.

In the end, she turned down the invitation. She remembered her mother and her promise of a treat for her birthday, and decided that she would go home and endure the sticky buns and 'special' dinner she supposed her mother would have cooked.

She walked along the Esplanade at Island Bay before turning up the steep incline of Brighton Street. The house was close to the sea. The sky was dark gold; beneath it a fleet of fishing boats cruised into the harbour. She heard the snatch of a song. Although she had lived for a long time among fishermen and their families she knew hardly any of them. At school, some of the children who were not Italian talked in whispers about how the fathers had been locked up in the war because they were Italian, only nobody said it out loud because, it was said, the Italians wanted to forget. In summer, she saw bright rows of vegetables over the fences, red and yellow peppers shaped like inverted bells, and purple aubergines. Catholics, her mother said, and left it at that. Jock was more blunt. Leave the Eye-ties to themselves, he told her. You don't want to go running with spies, just because you're getting educated. His voice was heavy with meaning: keep your mind on your work. It occurred to Jessie that her mother and Jock could be wrong about the Italians although she didn't deny they seemed dangerous — that was the only word she could think of. She thought the Italians at the bay were beautiful, the women luscious, olive-skinned and curvy, the men stocky and hard-muscled.

One of the men called out to her. Gidday, Jessie. He had been in her class at primary school, although he was older. Hey Jessie, how you going? Hi Antonio, she called back, and kept walking. Even though the wind was cool his shirt was open three buttons down, showing the soft curly black hair that sprouted on his chest. A gold chain quivered against his throat. He had special help with reading and mathematics when they were in school. Now he looked prosperous and certain. She had heard he was already promised to someone. She decided, for no reason that she could fathom at that moment (except that it was her birthday and she was eighteen), that she would ask her mother for the photograph of her real father, which she knew she had hidden. She would say it in front of Jock. The photograph would stand on her dressing table.

The last time she had seen it, it was stowed at the bottom of her mother's underwear drawer, beneath the frayed bloomers and cavernous brassieres and shrivelled woollen singlets, the one place where Jock might not be expected to search for a missing sock (though in truth, there were some of those too, bundled in with laundry that had been folded too quickly or carelessly). Jessie hadn't dared look in the drawer since she was last caught by her mother when she was eight. There was something else private in there, a small black box containing smooth rubbery pellets that looked like bad sweets. Uncharacteristically, her mother punished her, first with a slap, then with banishment to her room and, finally, as if to make the point absolutely clear, the cancellation of the school picnic. (But — there was always a but in the stories about her mother, the qualification that made her wince and yearn for her real mother, whoever she was — it was probably her mother's failure of nerve to appear at the school picnic where other mothers with slim bodies and long legs wore smart slim line bathing suits. Jessie knew now what the suppositories were for but she sighed when she thought how useless they were. Jock Pawson's sperm had too often found its snaky way into her mother's uterus. Jock worked as a clerk in one of the government ministries in town, Internal Affairs, which Jessie thought sounded unhappily like the story of her mother's life and her sorry body, in its increasing state of collapse.

That night, that last night at home, Jessie's mother met her at the door. Jessie saw at once how dressed up she was. She wore a polished cotton dress, drooping a little in the hem of its circular skirt, and a white cardigan. Her eyelids were painted an odd hectic green, her mouth scarlet with lipstick. A handbag dangled by its strap from her wrist and she clutched a pair of white gloves. At forty, Irene Pawson's complexion was too pallid to be healthy; her black hair, cut straight across the bottom, was pushed back behind her ears and held in place with hair clips. Jessie felt a sudden rush of love and moved to give her mother a quick hug. But even as this tide of affection was welling up, she felt, also, an anticipatory dread.

She saw that everyone else in the family was wearing their best clothes too. Grant, Belinda and Janice stood in a row, full of expectation, Grant's hair slicked up in a cowlick, the little girls wearing starched blouses with their tartan skirts. Behind them stood Jock, still in his work clothes, his tie in place, the newspaper unread on the dining room table.

'I've ordered us a taxi,' her mother said, her voice excited. 'I've booked us a table at Garland's for six thirty. We're going *out* for tea.'

Jessie's heart sank. 'Mum,' she started. And stopped. How could she have thwarted a plan so artfully conceived? Besides, the ugly chintzy room was full of unfolded washing and the children's toys and her mother's piles of half-read books. The air was thick with a familiar smell that made her want to throw up, the dark and horrible contents of her mother's gut that she flushed down the lavatory several times a day. Nothing to be done about it, the doctor had said, an irritable bowel won't kill her. Tell her to get more exercise, he'd advised

Jock. Irene's ailment seemed worse when she was tired, which was most of the time, or like tonight, plain excited.

'Your mother's been expecting you for hours,' said Jock. He was a tall man, slightly stooped, with sandy hair and a gingery beard that he pulled when he was displeased. He had married in middle age and had money to pay for the house they lived in. The record of his life he brought to them was one of saving and frugality. He was the kind of Scotsman who was born counting money; he did not expect to change when he married and he hadn't.

'I should change my clothes,' Jessie said.

'Throw a scarf on, darling,' her mother cried gaily, 'you'll be just fine. Oh, isn't this fun.'

Garland's was upstairs above Manners Street, near that part of Wellington where drunks and derelicts quarrelled and took shelter. The room was brightly lit by hanging shades that threw a merciless glare on the diners. You could choose roast beef or roast lamb with three vegetables, or fish and chips, and for dessert apple pie or ice-cream sundae — three scoops of ice cream in a boat-shaped glass dish with a choice of strawberry or chocolate topping. The children banged the handles of their knives and forks up and down on the table and sang a song they had made up that went *Cabbage, cabbage, never mind the damage/cabbage, ca-BAGE, never mind the DAMA-AGE.* They sang this regularly at home even when there wasn't cabbage. Between the main course and dessert, Jessie unfolded the presents that the children had dutifully wrapped: from Grant, a small bottle of rose-water that Irene must have helped him to buy, from Belinda, a crochet-covered coat-hanger (had she done it herself? Belinda wriggled and blushed), a handkerchief and an impressionistic drawing of a boat on a flat blue sea from Janice, the baby, who had started school at the beginning of the term.

'They saved their pocket money for those,' Jock said, pulling furiously at his beard. (Not true, not true, Irene had saved for the rose-water, the rest they had made.) He wiped the corners of his mouth with a napkin and sat back. His sister Agnes, whom Jessie was expected to call Aunt Agnes, had joined them by now. Her present was a small silver-plated spoon with an enamelled picture of the Milford Hotel at the top, wrapped in tissue. 'One of my treasures,' Aunt Agnes remarked to them all. 'I went there when I was a new bride. You don't see things like that too often in a lifetime.'

Thank you, thank you, and thank you, Jessie said to each of them, you're all so sweet to me, so kind.

'She could just about pass,' Aunt Agnes said to her mother, with almost a hint of approval. 'She could just about be Jock's own daughter. You can see her and Belinda, they're quite alike.' As much as anything, Jessie might eventually blame her defection on her mother's children who held traces of herself.

'Happy birthday, darling,' her mother said, her face flushed from its usual pallor. She had eaten off all her lipstick with the roast potatoes.

'Well,' said Jock, 'I suppose you expect me to pay for all this lot.' It was meant as a joke even though Jock didn't think it was really funny. Jessie could see that.

'Please,' her mother said, in a low voice. Jessie could see then the effort it had cost her mother for them to come on this outing. Jock scooped some of his leftover ice cream onto Grant's plate.

'There, then,' he said, pleased with himself.

Everything her mother did had a cost. Jessie didn't know why she hadn't seen this before. But now she understood in an instant that this was how it had always been, ever since her mother married Jock. If it hadn't been for her, perhaps her mother might have married better the second time round.

Jock, she could see, was the price her mother paid for being alone and having a child, for not always living as a war widow. Her mother might have been in love once, but not twice. All the same, here she was, married with four children — because, however reluctantly, Jessie had to include herself — turning to Jock Pawson for his charity, even on her daughter's birthday.

On the way home Jessie stared out of the window of the taxi at the hearse-black sky. Of course her mother would be better without her. And yes, it was true, she hated university, or at least legal studies. What arrogance, what a cheek, to think she might become a lawyer. Your Honour, heaven's thought was otherwise; I should have stuck with Virgil. How many women had been admitted to the bar? Why should she make history?

In the morning she said she felt ill and stayed in bed. She waited until her mother left the house to walk Janice to school, because the older children got impatient and didn't wait for her. When the house was empty, she got up and pulled on the clothes she had worn the day before. She went to the main bedroom. It felt like theft, just being in the room, as if she were invading the last vestige of her mother's guilty secrets. The room smelt heavy and musty, the bed unmade, the pillow on Jock's side stained with Brylcreem. The dressing table was thick with bobby pins and talcum powder, as if the room was all too much for Irene to manage, but then most of the house was like that. When she is older, Jessie will sometimes think that if she had just stopped and tidied up that day, things in her life would have been different.

Opening the bottom drawer where the underclothes were kept, she ran her hands along the bottom. The photograph had gone. She tried the upper drawers, hurriedly turning over cardigans and folded blouses, then the top drawer where Irene kept her make-up and old ropes of fake pearls and hat pins.

Nothing.

Jessie decided to take one last look in the shelf where her mother stored a hat box, some out-of-season clothes and a few knick-knacks of baby clothes and mementoes. She came across a small suitcase, one she remembered her mother carrying when they shifted from one place to another when she was a young child. For a moment she weighed it in her hand, before opening it, as if measuring her own presence in the house. She was possessed with the idea that her mother's life could only get better if she left. Jock was not even a bad man. He tolerated her. That was the hardest part. In the suitcase she found some papers: her own birth certificate, a death certificate for her father, copies of Jock and Irene's wills, which she didn't open, some old stored accounts bound up with a rubber band. She took the first two items and emptied the rest on the crumpled blue satin eiderdown.

Jessie sat in an olive and mustard-coloured Road Services bus as it trundled through rolling plains, then the wasteland of desert space in the centre of the land, the starry tussock glinting under an erratic sun, the mountains leaning towards her from the west. It had been the first bus leaving Wellington with a spare seat. Her purse contained three pounds ten in notes and loose change and her Post Office savings book showing thirty-five pounds, her entire life savings. As the bus pushed north she saw a line of army tanks ploughing through the grass, firing practice rounds of shells that made puffs of dark smoke, and then the bus descended towards the lake country, the dark iris of Lake Taupo trembling on the horizon, and on past it, until they reached their destination, a town straggling along the shore of another, smaller lake. Had it not been so close to the water, it would have been a plain town, although as she walked its long main street Jessie saw that there were some charming facades on some of the older buildings, something more cosmopolitan than the places she had passed through earlier in the day. She would look back on that long walk through the town and see a reflection of those houses in unexpected places, not just in Sydney, or Island Bay, where she had lived, but in suburban Chicago perhaps, or in the crumbling streets of Asia, in the French arrondissements.

The town unfolded itself before Jessie Sandle and just when she thought there was nowhere else to go, it revealed to her the Violet Café. That evening when she met Violet Trench it was as if nothing of importance had happened to her before and everything from now on would matter.

SYBIL AND MARIANNE

Derek said that, if it was all right with her, he would come around about seven and Sybil Linley said yes, that was quite all right, she was sure Marianne would be pleased. Sybil liked the way this young man of her daughter's studied the arrangement of roses on her desk, appearing to absorb their fragrance, not exaggerating his interest or pretending to know about flowers.

'I just never know when she'll be working these days,' he said. He had an athletic grace about him, a ball clutched under his arm, like a schoolboy who couldn't wait to be released.

'Violet Trench keeps those girls on their toes. A very temperamental woman,' Sybil said. She took a delicate bite of her cheese and grated apple sandwich and eased a crumb from the corner of her mouth with one fingertip. Derek came to see her often. The phone in the house where she and her daughter lodged belonged to their landlady. It was not possible for Marianne and Derek to phone each other casually. Their arrangements often had to be made through her. Marianne sometimes came to town to meet Derek during his lunch hour, but other days she slept late. The hours she kept at the Violet Café were unpredictable. This was why he came by the office most days, to see when Marianne would be free.

Sybil pushed aside the bill of sale she was studying while she finished her lunch, giving him a look she hoped would be disarmingly frank. At forty-five, Sybil knew she was one of the most attractive women of her age in the town. Her large amber eyes were lustrous and faintly slanted at the corners beneath dark impeccably formed brows, and her skin, despite a tiny pouch that had recently formed under her chin, still possessed some of youth's delicacy. She wore, on that late autumn day, a liquorice woollen dress nipped in at the waist, which gave the illusion of a girl's figure. People still thought she and her younger daughter, Marianne, were sisters when they saw them out together. Her older daughter was already married and had two children of her own. Sybil was grateful that they lived on a farm down south at Featherston.

Sybil didn't consider men a weakness. She worked for a land agent. Selling houses was a business where a woman had to stay on her toes. Men thought they knew more about property, but she had some tricks up her sleeve, or both of them if it came to that, that they never thought of. Things like an appreciation of the finer points of kitchens and the convenience of laundries — all the simple obvious stuff. Perhaps they did think of it, but they didn't know how to present it through a woman's eyes and of course it was women who made the decisions about buying houses, even if the men did make the deposit and sign the mortgage agreements. She had long ago learnt the fine art of allowing men to believe they were making decisions while maintaining the utmost complicity with their wives. Men had their limitations, she believed, but that was no reason to dislike them.

'I wish Marianne would leave the café,' Derek said. 'She could get a proper job.' Derek himself worked in the bank across the road. He was head teller but soon they would be moving him up to accounts.

Sybil saw why her daughter yearned for this young man, his murmuring in her ear, and no doubt the sex she assumed had already begun. She could see them together if she imagined it, and she did. He was slightly shorter than Sybil, and than her daughter for that matter, but he had hard young muscles and a strong chest. He played rugby in the weekends. The local newspaper had singled him out as a prospect for a provincial side. She liked men that shape, like barrels with slim hips, especially when they were clothed in nice suits. In some ways he reminded her of Lou Messenger, until recently her lover, although Lou was a more casual sort of man. Thinking of Lou made her heave a small inward sigh of regret. He sold sports goods and fishing tackle, and he was afraid his wife was getting suspicious. That's what he told her. She understood. This sort of thing happened.

'Well,' she said. 'Well. The way Violet Trench talks you'd think she was offering the best job in the world down at that café. Of course, Madame's decidedly above herself, but still she's got class, I'll give her that, a bit of style.'

'Marianne might as well work in the pub. All sorts of things go on at that place.'

'Oh come on, Derek, it's not so bad.' Her lunch finished, Sybil folded the brown paper bag into a little square and dropped it in the rubbish bin at her feet. She considered her fingernails, which were buffed and smoothed, the cuticles pushed back to show her strong crescent moons. It was better to take things slowly she decided. This man is not in a hurry to marry, she thought, rubbing the nail with the pad of her thumb. 'Anyway, what would Marianne do?'

'She's artistic,' he said, with a touch of irritation. 'Perhaps she could try teaching, they do lots of art and stuff.'

'She'd have to go away to do that, go away to get trained.'

'Yes I suppose she would.'

'What you mean,' said Sybil, 'is that you want a long engagement. I'm surprised.'

'I don't know whether she's ready for all that stuff yet, settling down and everything.' Derek's tone was flat.

'You know she's mad about you,' Sybil said. 'I mean, what more do you want?'

When he didn't reply straight away, she said, 'Well, it's solid work, banking. A good career.' What she meant was, he was respectable and careful. He would become a pillar of the community. He might settle for less than her beautiful daughter, someone with two parents who already had a pastel bathroom of their own. While she was still looking and wondering how far she could stretch the deposit, and how long it would be before she was free of Marianne and could buy one of those nice little one-bedroom flats that she came across now and then in the course of her work. It occurred to her that Derek wouldn't play rugby for much longer. If he had really wanted to be a top player it would probably have happened already. What he wanted, she believed, was to run a bank. If she was any sort of mother, she would warn Marianne, tell her to do something about it, get pregnant, anything at all. She felt a momentary pang of profound regret. It was not Marianne he had to fear, but a mother without scruples, a divorced woman. Sybil pushed her gold bracelets up her arm and smiled sideways at him. 'Seven o' clock then, we'll expect you.'

Only, when she got home, Marianne had left a note with the landlady to say she had been called for work. (The landlady took calls if they concerned work. Her tenants did have the rent to pay.) This was more or less what Sybil had expected, given that Belle, who cleaned the café, had become so erratic, as Marianne had described it. She didn't like it, any more than Derek, that Marianne sometimes did cleaning work as well as waitressing at the Violet Café. Sybil knew she should throw herself upon the landlady's forbearance, and ask to use the phone. But the house was quiet, as if she had gone out. There were other tenants in the house, but she thought they must be out too. At least it was a relief not to hear the bad-tempered woman banging around in the kitchen while she boiled meat. Sybil could have gone down to the telephone box on the corner and phoned Derek. He would have had time to go home and change out of his suit into slacks and a pullover as he did most nights before he came to see Marianne. Sometimes the couple would go to the pictures, or they would just go for a drive in his Hillman Hunter. When she came home, Marianne's eyes were always alight, her perfectly shaped top teeth taking excited little bites of her lower lip, as if something momentous had just taken place.

Sybil knew she shouldn't let him visit for nothing. She sat down in a wicker chair with a big cushion behind her and took off her high heels, stretching her nylon-clad legs in front of her. There had been two near sales this week and she was tired of showing people the master bedroom and raving about the size of the linen cupboard. Soon she would have a gin and tonic. She should have something to eat. In the meantime, she would sit for a while and let things take care of themselves. Later on. She couldn't pretend she wasn't waiting for his knock.

When she opened the door to him, she told herself it was all part of an old, old story and you could make up different endings to suit yourself. On another day it would be different. Sybil lay down on the bed in her room with her daughter's lover and spread herself beneath him, her voluptuous mouth covering him in kisses, and that was where Marianne, who had forgotten her flat-heeled shoes for work, found her very soon after.

That was last autumn and now it was nearly spring and Marianne hadn't seen her mother since. In the evenings, Marianne told herself it was good to be free, not tied to anyone.

WALLACE AND BELLE, AND LORRAINE SEEN
FROM A DISTANCE

When Belle's fiancé, Wallace, had found God it was as if a
great white light had been turned on. The light just kept
burning and burning with an intensity that made him feel
as if he glowed when he walked down the street. Perhaps he
felt this way because he was an electrician, used to switching
light on and off, understanding and yet not understanding
the amazing current that illuminated the world. It seemed
natural that he saw himself in terms of light, as if a great
neon sign had been erected above him. He was surprised
people didn't see him coming. The Lord is truly my Shepherd
he said to himself every day. His conversion had begun one
night years before when he had gone to hear the word of God
preached by Billy Graham, in an Auckland park. At the time,
Wallace was hanging out with motorcycle gangs and wore his
hair slicked up in a comb. Years later, he learnt about movies
like *Grease* and thought them profane, as if glamorising all
that bad side of his life was unacceptable. That is just the sort
of thing that corrupts people, he would say now, although
he knew that sin and corruption crept up in many guises.
When he preached, there were things in this life he could
draw upon that would make people sit up and listen. They
would wonder how he could know as much as he did, a man
who kept himself so pure and at one with the Lord. It was
that mysterious well of knowledge and understanding that
drew the sinful to tell him their innermost secrets. Just like

Billy Graham himself. Wallace was with a gang up north at the time Billy Graham came along. This was 1959. There was a girl who used to cruise with the crowd and hitch rides on the back of motor-bikes. She never had much to say for herself but Wallace could tell that he was the one she had set her sights on — she used to gaze at him with adoring eyes. One night when he had been drinking beer at the waterfront, she sat staring at him, tilting her breasts this way and that under a shocking pink sweater and dangling her legs over a bench seat in the park. He remembered her legs in particular, clad in diamond-patterned matador pants. She was looking and acting like a bad girl; it was time he gave her a lesson and showed her how really bad he was.

'I'll take you out then,' he said. 'What do you want to do?'

She had suddenly looked nervous. 'I have to be home by ten. I'll get it if I'm not.'

He hated the way she was backing off. Teasing him, he reckoned. 'Decide for yourself, we can get together or go to Billy Graham at the park.'

He could have sworn she would have opted for sex, she had been hanging out for it now for months.

'I'll take Billy Graham,' she said.

His mates jeered when they left. He tapped his forehead and grinned so that they would know she was about to get what was coming to her. Only, he knew he wouldn't do it to her. He just didn't fancy her enough, or perhaps she scared him a little. She was an unknown quantity, the sort who might make trouble if you called her bluff.

At the gates to the park, thousands of people were moving forward. The girl reached for his hand but he didn't pick it up, didn't look back to see where she went or whether she would go into the park without him. But a current of excitement in the air was infecting him, like that feeling of electricity that seemed as normal as breathing when he worked with it; it was just that when he put down his tools for the day and folded away the wires, there seemed to be nothing there inside him. He felt in his bones that something was going to happen, as if the vacuum was about to be filled.

When he saw the grey-suited man with the handsome lantern jaw (this was how the newspapers described it), and heard him begin to speak, he knew he was right. I'm going to ask you to do something hard, the man said. It's hard and it's tough but you can do it. I'm going to ask you to get up out of your seat, and come on this field and stand here quietly, reverently. Come now, it won't be difficult. There will be hundreds of you, and you know as I speak that it is not me who speaks to you, but God. God has spoken to you. You get up and come. I can hear it in your hearts. You want a new life.

Wallace looked around for the girl but she was not there. She had brought him here and she should, he thought, at least share this moment. He looked across the sea of faces, intent, raised and watching the man. When he twisted around, seeking the girl, people raised their fingers as if he might break the spell. He was going to have to go to God on his own. You want to be clean and wholesome for Christ, Billy Graham said. The Lord has spoken to you. Now you just get right out of your seats and come on … come on … you are not on your own, your friends are coming with you.

In the background a choir robed in white had begun to sing *Just as I am, without one plea, dear Lord* and dear Lord, he was on his feet and going towards the man.

And, after one quick glance backwards, he never looked back. After that, he knew only pure women and girls, like Belle Hunter, the pastor's daughter.

Once he had walked off on his journey towards eternity, his old friends behind him, things happened quickly. He bought himself a grey suit of his own and several snow-white shirts so that he could be sure of having a clean pressed one every day, he put a carnation in his buttonhole, and had his fair hair, which his mother used to call golden when he was a child, cut short back and sides. Preaching was a gift he never knew he had in him. When he stood up and told people about the things he saw, about the magnetic forces of electricity and the way it was all part of God's plan to light up every corner of the world, from the darkness of Africa and its benighted people to the black soul of the big cities where evil resided, it was like magic.

He was invited to preach in a town further south, where a man called Hal Hunter was conducting a prayer meeting. It was winter and there was rain in the air, which combined with the rising volcanic steam at the edge of the racecourse, where the meeting was being held, to create eerie mists and shadows around them. He shivered inside the new double-breasted coat that he wore over the grey suit. Then Hal began to speak and told them about the Church of Twenty, which was his very own creation.

Twenty seeds are all I need, he told them. Each seed will go forth and find twenty more, and each of those another twenty, and the word of God will spread like wildfire. You'll hear it in the streets and from the mountain tops, you'll hear it spoken by the wise old men (not a word about wise old women) and children. It will be the song that carries us all forward until the end of time and the new creation. You hear me?

We hear you, the crowd called back. Then Hal called on Wallace to speak of his experiences, and the way the light had been turned on for him, and before long everyone was shouting *Praise the Lord* every time he paused for breath. He knew just how well he had done when Mr Hunter invited him home for supper. His daughter, who was called Belle, was only fourteen at the time but he fell in love with her on the spot. Belle rode in the car beside him on the way back to the Hunter place, Mr Hunter driving and Mrs Hunter beside him. Belle had big blue eyes that you noticed straight away, very fair hair that she wore long and wavy round her shoulders. As soon as they went into the house, she went to the kitchen and began helping her mother lay out a supper of sausage rolls and custard squares.

'Sir,' he stammered, unable to find the words to express how delighted he was by Belle's appearance, without giving offence. He saw how young she was.

Hal looked him in the eye, as if seeing right inside him. Wallace blushed, aware that what the pastor saw might be interpreted as carnal desire, a terrible shaming lust for the child, and that the recognition of this stain on his soul could be his undoing. 'She'll make a good wife for someone,' he said.

Belle's mother, whose name was Lorraine, paused from her work for an instant, tight-lipped. 'She's too young to make a promise,' she said, in a low quick voice.

'I beg your pardon,' Hal said, a blaze in his eyes. When she didn't answer, he said, 'I think you should go to your room, wife.'

Immediately, and without another word, Belle's mother laid down the last of the food and walked out of the room. Wallace glanced at Belle to see if this had upset her, but she seemed undisturbed. She knelt by the fire and poked at a log of wood. Wallace felt excited and stirred by what he had just seen. He could tell that Hal was a man who knew what he wanted, what was best for everyone.

'She's a very good girl,' Hal said. 'You like this man, Belle?'

'Yes,' said the girl, keeping her eyes downcast, but Wallace saw a smile hovering at the corner of her mouth.

'You'll have to teach her to be a good wife,' said Hal.

'Yes sir,' Wallace said. He wondered how much he would be allowed to teach her before his marriage and how soon her education would begin.

'You got any money?'

'Not much, sir.'

'I thought as much. You need money for a ring when she leaves school. A girl needs a good diamond, tells the world she's worth it to a man. Like a down payment,' he added, grinning. 'You have to be able to support her.'

'Oh, I can save up,' said Wallace. 'I've got a trade. I only preach weekends and evenings as a rule.'

'Good man. Don't take any nonsense from her. I take too much from that woman down the passage there. She had too much freedom before we found the Lord.'

Wallace just nodded. Now that the washing up was finished, Belle picked up a piece of needlework and sat down beside the fire. Wallace felt helpless, already so in love with his child bride.

'And you keep pure for the wedding, you hear me. No messing around. A goodnight kiss is quite far enough.'

'Yes sir.' Wallace couldn't believe God was being so good to him. Later in the night when the house should have been settled in sleep, he heard a thud and a scream inside the house, a voice muffled. He understood that the man was the head of the house and Belle's mother needed discipline. Belle, swaddled in a long winceyette nightgown, had come to him and demurely offered her cheek for the first of his kisses. He wanted to kiss her and kiss her until she fainted in his arms.

Out on the street or even in the house helping her mother bottle preserves and cook and clean, she was so quiet you couldn't hear her move from one place to the next. Her mother had bruised and brooding silences of her own, but Belle's silence seemed to reflect a happiness he hoped he had inspired. She let him kiss her a great deal, on her lips and on her neck and on the tops of her sweet white breasts. The day before she turned fifteen he gave her the ring, because she was finishing school the next day and she wanted the girls there to know that she had her future mapped out and waiting; it was the first and last triumph of her school days. By this time, Wallace had given up his trade and only did jobs for friends of Hal's. The rest of the time he spent learning the Scriptures and preaching with Hal here and there around the countryside. The husbands of Belle's older sisters were his new friends, amiable smiling young men called Joshua and Albert. One of them was a drainlayer and the other worked in a menswear shop, and when they weren't at their jobs they helped to find more seeds for the Church of Twenty. Already the sisters and their husbands had seven children between them.

Wallace had enough money saved in the bank for a deposit on a house when he gave up regular work, but there were weeks when the ministry didn't offer much by way of a living. Hal said Belle could take a job for a while, as long as it was something humble. She first took a job at a boarding house near the end of the main street, cleaning bedrooms after the guests left. In the evening she came home smelling of carbolic soap and toilets. When she heard about a job washing dishes at the Violet Café on the waterfront, she asked her father if she might try out for that. It was a den of harlots, her father said; he'd heard about the kind of women who hung out around that place. Then there was trouble in the boarding house. A man ran amok with an axe and Belle nearly got her head sliced in two. Hal and Wallace went to see the woman who ran the café. The woman was all lip and very impudent in Hal's opinion, although Wallace rather liked her. I make the rules, she told them, and Belle will obey what I say when she comes to work at the Violet Café; she could worry about their rules when she went home. They waited for her to show them around but she didn't, just waiting for their answer with a take it or leave it look in her eye. In the end, Hal said Belle could go there and work for a few months, until she was married, now that they had set a date for the wedding. Belle was sixteen by then. Her older sisters were thinking about their matrons' outfits already.

'I reckon she's about as ready for things as she'll get,' Hal said, as they drove home from the café. He looked at Wallace speculatively.

That night he did take her at last. When they first lay down together he thought she would be afraid but she put both her arms around his neck and pressed her cheek against his, as if being in bed was the most natural thing in the world. He plunged into her with the urgency of a man who has come to his last gasp, yet with a tenderness that surprised even him. Only it didn't feel like breaking and entering, and afterwards he sensed that she might have been disappointed. He told himself this was only natural, he supposed the reality was not what most girls expected. All the same, this is what they did every night from then on. She would rest her head on his shoulder while they slept, her hand sometimes stroking him as if to give him comfort. Nobody seemed to mind, although he couldn't be sure what her mother thought, as she never said. Sometimes he sensed her, when he was drifting off to sleep, walking up and down the house.

It surprised him how much Belle liked her job in the café. One of the girls was getting married soon, just like her. Hester said she could help Belle with the dresses for her wedding; she was terrific at sewing. They were ever so busy at the café.

Everyone, except one girl called Marianne, was pretty nice to her, although the boss kept them all on their toes, and you had to be quick with the pots and pans or the cooks shouted at you. But that was all part of the job and you had to understand the pressure everyone was under to get their jobs done in time and keep the customers happy. He wondered about the place then. His image of a kitchen was a plain serviceable room with a sink and dirty plates, much like the one where Belle worked alongside her silent mother. What could be different about it? Sometimes when Belle came home late at night and he was lying in bed waiting for her, he heard her kick off her shoes and hum to herself, or even sing little snatches of song. It unsettled him, knowing that Belle was moving out there in the world beyond. He remembered the wicked girl who had tried to lead him astray. Or had she been wicked? She had led him to God and then disappeared like a phantom. Perhaps she had been some kind of angel. At any rate, he had been led there to Belle and her people and her people's people. Belle was his star, his private beacon, his dazzling little mistress. Untouched by the world.

'You should give up work now,' he said one morning, after her third late night in a row.

She was washing dishes, running them under the hot tap to rinse them, polishing them on the tea towel with painstaking care, as if washing dishes was the most important thing a girl could be doing.

'I like it there,' she said.

'You'll have to stop soon.'

'Why? It's money in the bank.'

He knew she was proud of the growing line of figures in her Post Office book. 'You'll have the wedding to see to. And we might have a baby next year.' This had just occurred to him, but he was enchanted at once with the idea, seeing it

71

immediately as the thing they needed to do very soon.

'We're not even married yet,' she said, scoffing at him.

Her overbright stare embarrassed him, her eyes were so big and blue. 'We could have. I mean, we could have any time.' Now that he had started on this train of thought, he could see that it was one thing to have sex with Belle; it was another for the young pastor and his bride to be with child (how he loved that biblical phrase) on their wedding day.

'I've got a diaphragm,' she said, 'didn't you know?'

'You didn't tell me,' he said, stunned. He didn't think unmarried women could get contraception.

'Well, somebody had to do something, didn't they? I mean, you didn't think about it, did you?'

Wallace smacked Belle then, first under her eye and then across the mouth, and when he had done that, he took off his belt and hit her on the buttocks three times, each time harder than the last. He loved it, the power of it. She didn't make a sound. Afterwards he put his arms around her and said that he was sorry.

'I'll put you to bed and make you a cup of Ovaltine,' he said.

She pulled out of his grasp. 'I've got to go to work,' she said. 'Now.'

He heard her running water in the bathroom and soon after that she left the house.

It had begun like that, back then.

RUTH AND HESTER

The bookshop was long and narrow and full of wood panelling, like a miniature version of those famous Fifth Avenue bookshops that Ruth Hagley had visited when she was young, although they had come to seem like a mirage. She loved the books sitting in orderly rows on the shelves. There were days when she almost wished nobody would come into the shop and interfere with the straight organised way she pulled their spines forward to the edge of their shelves, their colourful covers which she could interpret without reading the book, the lovely spicy newness of their smell when they were laid open. Ruth banned children from the shop, even though parents complained from time to time. One had even written to the local newspaper, claiming she was inhibiting the educational growth of the youngsters in the community. It is my shop, Ruth said with implacable steel, to a reporter intrigued by this brisk ample woman with a narrow sideways glance, wearing a black cardigan, one of those long ones with deep pockets, and a checked skirt that reached her ankles. A stifler of knowledge, the letter writer said, someone who doesn't enjoy and understand the company of the young. What sort of a person is that to be running a bookshop? But Ruth Hagley told the reporter, 'Children may go to the library. That is what a library is for, a place where people may use jam rolls for bookmarks if they wish. Bookshops are for the preservation of newness and originality until someone pays for the privilege of owning a book. Then they can do what they like with it.' The newspaper ran a short puzzled piece over a headline that said 'LOCAL LIBRARY BOOKS FILLED WITH JAM'. It wasn't great for business. A new bookshop was opened on the next corner, by a man with hair like an oiled raven's wing who was in love with another man, and in touch with people's feelings. His business was doing very well.

Ruth found herself capitulating to the demands of commerce. A publisher's representative (a rep, as he vulgarly called himself) came round and persuaded her to invite an exciting young author who was onto his third or fourth highly successful novel to come into the shop for a signing session. Ruth had never held such an event before, but if she sometimes offended people, she considered herself astute, and times were difficult.

'Are you suggesting a little gathering?' she asked.

'Oh that would be simply divine,' said the young man. Ruth thought people only talked like that in West End stage plays.

'What do you think I should serve?'

'Gary's partial to a beer or two.' Gary wrote about the life of men in the bush, hunting and fishing, that kind of thing, of which Ruth knew absolutely nothing.

'There won't be any beer in here. Think what it would do to the books.'

'Well, perhaps a little glass of bubbly, something nice and sparkly. Up near the counter away from the books.'

'It would be after six o'clock. I'd be arrested.'

'Mrs Hagley, it's not as if you're a hotel.'

'I should think not. It's a public place though. Anybody can come in here.' Her expression registered how unfortunate this was. 'A cup of tea or a glass of lemonade, perhaps.'

'Well, I suppose so.'

'It'll be expensive enough as it is. Are you going to pay for these refreshments?'

'My firm could make a contribution,' he said uneasily. 'We'll help with the advertisement for the paper.'

'Advertisement? Definitely not. I'm not putting an advertisement in that paper, and besides, if it's to be a party I don't want just anyone turning up.'

'You don't advertise at all?'

'Only on radio. Now and then.' Ruth loved the radio.

'Then how does anyone know what you've got in stock?'

'They know I'm here.' Her voice was regal.

'Well, I don't know whether that would work.' The rep turned towards the door as if he might go away. She guessed he would walk on up the street to the sleek sad man in the corner bookshop, whose lover had recently betrayed him.

'A flier to all my regulars. I have five hundred people on my mailing list.'

The rep turned back, his eyes lit up with surprised admiration. 'Now you're talking.'

'You'll pay for the postage?' she said, her voice as smooth as ball bearings. When he nodded, she said, 'My daughter will attend to the food.'

'I think we should make provision for one hundred and fifty,' Ruth told her daughter that evening.

Hester looked up from her task, sewing seed pearls down the front panel of her wedding dress, and flushed. Her mother was used to Hester's flushes, the dark maroon stain that started at her throat and travelled upwards. This was almost the only sign her daughter ever gave that she was annoyed. Sometimes Ruth wanted to shake her and tell her to shout back at her. She knew very well that what she was asking was an imposition. Hester had so little time off from the café where she worked, because the woman who ran it was well known for being difficult and imperious and expected her staff to work longer hours than anyone in town. Violet Trench was the nearest Ruth had ever come to meeting her match, and when it came to Hester she had a way of winning that Ruth could never fully comprehend. Hester was twenty-eight and her only child. They had gone through so much together. There was Hester's birth when Ruth was forty-six years old and the thought of a child was so unlikely in brief late marriage that the idea simply never occurred to her until one day her clothes wouldn't fit and then a few days later she was bleeding almost to death in hospital and Hester was breathing her first heart-wrenching gasps, her face as blue as anemones, and there Ruth was, a mother. As if that were not enough, widowhood and poverty followed in short order, and then, when it seemed she had nowhere to turn, in one of those sudden reversals of fortune that seemed to follow Ruth, an inheritance came from abroad.

Ruth considered her young life as dense, packed, virginal. I've had an interesting life, she was wont to say. She would describe it as genteel and a little impoverished with some treats thrown in (her father was a professional soldier; he moved his family often). When she immigrated to New Zealand with Monty, a retired civil servant who had wanted to see the world before he died, as he put it, and had fallen in love with Auckland on a blue summer's day and wouldn't leave, she decided that she would take things as they came. But then there was Hester and everything changed so quickly. She moved south and bought her shop from the money that had fallen like a merciful rain from afar. Hester grew up surrounded by the smell of new ink on the page, counting stationery packs after school. A girl of quality, her mother believed. She expected her to go far. Hester would win scholarships and go to university, she too would stay clear-skinned and virginal. Instead, Hester grew more quiet and shy as one year followed another. When she was fifteen her frothy brown hair became mysteriously streaked with grey, as if she was already old.

Cooking and sewing were all that interested her. Rather than study classics she propped recipe books above the sink and cooked. *Le Guide Culinaire* by that Frenchman, Escoffier, was thumbed and stained beyond recognition. It made Ruth shudder to see the disgusting thing, but when she arrived home from the shop, dinner was always waiting. 'You shouldn't have done this, dear,' Ruth said each evening, but the fact was her own dinners were always late, the potatoes not properly cooked. It was a comfort to sit down to Hester's inventions. The aromatic scent of spices and herbs that Hester wrote away for reminded Ruth of school trips across the Channel, the week in Provence, the little cafés in the south of France. While other girls were still chasing hockey balls, Hester took up ballroom dancing and met a boy called Owen. They had been engaged for five years. An impossible match, her mother declared. A farm labourer who came from common stock. Don't go ahead with this, Ruth warned her daughter. I'll cut you off without a penny. By this time, Hester worked in the shop because Ruth could see that the girl had no ambition at all. Hester sewed ballroom dresses by the dozen. They accumulated like giant glittering puffballs in her bedroom. When there were too many she sold off the last year's lot and made a small profit. This was her dowry, she said, so her mother needn't bother herself about the money, she and Owen would manage. You'll get over it, Ruth cautioned, you mark my words.

'Would Violet mind if you stayed home and ran up a few sandwiches?' she asked her daughter the night of the book rep's visit. Because Hester no longer worked for her mother.

Ruth still didn't know how she had met Violet Trench. It seemed as if some act of seduction had taken place. One day Hester was pricing paperbacks and the next day she was working as a cook at the Violet Café at the edge of town. As far as Ruth could make out, Hester had begun talking to Violet about her passion for cooking and recipe books in the shop one afternoon, and Violet had followed up with a dinner invitation to her flat. Only it was Hester who had cooked for Violet, and Ruth who had had to do with cold pressed tongue and salad. To make matters worse, Hester was now going through with this disastrous marriage. Ruth blamed Violet Trench for that. It was as if an alien had landed in Hester's brain. She had been to see Violet to enlist her help in preventing it.

'She could do worse,' Violet said. 'She could kill herself. If you don't mind, I've got work to do.'

'Mother, you know how busy we are,' Hester said now. 'Mrs Trench needs me.'

'She owes me some consideration. Taking my staff away, the way she did.'

'Don't start that again. Please.'

'I expect I can manage on my own.'

'You could get someone in to help you. You could afford it.'

'I'm not sure that I could.' Ruth allowed her voice a quaver, but there was just enough of the real thing there to make Hester pause. 'Well, it's the new bookshop,' Ruth said, looking at her hands, well-kept hands but thickened these days and mottled with liver spots. Her single worn ring was embedded in a swollen finger.

'I'll see what I can do,' Hester said, sighing. 'I might be able to run up some sandwiches in my break.'

'Some nice little savouries?' Ruth picked delicately at the

encrusted satin Hester was sewing. 'So pretty, dear.'

'I'll make them the night before.'

'You couldn't possibly help me to serve them?'

'No, I couldn't. Oh damn you, what time is this bun fight of yours?'

'Hester. Language.' Her daughter had developed a habit of smart talk since she began working at the café. 'Five till six. Really, that woman rules your life, you don't have customers until six thirty.' Her eyes filled with real involuntary tears which made her ashamed. Age was not a pretty sight for the young. She lifted her chin.

'I'll go in and do my prep early,' her daughter said, her scissors moving smartly over loose threads.

'I think it will be quite charming,' Ruth told the radio shopping reporter, Freda Messenger, the following morning. Freda was a nervous rushing sort of woman, who darted from one shop to another gathering material for her programmes, which she delivered during the afternoon in an austere polite voice. Her hair was a neutral blond, occasionally tinged an odd shade of green when her regular dye needed freshening; her long upper lip wore a heavy down if allowed to go unchecked, although she had taken lately to electrolysis once a month. On this spring morning with its cool wind, she wore a pale mustard jacket over a silk blouse and scarf, a tweed skirt and sensible brown brogues, as might be expected of someone who pounded the streets all morning. An astute woman, Ruth considered, the nearest she had to a friend these days. If they had been more of an age, they could have been close, she sometimes reflected. Freda was like her, a woman of quality who had fallen on hard times, married in haste but, unlike Ruth, had had time to repent at leisure. They were both the mothers of only children, both girls. The resemblance ended there. Freda's daughter, Evelyn, looked as if she might have the success Ruth had dreamed of for Hester; next year she would go away to university.

Her husband was younger than Freda by some years, a sparkling devilish man about town who made quantities of money and spent it all on horses and, Ruth suspected, women as well. A man who hung around bars when he should have been at home with his family, or who fooled about at the Violet Café. Ruth asked Hester what he got up to down there, but Hester closed up on her. What people did at the Violet Café was their own business. Ruth considered asking Freda about the café, as if with a passing professional interest, for often on the radio, which she kept switched on in the shop to the local station, she heard Freda talking in an animated way about the café, its charming ambience, the quality of its unusual menu, and the warm welcome patrons (oh what had happened to customers, Ruth wondered) would receive from its increasingly famous owner, Violet Trench. In the end, she always ended up deciding against it. She knew from Hester that Evelyn had a job at the café, filling in until she started at university.

'I don't like to mention this,' Freda said, 'but the new shop is putting up a special display of guns and deer heads in the window.'

Ruth shuddered. 'Good luck to him, I say. The customers will get a nice bite to eat when they come here.'

'They're something of a novelty, these book signing sessions,' Freda observed.

'Oh, people have book parties in the cities all the time, these days,' said Ruth airily, 'One has to move with the times.' Privately, she thought how tired Freda was looking.

FREDA AND EVELYN, AND, IN HIS ABSENCE, LOU

Freda Messenger sat in front of the microphone, her finger poised on the button, waiting for her voice level to be taken. The studio was like a small cell. No natural light intruded. Between her and the technician stood a soundproof pane of glass. In these moments before the broadcast began, she was aware that intangible airwaves were her only connection with the world beyond, and this was when things always seemed as though they might slip out of her grasp. It was not that she didn't enjoy her work as a shopping reporter. If she was asked she would say what a great privilege it was to be part of the working lives of so many people in the town, and that in return she made a valuable contribution to their businesses. But she always felt fearful just before she started, as if some secret act, more private than love or sex, was about to be performed in public. Some would call it stage fright. In preparation, she repeated a ritual that worked for her week in and week out, breathing deeply through her nose, expelling air with a slight aaaahhh, in and out, until her terror abated.

Only today she couldn't breathe at all. Her in breaths emerged as choking gasps. Her nose was blocked and her eyes so swollen she had kept her dark glasses on. Any moment now, she would have to take them off because under the fluorescent light tube it was impossible to read her script.

A red light on the panel alerted her.

'Try a level now,' said David Finke, the technician. He was a spiky-haired youth with a white face and red-rimmed eyes.

He boarded in town and slept between shifts. That was all he did, he told her. Never went out, just slept. What else was there to do in this hellhole of a town, this pit of a place, reeking of hydrogen sulphide? Where would he go? If he went out he was just as likely to fall down a vent hole and be boiled in a pot like puha, or get eaten by the Maori who lived at the waterfront. He'd done science and a little music at school, before he came here, but neither of them well enough to take up a career. On his way home to his boarding house his only distraction was to check, with a long, thin laboratory thermometer, the temperature levels of the hot pools that dotted the park. Sooner or later he would get away from this place, go back to Hamilton where he grew up. This whole town was just waiting to explode. This apocalyptic view was the main topic of conversation he ever engaged in with Freda.

She steadied herself, took a grip on the edge of the table. 'Testing, one, two, three,' she said, and was surprised that her voice sounded normal in her ears.

'Stand by,' said David.

'Good afternoon, shoppers,' she began. 'In today's programme we bring you an exciting range of what's new around town. We've got brand-new summer knits in vibrant colours in the fashion stores, a uniquely blended line of carpet at the flooring shop and, as a special guest today, we've got the town's newest bookseller, Patrick Trimble, a man who'll tell you all about the author in town, Gary Lord, that Tarzan of the literary world, and much much more.'

So far, so good. Now it was time for David to play a track. Freda found herself crying all the way through Pat Boone singing 'Love Letters in the Sand'. She must pull herself together. David pushed the studio door open, which was against the station rules, once the programme had started.

'What is it?' he said. 'Is there something wrong?'

As if the poor fool was blind. 'I'm perfectly fine. Get back in that control room now or I'll have you dismissed. D'you hear me?'

It was a little station, so she didn't have a producer. All she was supposed to do was read the script, sound chirpy, and ask a few questions of enthusiastic retailers. She knew she had overstepped the mark.

The red light flicked on again. 'Stand by,' David said, his voice croaking with anxiety. Deep breaths. Now she had to talk for a few minutes about the surge of retail activity in the town. This was unbearable, the ugly face of her problem. When she had gone home at lunchtime to pick up her mail, there was the bank statement, the joint account she shared with her husband. Louis (Lou to others) had spent all their money again.

'What is it this time?' asked Evelyn, as she sat in her dressing gown rubbing cream on her face. There was something cold about the girl, the way she closed her dark eyebrows together when she frowned, and yet Freda loved her so much that it hurt.

Freda had placed her hand over the statement. 'Nothing for you to worry about.'

'It can't always be my father's fault,' Evelyn said.

But it was Lou's fault. A little cash here, a bit there, nothing you could point to and say what an extravagance, until you put it all together. Not even some special thing he could exult over. Freda had known money when she was young; it hurt not to have any now. More than that, it was painful to consider how he had spent the money and who had helped him part with it. That was at the heart of the matter.

Now there was time for a short news update, the weather forecast and a pre-recorded commercial. Ten minutes for Freda to weep uninterrupted. David's voice from the control room cut through her sobs, the awful heaving she couldn't seem to stop unless the red light was on.

'Your guest's here.'

For a moment she had forgotten what her interview was about. She looked at her notes. No, those were from her conversation last week with Ruth Hagley. Don't forget the sandwiches. Cucumber and thin ham, nice brown bread. Never mind the book, in this case it's an irrelevance. Ruth thought of herself as old but shrewd. Perhaps she was. The new bookseller came in, his hands clasped in front of his light grey suit. This was Patrick Trimble who, in the beginning, everyone said didn't have a show of getting his shop off the ground in opposition to Ruth. But, of course, he was proving them wrong.

When he sat down opposite Freda, the microphone poised between them, he folded her trembling hands in both of his own. 'My dear Mrs Messenger,' he said. 'What ever can the matter be? Let me get you a glass of water. No? Well, here, you must have this.' He took out a white folded handkerchief from his pocket and gave it to her.

'Forgive me,' she said, wiping her eyes. 'So unprofessional. There, it's nothing.'

'Grief is never over nothing,' he said.

'I know, but this isn't the place for it.'

'Surely it doesn't choose a time and place. Grief, I mean. Well, if it did,' he said, stumbling a little, and she could see what a shy and awkward man he really was, but that he had pleasant sad brown eyes, 'if it did, why then we would choose to be in some other place, some other life. But it's never like that.'

The light was on again. 'Stand by,' said David, in a low excited squeak, as if he were expecting his anticipated explosion to take place now, at this very moment. A relief from boredom. Freda could see how he hated his job, that he saw himself as a failure. A lot of things were suddenly clear to her, but most of all, that she would live through the next hour, she would advertise and enthuse and sell for her customers, just the way she always did, starting here with Patrick Trimble. 'Perhaps you would like to begin by telling me about this astonishing book that's taken the country by storm. You've read the book of course?'

'Of course,' he said, picking up his cue like a professional. In a minute he was talking in a light entertaining way and she knew, with a pang of pity for the woman on the south corner of the street, that his shop was going to do very well, and that she was pleased for him. She put on her dark glasses and leaned forward, nodding her head and letting him do the talking.

When the interview was over, he said, 'Let me take you to dinner. There's a group of us going down to the café at the lakefront this evening after Gary's been into the shop. Some good friends of mine are determined to cheer me up, because I've been down in the dumps too. Perhaps your husband would like to join us.'

She would like that, she told him, because she hardly ever went out in the evenings and was often on her own. No, she thought her husband might be 'doing business' this evening, but she would get a chance to see her daughter, Evelyn, because she was working at the Violet Café. Just a fill-in job, but the wages were quite good. She would be going on to better things soon.

'I understand,' Patrick said. 'I'd heard your daughter was a clever girl.' The young people leaving town for their education made him pine for his own university days, he explained, warming to his theme. That had been a long time ago.

'Everything was a long time ago,' Freda said, miserable again. 'Everything that mattered.'

THE BOOK PARTY

Jessie walked through the town with little curiosity at first, for she didn't intend to stay long. A red brick bank occupied one street corner. A young man wearing a suit emerged, his face merry, an attaché case in one hand, a football in the other, almost dancing as he descended the stairs. As soon as he hit the street, he drop-kicked the ball a short way and ran to catch it. A woman across the road waved to him and he hesitated and waved back. He looked up and down the street as if reminded of something or someone, almost as if he was being followed, then resumed his journey down the street in a quieter fashion, his expression thoughtful. Opposite the bank stood a milk bar. Girls in tight skirts and spiked heels leaned against dark-skinned youths in leather jackets. A youngish man in a suit, with a Bible in one hand, was offering them pamphlets. One of the swarthy boys took one and made a lazy paper dart that flickered momentarily above his head and fell at the feet of the preacher, who appeared not to notice this desecration of the Word.

Suddenly a commotion erupted as the town began to close down in the late afternoon. The noise Jessie heard issued forth from one of the town's bookshops. It looked as if a scrum had developed, the sort Jessie associated with the department store on sale day, people shoving and elbowing each other aside as if anxious they might miss the very last item. A huge banner hung from the bookshop roof, right down over the street. GARY LORD COMES TO TOWN — ALL WELCOME the sign read in three-foot letters. Gary, shouted voices. Over here, over here. A man with tousled hair and a roll-your-own cigarette hanging from his lip sat at a table in the centre of the mêlée, a young woman with large eyes clutching his arm or handfuls of air when he moved away. The man was signing books with such speed that once the signature had been received the recipient was ejected from the shop by the force of the crowd pushing forward to replace them in the queue. On the footpath, these people were forming a small throng, wondering what to do next. Then someone turned and began walking further along the street to what turned out to be the next bookshop. The others began to follow. Jessie could see from the street that the second shop was more or less deserted, except for a tall older woman, and another one of indeterminate age with pink cheeks and a flustered expression, who was fussing over food laid out on the counter. A short row of the famous author's books were lined up across a centre shelf in the window, between textbooks on the bottom shelf and some romantic novels with bright swooning covers on the top.

The book buyers from along the street bore down on the shop, clutching their parcels and talking at the top of their voices. Jessie followed them inside as they swept through the doors, hardly seeming to notice the proprietor or her assistant, and began attacking the sandwiches.

'What can I get you?' the older woman asked, in an unfriendly voice.

'Nothing,' said Jessie.

'I don't sell nothing,' the woman said.

'Mother, let it go,' said the other. 'I'll stay and help you clear up when they've finished.'

For hours, Jessie had been aching with hunger. She considered going into the milk bar and ordering a milkshake but decided against it. She wasn't afraid, she felt different. Her reflection followed her down the long mile of shop fronts. A man closing the doors of what appeared to be a sports goods and fishing tackle shop, turned and half whistled, a low sizzling sound between his teeth. His mouth was strong and curved, and his colouring was not unlike that of the young Maori men outside the milk bar, but a lighter shade of copper. He wasn't tall, but dapper in that chunky middle-aged way that happens to handsome men. He wore a brown hairy jacket, moleskin pants, a small hat tilted over his eye. She met his glance without meaning to, and saw the beginning of a smile. An older woman might have thought him vulnerable.

This was the man with whom Jessie fell briefly into conversation, the one who suggested that if she were looking for a bite to eat, she could do no better than the Violet Café, down another block and turn left.

Part Four

The Violet Café

1963–1964

THE WAITRESS

The café was situated in a white stucco and wood building on the edge of a lake. The address was Number 8, Lake Road. A green picket fence surrounded a garden of white daisies beneath a magnolia tree, its lemony-scented cups of bloom, speckled with recent rain, so perfectly formed that Jessie found them almost heart-rending. At the end of the path a black door with a brass knocker stood ajar. Jessie pushed it open because the sign outside and the smell of garlic promised food. At once, she found herself in a large L-shaped open space that seemed to be full of reflected light, for a part of the room was flanked by french doors that opened onto a verandah facing the lake. A woman sat behind a low reception desk, her head bent over a large reservations book.

She was an older woman, dressed in an impeccably tailored navy-blue linen dress that might have looked mannish had it not been for the drawn threadwork across her breast. There were no rings on her fingers but she wore a heavy silver bracelet on her right wrist and a square-faced watch on the left. The woman looked Jessie up and down, a slight contempt lurking in her cool blue gaze.

'I have no vacancies,' the woman said, before Jessie had a chance to speak. Her astonishing hair, the colour of a pale hydrangea head, was drawn up in a chignon, giving the effect of a halo of flowers or blue smoke. On the dark wooden bench stood a small sign bearing the name 'Violet Trench'.

It registered then with Jessie that she had passed another sign outside which read VACANCIES, APPLY WITHIN. She placed a tan leather suitcase on the floor beside her. Stamped with the words 'Warranted Bullockhide', it had brass clasps, white saddle stitching around the handle — it was the same one her mother had carried on both her honeymoons. She said; 'I haven't come about a job.'

At the far end of the café, a young man with slanted almond-shaped eyes, and wearing a striped apron tied over his impossibly slim hips, stood in front of an upright piano. He fingered the keys idly, nothing more than a line of scales. His gaze rested on Violet Trench and although he appeared very young, and she was not a young woman, there was a lurking heat about the way he looked at her. Jessie, glancing away from the woman's insistent eyes, saw that the whole café was white, broken only by stained wooden ceiling beams and the polished lacquered surfaces of a dozen or so tables, and chairs made of black wrought iron. The tables were laid with dark green place mats with raffish fringed edges, and modern stainless-steel cutlery. Alongside Violet Trench's name on its stand stood a small cut-glass vase containing a clutch of white violets, and straight away, Jessie thought, how clever, how unexpected. White violets, even though the woman herself was blue from head to foot, except for her fine lined skin and a hint of pale lipstick.

'I usually depend on word of mouth,' said the woman, and shrugged slightly, leaving it there.

'But it's early in the season,' said Jessie.

'I may have someone starting tomorrow. I should have taken the sign down earlier.'

'You could do worse than me,' Jessie said. 'I'm used to waiting on people.'

'Tables?'

'China department,' Jessie told her, naming the Wellington store.

'You can't eat china.'

'You like it though,' Jessie said. 'Nice china.'

The woman looked her over again, her eyebrows raised. Jessie almost turned away, seeing herself through her eyes. Five foot eleven, thin as a broom, with a flat chest. Her hands had always seemed disproportionately large, compared with her wrists and ankles, her skin pale beneath its mosaic of freckles. Although she wore her long hair pulled back from her face and clasped with combs on either side of her head, curly tendrils, the colour of gingerbread, escaped round her face. She wore a duffel coat over a red jersey and a pleated black and green skirt. Her legs were clad in red stockings, her feet in black buckled sandals.

'I don't take on complicated girls,' Violet Trench said. 'Not if I can help it. Let me look at your fingernails.'

Jessie laid her hands out on the counter. 'Clean enough?'

'Soft. This is hard work.'

Jessie straightened herself. What on earth was she thinking of? 'I didn't come about a job. I wanted something to eat. Although I thought this was a coffee bar.'

'We have a continental influence here — we serve meals. Anyway, we're fully booked.'

'Then who's taking Belle's place tonight?' The young man had abandoned the piano, and approached cat-like, to hover in a shadow just to the side of a slanting band of light.

For an instant Violet's composure seemed about to desert her. 'Oh, what's wrong with Belle tonight?' she asked on a long exhaled breath. 'No, don't tell me, I don't think I could stand to hear it again.'

The sky, which had seemed thin and watery when Jessie

was out on the street, was turning purple, a dangerous eerie light. Violet turned to Jessie. 'Ten shillings for the night. Cash. Don't tell me you're not interested — it will give you something to do for the evening, something to write down in your notebook. Oh, it's all right, I saw you for what you were as soon as you walked in: a poor university student on the lookout. Make some notes, write an essay about it — my night in the provinces, how quaint we all are. What did you say your name was?'

And when she told her, the woman looked pleased in a way Jessie couldn't read. John, the young man in the apron, took Jessie's suitcase as if she were a hostage.

'Give her something to eat,' Violet instructed him, and turned back to her reservations book as if there were nothing further to discuss.

'This is the kitchen,' John said. Pristine counters gleamed in two rows before her. A large pot simmered on the stove. On one side, the food preparation had begun, little mounds of uncooked ingredients stacked side by side in china bowls: potatoes pared of their skins, mushrooms with their spiny hearts gutted and open, staring at the ceiling with their one vacant eye, a satin-red capsicum and moss-like mounds of parsley and thyme. In a separate glass bowl she saw what looked like three lumps of coal covered in warts.

Gently touching one of these, John said, 'One of the rarest ingredients in the world, pity they're so ugly.' He lifted the lid of the pot. 'See this chicken, it's got morsels of them packed under its skin. We'll serve this chicken cooled a little as an entrée, with a touch of mayonnaise.'

'What are those things?'

'Truffles.'

'Where do they come from?'

He touched the side of his nose with his finger and gave a

little whinny of laughter. 'That's the secret. You'd have to ask the pigs. You don't know what I'm talking about, do you?'

It was true, of course, she didn't understand a thing. This sweet-looking funny young man, with his slightly bookish way of speaking, made no sense to her at all.

'Truffles are a type of little fungus that grows underground on the roots of oak trees. They smell very strong, like perfume I think, although you might disagree. The farmers use pigs to smell them out when they're ripe. You send a sow after them, and the smell of a black truffle is the same as that of a boar, so the sow goes on heat when she's looking for truffles, wondering where her lover is hiding.'

'So they're under just any old oak trees?' She did know about truffles. Third-year French, after you'd learnt the nouns and the grammar. There was no harm in having him on a little too.

'Oh no. Not at all.' He looked alarmed and evasive, as if he had given away far too much. 'Truffles come from France. Mrs Trench lived in France and Italy, so she has European ideas about cooking — not that the peasants round here have a clue. We have to cater for everyone in this backwater.'

'But you've got truffles all the same.'

'Tins,' he said, 'Mrs Trench's father was in tin canning. About the dishes — that's what Belle does, washes dishes — it's a complicated job. You have to have enough pans ready when we cook. It's not the plates that matter most, the customers can wait a few minutes but the cook must have four pans on the go at once, and soon you'll need even more. I'm in charge of the kitchen here.' He stopped, correcting himself. 'Hester and I, that is.' Jessie sensed reluctance, as if he would rather be in sole charge. 'I can't take it if there aren't enough pans. They're the top priority, you understand.'

'I understand.'

'Good, I can't cook without them. Will some scrambled eggs do?'

'Thank you,' she said. The sense of having been captured was growing stronger. He led her back into the restaurant, showing her a seat. Something filmy clung to him, the smell of garlic and a feeling of heat. Jessie had never been in love though she had thought of love's possibilities. Only, whenever she did, she thought of her mother and felt desolated. Her mother had once told her that she was not to worry if she didn't get married. You're clever, darling, that will see you through.

Jessie took the table beside the window John had taken her to, and gazed out at the darkening lake. While she waited for her food, she looked at a menu, even though she hadn't been offered one:

Soup of the day

Entrées

Foie de Volaille au Beurre
Chicken livers delicately sautéed in butter

Fritot de Cervelles
Fritters made of brains marinated in lemon juice,
cooked in a pale ale batter

Quiche au Crabe
A delicately flavoured crab quiche

Mains

Fish of the Day

Tournedos Henri IV
*Fillet steak served with sauce béarnaise, accompanied by French
fried potatoes and salad*

Escalopes à la Crème
*A melt-in-the-mouth veal fillet, served with cream
and flaming brandy*

Coq au Vin
*Violet especially recommends this classic chicken dish, made
with mushrooms and tiny onions.
We use only the finest cognac*

Desserts

Crème Brûlée
It speaks for itself, ours is incomparable

Tarte aux Framboises

*Please do not ask our waiting staff for wine.
Sadly, it is illegal to sell alcohol on these premises.
C'est Nouvelle Zélande.
Bon appétit.*

It seemed that one must be in the know to ask for truffles.

CHEFS

John had propped open the swing door between the kitchen and the dining room, so that he could see the girl. She was like an awkward gazelle, and he found himself liking her without knowing why.

From the moment he began working here, John felt he fitted into the Violet Café. He felt half in love with the woman who employed him, although he couldn't explain this to himself, didn't understand why he liked to be near her. It was important that he pleased her because she was the best thing that had happened to him so far. She treated him more like a business partner than her cook. The business had grown from two or three of them, including Hester, to a staff of six. There were days when he wondered whether Violet hadn't let the business become too big, because the girls who worked there were a lot to handle. But difficult rebellious girls were the kind Violet seemed to like having around her, as if she could mould them into something different.

And, looking out of the shadowy kitchen, he guessed that Jessie was about to be subjected to the same kind of makeover, although Violet would have been more inclined to describe it as a chance to make the best of herself. Something more than physical appearance, a remoulding of the spirit, as had happened to him when he came to work for Violet. Now that he'd been remade though, he'd begun to wonder whether all his life would be spent cooking at the Violet Café. He didn't want to admit to his sense of restlessness but, just lately, in the moments before sleep, a question had been flashing through his brain. What happens next?

She's too gullible, John thought, engulfed by a wave of tenderness for the girl with her pale face and freckles, her wrinkled tan hair. She needs someone to look after her.

This was the moment when Jessie might have got up and left, when she could have gone to the kitchen and demanded that her suitcase be handed over at once, and turned and gone back the way she had come. But already she knew that she didn't want to go back. It was the moment, too, for John to return with a dish of scrambled eggs, sprinkled with croutons, and a small yellow glazed bowl of salad. He placed a glass beside her plate and half-filled it with golden wine, poured from a china teapot. She felt a thrill, a frisson of something illegal. When he laid the food on the table, John's fingers looked like bamboo stems. The scrambled eggs were stained with some unidentifiable flecks, the texture of mushrooms. Each mouthful was accompanied by a scent, like nuts, or musk, perhaps like vanilla, or again, something darker and earthier, more like buried rubbish, which would have made her recoil had she not been so ravenous. She felt dreamy, as if she had been drugged. You heard of things happening to girls when they went travelling. Carefully she sipped the cold unaccustomed wine; it ran like a sweet riff beneath her breast bone.

'You like that?' asked John, hovering over her. Shouldn't he have been out in the kitchen?

'It tastes strange,' she said, 'not like scrambled eggs.'

'*Les truffaux*. They smell sexy, don't they?' His accent wasn't French, but not exactly Kiwi either. Each word was perfect, yet sly with long vowels, as if he were mimicking language itself.

'You mean I'm eating those black things?' Although of course she knew without asking.

He laughed, a high sound in the back of his throat. 'I fancy you,' he said. 'You'll die of love for me before the night's out. You need to get ready for work or you'll have Mrs Trench on your back. You always call her Mrs Trench. Always.'

As she stood, Jessie felt a wave of nausea and for a moment the room swam. It felt as if John was poking fun at her, yet she couldn't be sure.

Marianne and Evelyn, and Hester the other cook, arrived in that order, one by one. Jessie thought Marianne might be about her own age, with skin that appeared transparent and sharply etched cheekbones. She dug her hands into the pockets of a wide flowing black skirt with black and gold flowers embroidered all over it; she carried a bag slung casually over her shoulder, her chin slightly tilted.

'Right on time tonight, Marianne,' said Violet Trench, with a note of approval. Jessie supposed immediately that Marianne was her favourite — you could tell who the bosses liked. But Violet's pleasure contained a reproach as well. 'I do wish you'd get changed before you come.'

Marianne disappeared through a door and reappeared a few moments later, wearing a dark green waitress's dress, partly obscured by a green and white checked apron. She still looked beautiful, her waist tiny beneath her heavy breasts, her hips swaying in a way that struck Jessie as insolent.

Evelyn was already wearing her uniform when she arrived. This girl had such black hair that there was something almost swarthy about her. Her dark glittering eyes showed no sign of welcome. She acknowledged Violet by raising one eyebrow, so thick and straight it might have been a man's, as if she didn't really belong in this place.

The last to arrive — for the time being at least — was Hester, a woman of indeterminate age, although her moist face was youthful at first glance. She was the younger of the two women from the bookshop.

Hester bustled through the café, brushing her hair behind her ears, her face pink and fraught.

'Hester, meet Jessie, our new dish-washer.'

'Where's Belle?'

John shrugged. 'Vamoose. Who knows?'

Hester studied Jessie, a tired frown resting between her eyes. She gave no indication of having seen Jessie before, except for a puzzled flicker of recognition, but yet Jessie felt that in the space of an hour or two, she had moved into another world where she was already known and knew others. Hester spoke past Jessie, as if she wasn't there. 'Mrs Trench won't get rid of Belle that easily.'

'You could say mercy is in short supply,' said John and laughed, another of his curious high musical peals.

Hester looked pained, finally acknowledging Jessie's presence. 'You can wash dishes, can you? I mean, you have had experience?'

'Yes,' said Jessie.

'You have to polish everything, not just a rub and a swipe.'

'Plenty of clean pans,' Jessie said.

'Exactly.' Hester wiped her arm across her forehead, displaying a wet armpit. She seemed reassured.

'You'll have to roll up your sleeves,' said Marianne. Hester had immersed herself in a conversation with John, their heads bent over a list, John speaking rapidly, as they planned the specials for the night, and about something else that made them lower their voices. 'You do get your hands wet,' Marianne added. There was a touch of malice in the way she spoke, a sort of anticipatory glee as if she foresaw Jessie's downfall. Marianne and Evelyn adjusted their waitresses' uniforms and straightened their curved caps. In the café beyond, the sound of voices rose as people greeted one another and chairs were pulled back, then moved into place. The staff in the kitchen stood poised with an air of readiness. This was the moment Belle chose to come racing in the door, fair ponytail askew, her prominent blue eyes frantic. 'I'm sorry I'm late.' She threw her jacket over a hook.

Hester spoke to her with a mixture of relief and reproof. 'What are you doing here, Belle? I heard you were sick.'

'Who said?'

'Your mother,' John said.

Belle blinked rapidly. 'Why does she do this to me?'

'Because she thinks you shouldn't be here,' said Evelyn, who had hardly spoken a word to anyone. 'She doesn't think you should be down in the muck with people like us.' Her tone was sarcastic and mocking, as if she believed what she said, but not about herself.

'She thinks we might defile you,' Marianne said. 'Belle's a Christian, you know,' she added, for Jessie's benefit. 'She should pray for her job, don't you reckon?'

'No,' whispered Belle, 'she wouldn't do that to me.'

'I'll pray for you. Lord have mercy upon us,' Marianne cried, throwing herself into a dramatic swoon on the floor, one hand trailing across the bench above her. '*La belle dame sans merci.*'

Hester's hand flew up to cover her smile. 'Stop it all of you. The point being, who is going to do the dishes, Belle or Jessie?'

Violet's face appeared at the door. Marianne scrambled to her feet, less gracefully than she had fallen. 'I can hear you in the café,' Violet said. 'The first person who speaks another unnecessary word this evening can leave at once. I mean it. Hester, I thought you had more control over the staff.'

Hester flushed deeply. 'I'm sorry, Mrs Trench. Ma'am.'

The room had gone quiet; the tension in the air was so palpable it felt as if something would break. Violet's eyes settled on Jessie. 'The girl I was going to interview tomorrow can't come. I'll try you out as a waitress. If you drop anything in a customer's lap, I'll dock your pay.'

Jessie collected herself. This was her last employer's trick — a little intimidation, a threat, the prospect of a shattered treasure on the floor reaping punishment. Miss Early had called her clumsy so often that she had come to think it must be true. The atmosphere in the room deepened. Jessie guessed that if she said no, that she was leaving, they would all suffer Violet's wrath. Much later, when she believed that her life was entwined with that of Violet Trench, she would think these were acts of protection. In all the times she would recall that scene in her head, she never remembered a phone ringing, or someone coming into the café to speak to Violet. So she couldn't think how Violet might have received a message in those few frozen moments. But then in that dreamy haze, an evening spent somewhere between her appalled astonishment at her flight from home, and fascination with her new surroundings, anything could have happened. She would learn, through something like osmosis, the way Violet held young women in the palm of her hand, and the power she had to make a difference in their lives.

For a moment, Belle's desperation, as she stood quivering beside the bench, infected everyone in the kitchen.

'I guess experience costs,' Jessie said.

She did, she told herself, have a brand-new life.

'Give her a uniform, Hester, if you've got one long enough, and a cap,' Violet said, when barely a beat had passed between her and Jessie. 'As for you, Marianne, you're behaving like a child. Get out there and take some orders. You're on a last warning.' She turned and walked back into the café. Belle tipped soap flakes into a stream of running water.

Hester took a uniform from a folded pile at the end of the bench and threw it to Jessie. 'We've got a table for eight coming, they'll all want their orders served at once. Marianne and Evelyn will take those — you can do the small orders. We've got a special guest coming tonight. He's a friend of Mrs Trench, her oldest friend in the world. It's his eighty-fifth birthday. He has a seat by the window overlooking the lake, the one you were sitting at when I came in. He's patient, he won't mind if you take a little while. All the same, everything must be done exactly right.'

Evelyn reappeared from the café. 'I don't want to do table six,' she said to Hester.

'Neither do I,' said Marianne at almost the identical moment, holding a sheaf of dockets from her first orders.

'Why?' said Hester.

'My father's out there.' Evelyn's enigmatic face faltered for the first time.

'Well, what's wrong with that?' snapped Hester. 'He's usually here.'

'You don't understand,' Evelyn said in a hopeless way.

'Poor Evelyn, always misunderstood,' Marianne said, almost too softly to be heard.

'But my mother's out there too, at table nine.'

'Girls,' said Hester, 'haven't you had enough warnings for one night? You'll go where you're told.'

'God's truth,' said Marianne.

Belle said then that Marianne shouldn't talk about God like that. Now that she was elbows deep in suds she seemed to have recovered. Her prominent eyes had acquired confidence since Violet's intervention. Out in the café, the noise level was rising. Marianne offered Evelyn an awkward hug, as if to say she was sorry.

104

AUTHORS

Outside, dark had fallen, blotting out all but a shimmer over the lake; inside, creamy lamps had been switched on. The café was full of humming life; to Jessie it looked like the set of a movie, full of people in a foreign place where everyone on the set spoke the language, but those off stage could only stand and watch.

'Could you start taking orders?' Marianne said urgently. 'Is that woman off her head?' Referring to Violet Trench. 'You don't have a clue, do you, Jessie? Did Hester tell you the specials?'

'She said there was a special guest.'

'No, the special dishes, you idiot.'

So Marianne had to stop then and show her how you took orders in turn from each person, not mixing up the dockets, so that the food flowed back to them in the order they had asked for it. Jessie found herself beside a table, notebook in hand, reciting the soup of the day, French onion, and our fish is terakihi, cooked very lightly with a delicate lemon sauce, our special tonight is grilled lamb with a Turkish sauce made from onions, tomatoes, capsicum and pine nuts blended with wine. How chic it sounded, she would remember. And for those of discernment, there was chicken with truffles, *poularde de truffée*. Marianne made her say it two or three times over and seemed pleased with her efforts. 'I've never seen a real French menu before,' Jessie said.

'An adaptation of the classics, I suspect,' Marianne said dryly. 'You've learned French, have you?'

'Just at school.'

'Same here. Not that the French understand me.'

'You've been to France?'

'Not likely. The French come here sometimes when they're visiting. As you know, this town gets a lot of visitors. Now, about the wine. People might ask for it. You ask them if they want a cup of tea, and if they say yes right away, you go out and ask her ladyship if they can have one. If they seem surprised and ask why a cup of tea when they've asked for wine, tell them straight — we don't serve it, we keep the law. You understand?'

'I think so. But if it's a Frenchman, mightn't he be surprised?'

'Ah well, that's different. You still ask Mrs Trench. I promise you'll get to know which is which.'

Jessie saw that Marianne had taken table six, after all, and that the man sitting there was the man who had spoken to her in the street. Evelyn's father. He winked when he saw Jessie, and grinned. His companions were a couple of men in their thirties and forties perhaps. A business dinner of some kind, Jessie guessed from words overheard. Marianne moved forward. 'What would you like, sir?' she asked, and he laughed. The men with Lou Messenger were not bushmen or farmers, but outdoors kind of men all the same, with smooth tanned complexions. They wore suede ties with coloured shirts and, out in the kitchen, Marianne said it was a business celebration, a good sale their company had just made. Hadn't Evelyn been told about the sale?

'It's not what I'd heard,' Evelyn said. 'Ask my mother.' Her voice was full of a startling bitterness. 'Tell the new girl to tell her.' Jessie overheard this in a snatch as she whisked away another plate in the rising heat of the kitchen, and shivered. A quick wink didn't go unnoticed in this place.

'Don't, Evie,' said Marianne, as if they knew each other better than they were letting on.

Jessie had, in fact, been delegated to the table where Evelyn's mother was sitting, because Evelyn wouldn't serve her and her assembly of surprising friends either. Evelyn seemed to be the one who got away with things.

Jessie tried to think of the menu as if it were a poem, or the law of torts, but found herself tripping on the *poularde de truffée,* because the author was playing with his spoon, banging it on the side of his water glass. It made her think of Grant and Belinda and Janice, so much so that she almost stopped. Evelyn's mother, whose name was Freda, stared at her in an intense kind of way as if willing her to get to the end. Jessie thought that this might be a job lived on the edge of desperation. Even so, at the end of her performance, the author slow-clapped.

Violet was there in an instant. 'There's a pie cart at the end of the road if you'd rather.'

'Oh please,' said Freda. Her eyes darted over to table six, but her husband didn't seem to be paying any attention.

Violet straightened her shoulders. 'You did well, Jessie,' she said, before she moved off.

Alongside Freda there was an odd assortment of men wearing cravats at the throat of their white shirts, smoking cigarettes in gold-patterned holders, a woman with an overloud laugh and bright lipstick who had come along because there was nothing in the fridge at home, a sallow youth with red-rimmed eyes, as well as the famous author in his checked shirt with the sleeves rolled up, and the frail-looking woman with big eyes and hollow cheeks. At Violet's insistence, the famous author had taken off his hat and put it at his feet. He said he'd like a beer — any chance of a beer?

'Would you like a pot of tea?' Jessie asked.

'Tea, for Chrissake, I don't want tea.'

'I think she means *tea*, you know, *tea*,' said his girlfriend. 'I think I'd like a cup of *tea*.'

It was like a complicated dance, waiting on tables in that crowded room. Marianne did it best, gliding among the tables with a feline grace, looking as if she was enjoying herself. Her broad shoulders bent again and again over the tables, delivering food with an accomplished ease. In the kitchen hardly anyone spoke to one another, although thighs touched and brushed as the chefs concentrated at the stove, and the waitresses flung the dockets on the spikes overhead. Once, later in the evening, Belle got in Evelyn's way as she dashed over to John with a sauce pot, causing a minor collision. Evelyn's dessert order, a *Crème Brûlée* wearing an exquisite net of spun sugar, teetered in mid-air before she saved it with a flick of her wrist. Evelyn turned a glower of rage upon Belle, and then shrugged her shoulders as if she was beneath her contempt.

Now that the café was almost full, Violet promenaded among her guests, dispensing a charming word here, or a cool stare where it suited her. For a while she stopped beside a heavy-set man with closely cropped greying hair, and his wife, a thin woman whose face was drawn into a pale mask, her hair pulled back tightly in a chignon.

'This is Dr and Mrs Adam, Jessie,' said Violet, although Jessie heard her call them Felix and Pauline. 'I want you to take care of them. I'm sorry the crowd is a bit noisy in here,' she said, appearing to refer to Lou and his friends, as well as the famous author and his companion. 'How do I begin to explain my restaurant to people who want fish and chips and a beer?'

'You don't allow them in,' said Mrs Adam.

'It's not always as simple as that,' said Violet. She glanced at her watch as if she was expecting someone. 'The doctor and his wife have travelled a great deal,' Violet told Jessie, as she leant over to clear their soup plates. As if that explained everything, and Jessie would instantly see the good breeding and aura of fine dining that surrounded them.

'So why don't you introduce us to your friends?' Lou called out loudly across the room to his wife. 'Your mate and I are in the same business.'

'Excuse me,' said Violet, getting to her feet. 'Lou, that's enough.'

'I'm in the hunting and fishing business,' Lou said, addressing the author.

'You are?' said Gary, a look of interest lighting up his face for the first time. Freda was holding a napkin to her bloodless lips.

'You can't do this,' Violet said. 'Stop it, Lou.'

'You telling me I can't talk to my own wife?'

'Not across my restaurant, you don't. A restaurant is not a place where people call out from one table to another. You know better than that.'

'Oh, is that so?'

'Lou, please,' said Freda.

Lou dropped his eyes. 'What a farce,' he muttered, and turned back to his friends as if nothing had happened.

The hush that had fallen for a few moments lifted and everyone carried on as before. Pauline Adam suggested to her husband that perhaps it was time they went home, but he said, not yet, not just yet, as if something else might happen.

Felix's eyes followed Violet.

Felix Adam was probably the only person in town who knew the year Violet Trench was born: 1907. April 12, to be exact. Doctors are able to find out that sort of information and, like priests, they can never tell. His wife, Pauline, had said to him more than once, that absurd blue she rinses her hair, it looks as if she's been in grandma's washing tub. Somebody should tell her. But Pauline, thin as a rake and as spiky, couldn't see how truly handsome Violet was, how utterly sensuous and appealing. Well why should she, and would he want her to? Not at all. He would like to bed Violet Trench. This private admission was shocking in itself, not what doctors were supposed to think about their patients. Felix did know she had had a child once, a girl she hadn't seen for nearly thirty years. This fact of child-bearing was something she couldn't hide from him at the time of his first examination. But it irritated him to think that, for all his position of privilege, there was so much more to know. He couldn't understand, for instance, the odd sad parade of girls, mostly end-of-war babies, whom she employed in her café. He mentally examined his files:

Hester Hagley d.o.b. 19 September 1935 (the exception)

Mother in advanced menopause at time of her birth, nervous temperament. Prescribe salts for blushing. To be married. Virgin. Hymen may require surgical intervention if coitus to be achieved.

Belle Hunter d.o.b. 5 June 1946

Girl in generally good health, annual tonsillitis. Early maturation, precocious development with sexual activity. Contraception supplied at mother's request. Police matter? Better not.

Evelyn Messenger d.o.b. 12 December 1945

Bright hard-working girl. Anaemia, suffers from depression and severe mood swings, may improve when she leaves home. Mother very exacting. Father periodically treated for gonorrhoea.

Marianne Lindsey d.o.b. 23 November 1945

Claims dysmenorrhoea, probably psychological. Showed up in surgery on a Friday night with pimple on her lip. The vanity of the girl. Gave her a good talking to, bothering me when I was about to go skiing for weekend. Mother came in on Monday morning with girl in tow, face blown up like a balloon with an abscess. Incorrect diagnosis? Very difficult to tell with flighty badly behaved girl like this. Mother took her to Rowe [his opposition, at the other end of town], said she'd complain to Medical Council. Woman's a tramp, make note to Medical Council to warn them of ill-informed outburst. Not seen either of them in months, and good riddance.

'And where are you from, girl?' he said to Jessie, as his wife grudgingly ordered dessert.

'Tipperary,' said Jessie. Just the sort of thing she'd always wanted to say to customers in the china department. Or her tutor in torts for that matter. That's me done, she thought, preparing to take off her apron, and found herself grinning.

She was saved by the appearance of a very old man, entering the café with the aid of a stick.

THE SPECIAL GUEST

Violet escorted the special guest to the reserved table by the window and helped him take off his black beret and raincoat, before he sat down. His face was beak-like, his teeth yellow; he smelt gently but not unpleasantly of unfiltered De Reszke cigarettes. Beneath his coat he was wearing an old carefully brushed hound's-tooth jacket with a hint of red in its chequers. Jessie saw the strings of his hearing aids around his neck, connected to the little pink enamel blocks behind his ears. His hands were bent and weathered, fingers knotted around the joints. He and Violet talked for a while, until she had to go to the desk and turn away latecomers who didn't have reservations. Violet took one of Hugo's hands in hers and studied a bruise. The light from a passing boat flared and was gone. She released his hand. 'Happy birthday, dear Hugo,' she said as she rose. 'Jessie, tell John that Hugo is ready for his dinner. I'll be back soon, when table twelve's guests have paid their bill.'

'You're new here, aren't you?' said the old man.

'It's my first night,' Jessie said.

'Ah well, then, sit down and tell me about yourself.'

'But won't I get into trouble?'

'Of course you won't. It's my birthday, and Mrs Trench will let us do what we like. Besides, John will bring me my dinner soon. Now tell me your name.'

When they had introduced themselves to one another, he said, 'So what brought you to the Violet Café?'

'I'm just travelling, really,' Jessie said.

'Oh travel. It's a great thing. I've travelled from one side of the world to the other, but when I got here I stopped. By the time I had the money I was really too old for that sort of thing. Now tell me, where do you want to go?'

'To China,' said Jessie, off the top of her head.

Hugo blinked rapidly, and peered at her, as if to discern something behind her words.

'My mother had a friend who went to China,' she explained.

'Oh, I see. Well then, so you should go to China. I would have liked to have gone there more than anything else in the world. I'd have liked to have seen the Yellow Mountain. I have a dream of it here in my head. A place of infinite beauty. But closed now to people like us. You'll have to think of somewhere else to go in the meantime, perhaps.'

This was the moment when Hugo's meal arrived, and Jessie, seeing that there were tables to be cleared, got to her feet. The food John brought was not on the menu. He placed before Violet's friend duck cooked the Oriental way, slick with sauce, sprinkled with spring onions, and accompanied by a small bowl of rice, and chopsticks. As if this was the most natural thing in the world, and in spite of people who stared at him as he ate Asian-style, Jessie saw the way Hugo enjoyed himself, chewing in an old man's ruminative way. When finished he wiped his mouth carefully and placed his folded napkin beside his plate.

Felix watched the old man with dislike. He was sure that Hugo knew more about Violet than he did. He was Felix's patient, but the boy in the kitchen, a mongrel kid, as he thought of him, had come between them. His birth that had gone unregistered for some years. Surprising, for the father was meticulous in most things. He had switched his boys to Rowe, too, as if he didn't trust Felix. And yet Hugo had stayed with him; Felix knew his asthma, his arthritis, his prostate problems and his in-growing toenails, but still there was so much he would like to have asked him, and most of it concerned Violet Trench.

'Violet,' Hugo said. There was something he had to say to her, before it was too late. But Violet was busy, one minute out the back scolding, the next charming the doctor. Hugo saw the electricity running between them, wondered how she would get Felix for herself, because it was clear that that was what she wanted, and it grieved him. Then, in the next instant, she was back chatting with Lou Messenger. He'd known Lou since he was just a kid who came on holidays to the big brick house round the bay. The Messengers were high fliers. Upper class, or that's how his lawyer father would like them to be seen. No, not quite right. Upper middle class, perhaps. Funny how it was all coming back now, the old shibboleths of his childhood. He'd thought it was all vanished, all gone long ago when he married the woman from Yellow Mountain. Lou Messenger, for the hot months of the year, was the boy next door, with an endless insouciance about him. He wanted more than anything to build a boat of his own. His mother, a bridge-playing woman with a laugh like a clatter of pans, thought the idea was ridiculous, when they already owned a launch. We'll help you build a boat, he'd told the boy, I'm sure we can find a plan. You can set it up in our backyard. He was fond of the boy, liked the way he joined in, didn't seem to notice people's complexions. His own was dark, anyway, his father a man with tight skin and a blue-ish mouth, perhaps Indian in his origins, although he kept that to himself. He was fluent in several languages, sometimes breaking off in mid-sentence and launching into French. The lawyer spent those summer months in a hammock under the trees, endlessly smoking and reading, and pacing up and down at night. And then his wife had died, and so had his own, his second great loss. His dear wife Ming.

He hears her. She is describing a river that widens between its banks, a river so slow that it might almost be a pond or a lake. The bare earth of the banks is a light yellow clay. All around are trees with feathery branches that trail down towards the water, reflected there. Between the leaves the sky is relentlessly blue. Something distinguishes this natural scene, this composition of water, light, foliage and sky — a scarlet bridge that spans the river. It has horizontal sidings, so that it looks like a red cage. There is a girl on the bridge, as she tells it, carrying a basket of ducks.

'See,' she says, 'that is me. That is my young life that you never knew.'

Now the girl has moved away.

But the red bridge is still there.

'Ex-*cuse* me,' the author's girlfriend said. 'Are we going to get a pot of *tea* tonight or not?'

'I'll have to ask,' Jessie said.

'I'm sorry, madam,' said Violet in an icy voice, at Jessie's shoulder, 'but we're not serving any more tea tonight.'

The author had eaten his dinner very quickly, while the others dawdled over their food, although Freda didn't seem to want her meal, and pushed it around her plate.

'Is your meal satisfactory, Mrs Messenger?' Violet asked.

'Very nice, thank you.' Her voice was almost drowned out by the laughter at table six.

'Our chefs are having a busy night. I hope you'll speak well of your meal here, next time you go to air.'

'Truly, it's excellent,' said Freda.

'It's been a bit of a rush for Hester today, she had to help her mother out this afternoon.'

'I know,' said Freda miserably. Jessie didn't understand why Violet was holding her customer to account for the fiasco at the bookshop, but clearly she was.

The bookseller said, 'Really, Mrs Trench, this is a business matter.' He was beginning to look tetchy and tired, as if the evening had been a mistake.

'I reckon it's about time we shot through, mate,' the author said to the bookseller. 'All very nice, but where does a joker get a good feed round here?'

The bookseller and Freda stood up and shook hands with the author, and agreed that they should go too. Everyone at the table decided to leave, except the skinny youth who had been sitting beside Freda. It was as if he could now declare himself, show that he wasn't really part of the group. On the way out, Freda said goodnight to Evelyn, while the author offered Violet his autograph, and seemed puzzled when she said no, but thank you.

'Bit haughty,' he said to his girlfriend, loudly enough for everyone to hear.

'Violet,' Hugo said. Or he thought he did, but perhaps he hadn't made a sound. Violet, who had changed his life, who had brought him another son, and, later, riches. It was hard to believe, looking back, that he and Ming had ended up wealthy, not that they let it show. All that produce, all the fruit and vegetables, the harvests they reaped. They were richer than Louis Messenger's father, an unhappy man who made bad choices in love. He wished, for Ming's sake, that Tao had gone away to university, but some things were not meant to happen.

'You were right not to stay with me,' said this voice that didn't seem to be speaking out loud, this floating apparition of words in his head. He could hear the words, felt them formulating in his mouth, it was just that somehow his jaw had gone rigid. It was a pity children had to grow up. So many children he'd known. Violet was the first of them. She'd grown up and gone away.

She stopped by his table. 'All right, Hugo?'

'But you came back,' he said and was pleased to have uttered this thought.

'Soon,' she said, 'I've got a few more things to do, and I'll be back.'

All those boys, she had said to him. He wished they were all here, but the restaurant wasn't their style. He'd like to make a speech for his birthday and tell them how happy they'd made him. How he wished all happiness for them. How they should honour the memory of their mother who had gone through great trials and hardship to give them a good life. But they knew that anyway, even the odd one for whom the brothers had found a wife, and who had children of his own. Perhaps it was as well that he couldn't get the words out to say anything now, to this assembled group of people. He would like to tell Lou that he was a good boy before the war, and where to look for his boat, the one thing he'd built with his own hands before he went away to war, and come back and got married in a rush, and became a puller of sharp tricks ever since, a poor man parading as rich. He wanted to tell John that his search wasn't over, that he had farther to go in the world than this. Even though this, this café, was a place that he loved, where some of his money had settled. Perhaps they knew this, perhaps they understood. Better not to go on about it now. Once he started, he had the feeling that the words would come out in a steady gush, like vomiting, something indescribably embarrassing for everyone there. Jessie, the new girl, hesitated by his table. She was a big uncertain person, a little untidy in her movements, yet resolute in the way she had tackled the evening's work.

'Tell her to come now,' he said to Jessie. 'Violet. Now is the time to come back.' At least, he thought he said that, but he couldn't be sure, because the girl's face didn't register anything, except a look of passing concern.

'How about some music?' called Lou in a loud voice from across the room. 'Where's the piano player?'

'We shot him,' said Marianne.

'Marianne, that's enough,' said Violet. 'Our last musician proved unsuitable.'

'You mean he hit the piss,' said Lou.

'Stop it, Dad,' said Evelyn, entering this conversation uninvited.

'What about John? John could give us a tune.' Lou looked like a delighted boy in his sudden quest for music.

'He can't play and cook at the same time,' Violet snapped. 'No more to drink, Lou, that's my last word.'

'Me, drink? Oh ma'am, you don't serve drinks here, do you?'

'I'm telling you, I'll send you home.'

'You'd throw me out, Violet?' In spite of his quick fury, he had quietened down. He glanced sideways at his daughter, who had moved on, her eyes straight ahead, her mouth set.

'I would if I had to,' Violet said. 'I should have done it when Freda was here.'

'No you wouldn't.' His smile had grown impudent again.

'I'll play a tune for you if you want,' said the skinny youth who had stayed behind. He had already seated himself at the piano.

He played 'Happy Birthday' and Marianne started the singing off. They sang *Happy birthday to you/happy birthday to you/ happy bi-irthdaaay dear Hu-go/happy birthday to you,* Marianne using a high girlish lisp because she'd heard about the way Marilyn Monroe had sung this to President Kennedy, and everyone in the café laughed and gave her a round of applause and joined in, except Jessie who thought bloody birthdays, there's too much made of them, and that she'd had more than enough birthdays to last her a lifetime. Not that she wanted to be dead, she just wanted to be happy.

'His name's David,' said Evelyn, who had learnt this from her mother, as she was leaving.

David Finke kept on playing. He started into a new tune, singing a few words of the melody, a melancholy thread of a song about violets that went on growing, even when it was snowing.

Violet looked up, with a startled expression. 'Where did you learn that?'

David answered her without pausing as he pursued the melody. 'My mother used to play it.'

Violet tapped her finger in time to the music, as Lou led a round of clapping, and even Felix Adam nodded his head approvingly.

'You're the boy from the radio station, aren't you?' Violet said. 'Do you want an evening job?'

'We could do with a piano player,' John said.

'Sure,' said David, 'yeah, I'd like that.'

Evelyn looked pleased, as if her mother had redeemed herself for the moment.

At some point, near the end of the meal, when the staff had gone back to the kitchen, and the diners were pushing back their chairs and looking for scarves and handbags, and Felix and his wife had already sauntered out into the night, Hugo seemed to sigh, and folded his hands in front of him. His head slipped slowly forward onto the table, his thin wisps of hair floating on the plate.

'I think he's dead,' Jessie told Violet Trench shortly afterwards, for Jessie had learnt first aid as well as French at

119

Wellington Girls', and she could see that it was impossible to revive him, even though, with the café cleared of its customers, she worked on him, breathing in and out of his old tobacco-stained saucy mouth until there was nothing more to be done and the ambulance came and took him away.

'My father. My father,' said John in a scarcely audible voice.

This was how Jessie spent her first evening away from home, listening to uncomprehending sounds of grief, helping to close down the restaurant under Violet Trench's stony instructions, and rinsing her mouth out with cold water at the basin. At roughly the same time her mother at last found the note she had left on her pillow back home in Island Bay in Wellington, and commenced her descent into illness.

Just before the ambulance driver drew a grey blanket over Hugo's face, Violet placed two fingers on his cooling face. She said, 'I hope he's hearing all the music in the world.'

You wouldn't believe how blue the lakes are here. Mum, I'm sorry I'm not coming home at the moment, but the woman I work for is very strict about time off. Don't worry about my legal studies mark — you knew I wouldn't get a pass because I wasn't there to sit the exam.

Love, Jessie

'You can't leave now,' Violet Trench said the day after Hugo died.

At first, Jessie didn't see why not. It was not as if she was going to the funeral and there was nothing more the police or the doctors wanted to know. Just a huge aneurism and the old man was dead and it was nothing at all to do with her. And yet something made her feel she couldn't leave, that somehow she was connected to the Violet Café. When Violet Trench asked her to stay on she said yes. There was a spare bed at the place where Marianne stayed.

Dearest Jessie,

I am glad you are well and safe. I must say it was a shock when you left but I know what a strain you've been under with your study. Nothing matters to me except that you are all right and there will be another year and you can change your courses. I can see now that you've got too much imagination for the law. Perhaps you'll be a famous writer like my mother's friend, that woman who went abroad, only one with a happier ending. It feels as if you're overseas now. We can talk about it all at Christmas time, which isn't far off.

Your loving Mother

VIOLET

Violet shopped early in the mornings for her supplies. First she bought the meat. She had been going to the same butcher ever since she opened the Violet Café. His name was Shorty Toft, or that's the name she knew him by, though there was a rumour that his real name was Nigel, and his window sign read N. Toft so perhaps it was true. He didn't look like a Nigel. The shop was painted red. It had been a scandal in town when he first put his bright colour on it, but then someone painted one of the hotels pink, and nobody noticed any more. Violet thought it showed a touch of innovation. She liked the cut of his meat, the way he trimmed back the fat, and how he could focus on the sweetest nut of a fillet, and the absolutely straight cut of a pork chop, so that that most difficult of meats could be cooked evenly. Shorty was not the dwarf the name implied. As he explained to Violet, he had been the youngest of three sons, and of course he was always the shortest of the family until all the brothers were fully grown, so that's what he was labelled by his dad, and he expected he'd take the name to his grave. She called him Shorty, he called her Mrs Trench to her face, and Madam behind her back, like most of the other shopkeepers in town. All the same, they had a line of banter touching on the ribald now and then.

'I'll give you a bit of meat all right,' he said, regular as the town clock on the mock-Tudor post office, with just a little emphasis on the word meat, but not enough to cause offence. She was one of his best customers.

'No tripe,' she said, when she was in a particularly good mood.

'I'm not a man to mince matters,' Shorty would say, when she asked him about his chilblains, which were cruel in the winters, his greasy fingers like pink cheerio sausages. The town had always been known for the heaviness of its frosts, and days of black ice, hard on people who must work in the cold. 'They're killing me.' But then he would laugh, a rough cheerful bark intended to tell her that life was never as bad as people made out. He was a widower, and that had been a pretty cruel cut, he told her one morning, rubbing the back of his arm across his face. Then he had straightened his back, and acted as if he'd just had an itch on his hairline.

Once a week, when Violet had finished at Shorty's shop, she drove her blue Volkswagen out into the country to the market gardens, where she was known. She and her cook John Wing Lee, who lived near the gardens with his family, worked out with his brother Chun, who was also known as Harry, and the other gardeners the quantities of fruit and vegetables in season that she would need. This was the special pleasure of her work, knowing that everything served in her restaurant was made from the very best and freshest products available.

'You drive carefully now, Mrs Trench,' Shorty said every Wednesday, which was her day for going to the gardens. Those days, he showed her out of the shop, as if to emphasise the care he expected her to exercise on her journey.

It was hard to know what to make of the new girl, Jessie Sandle, who sat at one of the tables in the afternoon sun, writing a letter. As a rule, Violet wouldn't let the girls sprawl around the place when they weren't working, but this one had come in and asked her in a polite way if she could just sit down for half an hour and get a letter off to her mother. It was on the tip of Violet's tongue to tell her to go to the library, but there was nobody about, and she guessed the girl hadn't got any space to call her own.

Violet looked at the girl, pen poised over her pad, a frown between her eyes, as if by sitting there and looking out over the water, she could work out what was troubling her. Not that Violet had any difficulty seeing what it was — an overpossessive mother somewhere in the background, she'd be bound. She sighed to herself. Jessie had that pinched look that nothing but sex would cure, and she was plain. They worried her, these young women she employed. One day they'd be up, another down, one would have her period and make all the excuses in the world not to work, as if she, Violet Trench, had never suffered women's ills. And then there'd be fallings out, and they wouldn't want to work in the same space. She'd made it a rule, right from the beginning: take the job or leave it, and do it my way. In the end, it was the best thing she could do for them, she'd decided. These girls came from the school of hard knocks and there would be plenty more problems out there waiting for them. Either they could learn to deal with the world and its gin traps or go under. None of them would thank her in the long run if she let them make excuses for themselves.

The girl leant over the pad and began to write again, a tear sliding down her thin cheek. That was the moment that John came in, and Violet saw right away how his eyes rested on Jessie. And she saw something else, that from where he stood, the girl wasn't so plain. Her frizzy hair was pulled up on the top of her head, and caught in a band, exposing her neck. The blouse Jessie wore was familiar, she'd seen it on Marianne, and although Jessie was taller by nearly a head, the garment was too big for her, sliding down to reveal her shoulder. Violet was reminded of one of Constable's rare figure paintings, the nape of a girl's neck, so sexy and vulnerable, so pale and faintly marked with downy hair, that you instantly wanted to reach out and stroke it.

John's eyes were fastened on the beautiful neck, and Violet thought, well, it wouldn't be such a bad thing. It could be worse.

When Jessie looked back, she would wonder why she hadn't simply left home and got a bedsit of her own, like the clever carefree girls she'd met in Wellington. Much further on in her life, she would conclude that she had stayed home for as long as she had because of an outraged sense of pity for her mother, and that she had left because she was eighteen and the thought of enduring pity, for herself and anyone else, was unbearable. Yet even on the bus going north, the day that she'd left, she had begun to regret the impulse that had brought her to this point of running away. Already, she missed the odd erratic loving mother who had transported her from one rooming house to another until they found sanctuary under Jock Pawson's roof. She sometimes believed she could remember whole conversations and stories that she had been told by her mother when she was a very young child, pushed against the wind in her pram, shopping bags flapping from the handle. Now when she thought about her mother, she found it hard to recall her face, as if some trick of memory had erased it and left nothing but her voice.

Dear Mum,

I wonder if you could send me some of my summer clothes. It looks as if I'm going to be here a bit longer. The postal note is to cover postage. The pay's not great but there's plenty of overtime. I should get some money saved up for next year.

Love, Jessie

For what next year, she wondered, as she wrote the Wellington address on the envelope and patched a stamp in the corner.

The house where Marianne had a room and a share of the bathroom, so long as she didn't take a shower more than every second day, was down a side street between the main street and the swimming baths. The carpet crawled with floribunda roses.

The night Hugo died, Marianne had said to Jessie, 'Well, you have to stay somewhere. There's a spare bed in the room where I stay.'

'I thought there might have been a Y somewhere, like in Wellington.'

Marianne had snorted through her finely flared nose. 'Young Women's Christian Association. You won't find that around here. Unless you want to go home to Belle's, which is a Christian association I'd be inclined to give a miss.'

The beds in the room they shared were covered by pink candlewick bedspreads with crisp worn tufts. The mattresses dipped in the centre when the beds were tightly made up. If Jessie and Marianne were to reach out their hands from their beds at the same time, their fingers would meet in the middle of the room. Not that they did this.

Three mornings a week, Marianne got up early and went out. She said she was doing some modelling work on the side. The assignments were a secret. All she would say is that it got damned cold out there in the dew, and that she was going to leave town as soon as she'd got some money together. If Violet found out she was leaving, she might give her the sack.

'Where will you go?' Jessie asked.

'I'd like to go on the stage, get some training in drama, if I can find someone to teach me. I was Columbine in the school play, and I brought the house down. You should do something about yourself, Jessie. You're really quite attractive.'

In the mornings, after Marianne had gone, Jessie tidied up the piles of clothing lying on the floor and used the Hoover the landlady left in the passage to vacuum up loose threads and face powder and hair clips that Marianne had left lying around, and wiped down the surface of the dressing table with a damp rag. It reminded her of home.

'Well, that's something,' the landlady said, watching her out of the corner of her eye one morning, when she replaced the Hoover. 'You should have seen the pigsty they made of the sitting room.'

Jessie didn't know who the landlady was talking about. There were two other boarders in the house, David Finke, the young man from the radio station, and Kevin who was the pay clerk in the Forestry Department. Kevin was a stubby middle-aged man with puffy cheeks. He was engaged to be married, and soon, thank God, he would be transferred away. Kevin used the sitting room nowadays, and Marianne not at all.

'It's a bit amusing,' the landlady said, watching Jessie at work with the Hoover, 'her going off to clean up someone else's mess, while you clean up hers. At least she gets paid.'

'But, I thought ...' Jessie began, and then stopped. The modelling was a secret.

'This is a quality house,' the landlady said, 'there'll be no more shenanigans.' So something had happened here, but Jessie didn't know what it was, didn't think it would be right to ask. She sensed Marianne's relief when she came back to the order she had created.

The house where Hester and Ruth lived spoke of faded affluence and charm, a bungalow with a Spanish Mission influence, its walls clad with white stucco. Although the garden was more or less abandoned, there were outlines of scattered vegetable garden plots, and late grape hyacinths sheltering beneath overgrown hedges. Inside the house, dark brown curtains with braided fringes almost covered the windows, creating constant dimness. The lampshades were strung with crystal beads, and their dull pumpkin light glimmered on round inlaid and brass tables from the East. A servery hatch divided the kitchen from the dining room and alongside it stood a tea wagon. Hester worked at her sewing on the oak dining-room table, with its barley-twist legs. Each day before she began, she laid a heavy felt overlay on the table to protect its surface.

Her fiancé, Owen, came in from the farm where he worked, which grazed a bit of livestock for slaughter, as well as running a dairy herd. He appeared mostly on Tuesdays when he was on his way to the cattle sales. Owen was tall and fair, and people seemed to think he was nice-looking, except for his lazy left eye, which made his gaze travel in two different directions. When he came into the room where Hester was working, she got up at once from whatever she was doing, putting her face up to be kissed.

Owen brought eggs, and sometimes a piece of meat from the farm, which he thought perhaps Hester and her mother could use. (He spoke with determined cheerfulness whenever Ruth was mentioned.) He stayed and made cups of tea and told Hester about butterfat and which paddocks he needed to put the cows in the next day. She asked him to measure windows so that she could start running up curtains for the cottage, and chivvied him along about deciding on his best man. She frowned and sighed over his first choice because, she said, he might be too short for Susan when it came to the photographs. Not that it really mattered, she supposed, seeing that it was Owen's very best friend, and that was all that mattered. Susan was a girl she knew at boarding school.

She lived for sport — hockey in the winter and cricket in the summer. What with practice and one thing and another, she hadn't had time to make the trip from the Waikato for a fitting of her dress. Hester was sure this would all get sorted out sooner or later. Soon her conversation with Owen resumed its normal rhythms, going round and round, as if they so liked the sound of each other's voices that there was no need to think of new things to say. They talked about ballroom dancing and tangos, and sometimes they stood holding each other and did little bouncing skipping sorts of dances, pointing their heads and arms from side to side, and humming under their breaths.

'What will you do when you've finished all this?' Owen asked, pointing at the froth of tulle and lace on the table.

'Well,' said Hester, stopping in the middle of a turn, 'there's this girl who's come to work at the café who doesn't seem to have anything to wear. I thought I could help her out.'

'Don't you have enough to do?'

'I feel rather sorry for her. I think she should go home, she doesn't really seem to fit in here,' Hester said.

'I don't think you should get involved,' Owen said, unusually sharp for him.

'Oh sweetheart, I only want to help.'

'It's time you got away from it all. I wish we could just slip off and get married now without a fuss.'

'Don't be silly, sweetheart,' Hester said, in a fond daffy voice. She and Owen had been engaged for five years, and she'd been looking forward to a summer wedding all those days and nights.

Mid-afternoon at the Violet Café, early summer perched on the lake, the blueness of the sky melting into the water. That water so still the black swans repeated themselves in perfect mirror reflection, their necks elongated in space.

Jessie came to pick up her pay because it was Thursday, the day wages were paid, and also the day her rent was due at the boarding house. Violet looked her up and down. 'You look as if you'll snap off in the middle. Cook yourself something.'

'Oh, it's all right,' Jessie said, blushing as she spoke.

'Don't tell me you're not hungry.'

It was true, Jessie did feel hungry most of the time, although she found it hard to identify this cavity within as hunger. It was more like rage, and a shapeless sense of desire. She would look back and think that this was what homesickness must feel like. She would never experience this feeling again; in the rest of her life she would become a person who was where she was in a given moment, someone who moved on from place to place, her home often just an address in a phone book in another country. For the moment, she was willing to put this feeling down to hunger of the old-fashioned variety. She and Marianne sometimes ate beans out of tins they heated on the kitchen stove at the boarding house, or leftovers at the Violet Café, scraping sauce from the pots before Belle put them in the wash, a cold piece of fish, the dregs of vichyssoise, washed down with black coffee or a slug of the teapot wine.

Now that she was being offered food of her choice, Jessie felt overwhelmed with a sudden longing for steak, one of those fat ones she served Violet's patrons.

'If you're sure,' she said.

'Yes, go on,' Violet said. 'Help yourself.'

Jessie opened the door of the purring Frigidaire and took out a steak, weighing up half a pound of beef in her hand. The meat was a lovely clear colour that she could only describe as meat-red, faintly marbled with fat. With a jolt, she remembered Jock Pawson's habit of saying, 'If a working man can't have half a pound of steak once a week there's no point in going out to work.' He had fillet steak on Friday nights while the rest of them ate mince. Jessie chose a gleaming pot hanging from the rail above the stove.

Violet followed her into the kitchen. 'You're not going to put steak into that cold pan?'

'I don't know,' Jessie said, almost dropping it. Had she been too greedy? Was she supposed to have chosen something less? An egg, perhaps.

'Cooking is about science,' Violet said. 'You learnt some science?'

'Yes, some. Although languages and history were what I did best.'

'And then you set yourself to the law?'

'It seemed like a good career.'

'And now it doesn't. Never mind. I learnt music when I was a girl, and you might say that's irrelevant now. Music. Poetry. The sciences. They're not so far removed from each other, though the science of cooking isn't taught as such, more's the pity. What do they call cooking at school — homecraft or some such? Something you take in the first year of high school unless you're considered dull, in which case you make a career out of baking cakes and stitching hems in preparation for the great day of marriage. Or you're so terrified of succeeding that, if you're like Hester, you immerse yourself in stitching up dream worlds. Cooking isn't just the craft of the moment, it's a lifelong commitment. To cook, you need some science.'

'Really?' Jessie said, her appetite receding.

'Cooking's a simple process of changing the physical and chemical character of certain foods by exposing them to the action of heat,' Violet continued. 'For example, what is a steak?'

'Beef.' The flesh in her hands was springy and smeared with a light skin of blood. She wished she could put it back in

131

the refrigerator and close the door. Violet took the pan Jessie had chosen, and placed it on the stove, turning up the heat beneath.

'Indeed, that's beef,' Violet said, 'but steak can be veal or ham or lamb, almost any large animal you can think of. If you reduce your steak to scientific language, it's protein or albumin. It's like the white of an egg. If you expose it to heat it coagulates and shrinks. Do you understand?'

'Yes,' said Jessie. 'Should I add butter?'

'Yes, good.' Violet handed her a pound of yellow butter, showing her where to cut off a chunk. 'Not too much. Now, let it melt until it begins to turn brown, don't mind a little smoke. The butter keeps the meat from burning, because fat is an insulator. The steak won't burn unless the fat does. Now, quickly, put the steak in the pan, for another minute. The heat will turn the butter into acrolein, which smells like a hot exhaust pipe. Hot but not too hot. If you start with low heat, the meat won't get that caramelised texture outside, the lovely juices.'

Her discomfort forgotten, Jessie was transfixed by the meat transforming before her, as if she was seeing food cook for the first time. The smell was making her dizzy with pleasure. Like that first day, when John had cooked for her. As the juices eddied round the sides of the pan Violet reached over and turned down the stove.

'Now it's ready to eat,' Violet said, lifting the steak from the pan with a slotted spoon. She scraped the sides, pouring the fragrant sauce beside the steak. 'A dash of salt, a grind of pepper — go on, take it.'

A shadow had fallen across the doorway. Violet stiffened, without looking up.

'What do you want, Lou?'

Lou Messenger leant against the reception desk, an amused

look hovering in his eyes, a cigarette balanced by the tip of his tongue beneath his upper lip. Jessie sat down at a table with her plate and began to eat.

'Whatever it is, you can't have it,' Violet said to Lou, her voice sharp.

'I was thinking of a float in a boat, that's all. It's a nice day out there.'

'There're no girls here.' Violet glanced across at Jessie. 'Only this one.'

All the same, Jessie did go out on Lou's boat, though not that day. It was an eighteen-foot kauri cabin cruiser painted white, with its name *The Wench* painted in scarlet letters on the bow. It had a square cabin and, beneath that, two big portholes on either side. The back was open, so that three or four people could sit outside.

Jessie had thought that Evelyn would come with them, but she didn't. Evelyn and Marianne's friendship puzzled her. Jessie had heard it said several times that they were best friends at school and that Marianne had often spent time at the Messenger house in the past. Yet Marianne kept her distance from Evelyn, as if she didn't really want to talk to her. Jessie saw how unhappy this made Evelyn, and couldn't work out what was going on between them. Often, Evelyn would speak to Marianne in a way that indicated some old easy familiarity, and Marianne would turn away. More than once, Jessie had seen the rush of tears in Evelyn's dark chocolaty eyes, which she blinked away, before her stony mask fell again.

The day that Marianne and Jessie went out on Lou's boat, it turned out that Evelyn and her mother had gone up to Auckland, so Evelyn could enrol for her university courses in the new year. Whenever she mentioned the word university in the kitchen, it had been with a tilt of her head, as if it were something unattainable for the rest of them. Jessie hadn't mentioned how she had spent the past year, and she didn't think Violet Trench had either.

Marianne was already on board the boat, her head wrapped in a long gold paisley scarf that also wound about her throat, the ends flying over each shoulder, sunglasses veiling her eyes, her mouth framed with fresh lipstick. In a few minutes they were joined by John, carrying a bag of clanking beer bottles.

'You need to be warm,' Marianne said, tossing Jessie a mackintosh from under the seat.

'I'm warm enough,' Jessie said, because overhead the sun was brilliant.

Marianne shrugged. 'It can get cold out here. You'd be surprised.'

It did too, with a quick wind slapping the water into short choppy waves that dissolved in the boat's long wake. Lou spun the boat this way and that, looking light-hearted and carefree like a boy, not like a man who had been away to the war. His dark hair, worn slightly longer than the fashion of the time, sprouted in a dark halo as the wind eddied around them. He threw his head back when he laughed.

Dear Mum,

I hope things are all right with you. This is an interesting town. Yesterday, the father of one of the girls who works with me took some of us out on his boat. There's a lot of history about the place, or I guess you'd call it folklore. Like the princess who swam all the way across the lake to the island, in the middle of the night, to find her boyfriend. She had hollowed out gourds strapped to her body, like lifebelts. The lake's really pretty but you have to treat it with respect. They say the water's very deep in places, and cold as a frog's tit even now, as we're turning into summer. (Yes, I'm getting some bad turns of phrase, that's Lou for you, Evelyn's father, the one who's got the boat. He's quite young for a father.) This whole bit of country's pretty wild, squeezed up out of the centre of the earth a few million years ago, like a big tube of toothpaste, and it's still oozing out. One day they reckon this whole place is going to blow again, like sitting on the top of a pressure cooker. The ground is heated in some places and I'm told carrots get cooked before you can pull them out of the garden. That might or might not be true, but it is a real fact that people are buried at ground level and the tombstones are built over the bodies, because it's too hot to dig down. Well, it was just the best day out. When we got to the island, we swam in a hot pool. Warm bubbles trickle up from an underground stream and run up your back. I could do with my bathing suit, because I had to swim in my panties and bra which made me feel really undressed, although of course I was perfectly decent. Anyway, I thought about you and wished you could have been here and seen it with me. Mum, it's about time you had a holiday.

Love Jessie

Was that how it really happened? Yes and no. By the time they reached the island, the sun had become clear and hot. Jessie swam in the pool the way she described it to her mother. Marianne and Lou and John swam without any clothes. Of course Jessie had seen Marianne naked before; the intimacy of their room meant that they had little to hide from one another, only, they tended to look away from each other when they shed their clothes. Now, Marianne stretched herself. 'Sunlight,' she said. 'That's what I want, a bit of sun on my face.' Her breasts were full and springy, her nipples curved upwards, a blue mark the size of a thumbprint or a mouth beside the left one. Lou glanced at her with a puzzled frown, and looked away.

The men cast their windcheaters and slacks aside, stacking them beside the girls' clothes, and slid one by one into the water, holding towels from the boat over their waists. Still, as they dropped the towels, Jessie saw the smooth way their penises hung between their unevenly shaped balls. As she crouched inside her underclothes, not wanting to be caught looking, she thought they looked strong and somehow touching. Lou stood above her for a moment with the green bush behind him, deep-chested and fit, his penis brown and heavy. John's was longer and creamier, reminding Jessie of a bud lily as it swayed in its nest of black hair. He could be a dancer, he was so slim. His hands fanned out in a quick dramatic gesture, covering himself.

'What green eyes you've got,' said Marianne. Jessie blushed and looked away. The two men stayed at the end of the pool while Marianne and Jessie lay against the smooth rocks at the other side.

'I like to have young people around,' Lou said, in a mock fatherly voice.

'You're not old,' said Marianne.

'Old enough to tell you when to go to bed.'

Marianne eyed Jessie sideways. 'Evelyn and I used to have midnight feasts at their house. He was always telling us off. Not that it will matter when I'm forty. People don't notice things like that, the older you get.'

'Steady on,' Lou said, 'a joke's a joke.' He changed the subject then, talking about the war instead, telling them how it was to travel in a submarine and know there was nothing except the skin of a machine between you and a million million tons of the ocean pressing down, and what it was like when you released a missile, and it hit, and you were so glad you weren't the poor bastard on the receiving end, the fear of the lights going out, and being left there in the dark, and what it was like to come back up to the surface after days near the ocean's floor.

As Jessie climbed out of the water on to the rocks, she noticed that her skin had turned a dull puce. I'm cooked, she thought, I'm boiled meat. Not on Violet's menu. She sat down and started to shiver, in spite of the warmth of the pool and the sunshine. John got out of the water, drying himself with one of the damp towels, his back towards her. She couldn't see Marianne and Lou, who were already out and dressed.

'Jessie,' he said, pulling his clothes on. 'What is it?'

'I don't know.'

'You need a cigarette.'

'Thanks,' she said.

'Where are the others?'

'Gone for a walk.'

'I don't know what's going on here.' The air was quite still around her, and somewhere she thought she heard a raised voice but perhaps it was something else.

'I think they were looking for nesting birds.'

'Are we doing couples or something?' she said.

'Would it matter if we were?' He had thrown himself on the grass beside the pool. Leaning on his elbows, he stretched a blade of it between his thumbs and whistled gently into it.

'Lou's married. He's Evelyn's father.'

'I wouldn't worry about it. Are you scared of doing things?' He hadn't made any move to reach for her. And, as he was speaking, Marianne and Lou appeared along the path. Lou's face was dark, the friendliness erased, and Marianne looked as if she had been crying.

'Come on, shake a leg,' Lou said, 'I've still got that stuff to pick up for her ladyship.'

On the return journey across the lake, they veered away from the town, towards the eastern apron. Two men stood at the water's edge, waving. Behind them was a ramshackle cottage, partly covered with vines, a window boarded up and a chimney pot broken. A row of trees grew near the cottage; in the falling evening light, it was shading a garden planted in neat rows almost to the rim of sand. Closer up, Jessie saw one man was covered with a thick red and black woollen shirt, black trousers and black waders. He had a big loose frame, and a fair open face. Both he and the other man, older and darker, carried wooden boxes on their shoulders. The second man was Chinese, dressed in old trousers, baggy at the knees, and a faded evening jacket. The men lifted the boxes up to John. The first was full of green lettuces. 'Be careful of this one,' the Chinese man said, 'it's Madam's salads.' When he spoke, a solid gold tooth glinted in his mouth.

The fair man splashed through the water and climbed on board. 'See ya later, Harry,' he called back to his friend. In a moment, the boat roared away from the shore, as they headed back to town.

'Owen, this is Jessie,' John said, introducing them.

'Oh yeah, I've heard about you,' Owen replied, his eyes resting on her, his expression not entirely friendly. His glance strayed to Marianne, sitting in the cockpit laughing at something Lou had said. Things seemed to be back to normal between them.

'Jessie's all right,' John said, putting an arm protectively around her shoulders. Surprised by this embrace, she let his arm rest, finding herself calm within its circle. She wondered what had made her afraid. They were all acting as if something had threatened them, and now they were working in concert to drive the thing away. Owen looked from John to Jessie. 'Okay,' he said, 'okay.'

'You and my brother getting things sorted out?' John asked.

'Sure. The wedding's going to be fine. Harry's new house is looking good, don't you reckon?'

'Yeah, he's doing all right,' John said. 'I might move in with him yet.'

'Sam wouldn't like that, would he?'

'Well, it might be a bit far to bike to work. Pays to have plenty of brothers, you can pick and choose your lodgings.' Lou had notched the motor up, and the boat began to fly along at a breathtaking pace, the waves going bang bang bang beneath them. John's arm tightened around Jessie.

'Did you say that was your brother?' Jessie shouted above the noise of the engine. 'Yes, that's Chun, but you can call him Harry. I live with Sam, the next one down.'

'But I thought Hugo was your father. The old man who died.'

'He was. My mother was Ming, and Harry is one of the sons she had in China before her first husband died.'

'I didn't realise.'

'That I was a Chinaman?'

'I didn't mean that.'

He took his arm away. She wanted to say that it was all right, she didn't mean it in a way that might offend him, but she couldn't find the right words. Her face was smarting with the wind on her sunburnt cheeks, and with embarrassment. She couldn't understand why she hadn't seen what was different about John before.

JOHN

They'd called him a pansy and threatened to cut off his balls, holding him against trees with their arms across his throat, blocking his windpipe, until he cried, in spite of himself, while girls stayed away from him, as if in deference to the masculinity of the boys they hung about with. He couldn't work it out, because he hadn't felt anything for anyone. He knew boys who fagged for prefects. One of them wore a cape, and sat on the knees of sixth-form boys with his arm around their necks, and everyone laughed. John never wanted to do that.

He tried to see himself as they saw him. The mirror showed him a fragile girlish beauty he couldn't change. You're a clever boy, his English teacher said. The mathematics teacher said, you should specialise with us. You've got the brains. You ought to be a scholarship pupil, the principal said. When his school reports came out he tore them up. They're too dumb, he said. You don't want to know what they think of me, he told his father. Only one day his father, who thought they must be getting it all wrong, took it on himself to go down and ask how his son was doing.

John couldn't forget the night his father came home, his face like whey.

'Why?' he said. 'What makes you tell me lies? Why do you want to squander your life in this way?'

'People don't like me at school,' he said, after a long silence, because something was required of him.

His father had studied him intently. This father of his was very old, and had four sons — two stepsons from his wife's first marriage, his own older brother and himself — but none of them was like him. They were sturdy men on the whole, although his younger brother, Joe, the one who should have been close to him, had trouble reading and writing and had been taken out of school when he was thirteen. He was a huge overgrown boy, nearly a foot taller than John, who stayed at home and dug whole paddocks by hand in an afternoon, lifting the earth as easily as if he was shifting dust. Strong in one sense then, although you couldn't hold a conversation with him. John wished he didn't feel ashamed of his family. His father had taught him many things when he was small that seemed to have escaped other boys his own age. In the evenings Hugo played recordings of Schubert's music on a shaky turntable, although John believed he could no longer hear the notes, and the boy knew that the music was intended for him. Mostly, he pretended he couldn't hear it either, sat whistling through his teeth, or staring at the ceiling, thinking how awful it would be if anyone could hear the music his father chose. He couldn't meet his father's eyes when he found out how he'd been cheating on him.

'Fuck,' said his brother. 'Fuckfuck. They want John to do fuckfuck.'

His father had stood up, ready to lash out at his huge son, but one of the older sons, Harry, in his thirties then, who lived next door with his wife and children, put out his hand and held him back.

'You want to listen to him, old man,' he said. 'The boy knows a thing or two.'

'Is it true, then?' his father asked John.

'No,' said John. 'Yes, perhaps that's what they want, but not me. That's not what I want. It's not what I do.' Although, in his heart, he knew that if he stayed there much longer, he would have to do it whether he wanted to or not.

'I can send you away to school,' said his father. 'Boarding school.'

'It would be the same there,' John said. 'It would be the same wherever I went.'

It was after that his father said he had a job for him to go to: the woman who ran the new café at the end of the main street in town was looking for someone to work in the kitchen. She could give him an apprenticeship. When he told John this, he had to squeeze his eyes tightly together as if to stop tears leaking down the seamy old parchment of his face; as if he had done the very best he could and felt that he'd failed.

'It's only as important as you let it be,' John said. 'Being one thing or another. Being Chinese. If you don't like it, go out with someone else.'

'That's not what I meant,' Jessie said. 'I should have known. Your father told me I should go to China.'

'He did?'

'Yes, he did. But then my mother said that too. I thought it was just something people said.'

SPRUNG

Up in the ranges, on a road that led through thick native forest towards town, Freda's small Prefect car had broken down. The problem was probably the carburettor, she and Evelyn decided. Evelyn flagged down a car and asked the driver to ring her father when he got into town, and send help.

The motorist did ring Lou Messenger, but he was not there. The man who answered the phone had just overturned a tray of trout flies and his mind was not on the call. Lou, he believed, was out showing clients some fishing trips around the lake. As soon as he came in, he said, he would give him the message. Only Lou didn't come in for the rest of the day, and besides, the man forgot about the call.

Freda and Evelyn took short walks to keep their circulation moving because it was getting cold. To pass the time they sang songs they both knew, like 'Ten Green Bottles', songs without special meaning, just words to take them through the hours. Freda sang 'Beautiful Brown Eyes' because this is what she used to sing to Evelyn when she was a little girl, and Evelyn seemed softer and kinder, more like the child she adored while Lou was still away at sea.

'Mum,' Evelyn said, when they had run out of songs, 'David's asked me out.'

'David Finke?'

'Yes.'

'Well, I don't know about that ...' Freda began.

'Why not? He works with you. Isn't anyone good enough for me?'

'Well,' said Freda, flustered, 'that's sort of the point, isn't it? I mean if anything goes wrong, it would be embarrassing.'

'Nothing's going to go wrong, Mum. He's just asked me to go to the pictures on Wednesday night, seeing as I've got a night off owing to me, though goodness knows, Violet Trench will probably dock me for not being there tonight.'

'Well, you have to get out, dear,' her mother said. 'I just don't want you getting involved with anyone when you're off to varsity so soon.'

'Mum. I'm not getting involved, all right? I'm just going to the pictures.'

'Yes, of course,' said Freda, who'd had to take a pee in the bushes near the road and stood in oozing mud slime. 'I'm sorry, dear,' she said. 'I love you so much. I love you more than anyone in the world.'

'I know,' Evelyn said, and sighed. She was the only person in the world her mother loved, and the burden was almost too much to bear.

By this time, with the moreporks calling in the dark, they'd worked out that Lou was not coming, and flagged down another motorist, using a torch to attract attention. This way, they got a lift back to town. When they arrived back at the house, it was empty.

'I never thought of my mother as vindictive,' Jessie said, when some weeks had passed and her mother hadn't sent on any clothes.

'Mothers always are, that's the whole point,' Marianne said. She was wearing a clay face mask, although it was difficult to see how her flawless complexion could be improved.

'Why do you say that?'

They were in the bedroom on a wet Saturday afternoon, and there was nowhere else to go between now and work. Down the hall, there was music. David Finke had bought a record player and he was playing music with an agitated quality about it. Any moment they expected the landlady to tell him to turn it down.

'What would you say if your mother slept with your boyfriend?' Marianne said, before she could stop herself.

'That's just crazy,' Jessie said. She had thought Marianne couldn't shock her any more but then she guessed she was easy prey, and it was too late to pull back and act as if this was a joke. Marianne was enjoying her reaction.

So then Marianne found herself telling Jessie what Sybil had done, and where, right there on the bed where Jessie slept, and how much Marianne hated her and would never forgive her. She showed Jessie the place where she had worn her engagement ring for nearly a year, and how the white part wouldn't disappear until summer was really here, and the tan would cover over it.

'I can't believe anyone's mother would do that,' Jessie said. Her mother and Jock and the whole business of being female — it had had something to do with her leaving home, but what Marianne was describing was too extraordinary for her to make sense of. Marianne shrugged and let her shoulders fall, so that Jessie could see that she meant it, although it was difficult to read her expression behind the stiff mud mask.

'Your mother needs treatment,' Jessie said.

'It's just a shag,' Marianne said, after a silence. 'When all's said and done, what's a shag? I've had lots of shags — I had my first one on my paper run. I just don't like sharing them with my mother.'

'But you were in love with Derek,' Jessie said, her embarrassment turning to outrage.

'Nah.' Marianne began to buff her fingernails. 'It's probably just as well. Who wants to end up like Hester and Belle, tied down to one man for life? Besides, now I've got a boyfriend who's married, and you know, it's different, it's just different.'

'You can't,' Jessie said.

'But I have,' Marianne said, smiling her perfect smile, even though the mask was cracking and flaking.

'It's not …' Jessie stopped. There were some things it was better not to hear.

'Nobody you know.'

'You never know, I might,' Jessie, said, in spite of herself. Because Jessie was getting like the rest of them at the café, knowing all the regulars and who liked their meat rare, and who wouldn't complain even if their arses were on fire, and who might surreptitiously leave a tip, although Violet Trench frowned on the practice.

'It's a secret,' Marianne says. As she would.

'I'll help you make some clothes,' Hester said. 'I've finished my wedding dress and I can't do any more to Susan's dress until she comes for her fitting.' Hester had swiftly and unexpectedly become Jessie's friend. She didn't know how this had come about, but Jessie sensed Violet's approval of her, and if that was the case, Hester would go along with it. All the same, invitations to visit were timed for when Hester's mother was away at the shop, as if perhaps Ruth hadn't been told about them. Jessie fell into a pattern of calling round to Hester's place in the afternoons before they began work at the café. Hester, her mouth full of pins, fitted cotton blouses, a patterned skirt and a straight-fitting dress with a scooped-out back because, Hester said, Jessie had a lovely spine, which seemed a nice way of saying she looked good back to front. Mrs Trench had remarked on it too, Hester said.

146

So Jessie knew she was being talked about and she found it at once discomforting and reassuring, as if she was achieving some place in this odd but mostly benevolent new family.

When Hester wanted Jessie to try things on, she took her to her mother's bedroom where there was a full-length mirror. The bed was covered by a blue satin bedspread with ruched edges, and a fat bolster where the pillows sat. On the dressing table stood pots and jars of Roget and Gallet talcum and Eau de Cologne 4711, and some rose-bloom rouge. An embroidered sampler hanging on the wall read: 'An egg in the box is worth two in the nest.' Like some coded message.

'What does it mean?' Jessie asked.

'Oh, that old thing. My mother has some rubbish, doesn't she? I can't tell you how much I'm looking forward to a place of my own. I'm going to paint everything white. Owen and I are going to have a cottage of our own on the farm. It's not very big, but there'll be two bedrooms. Perhaps you'll be able to come and stay with me. Owen's going to buy ready-cut furniture, that lovely blond pine, it's ever so smart. He's a real handyman.' Hester's own bedroom in her mother's house was more like a child's, or a servant's, with an iron-framed bed covered by a heavy white quilt. 'I like to keep things simple,' she said, although, to Jessie, this seemed at odds with the ornate patterned gowns she toiled over.

At first, Jessie had trouble reconciling the Owen who sat in Ruth Hagley's dining room, surrounded by fine frilly things, blowing on his tea before he sipped it, with the big man in the Swanndri and waders. But she believed the openness she had first observed in him was real, that he was an uncomplicated man with no sharp edges she could detect. She saw how perfectly he and Hester matched each other. There was something guileless about them, the way they slipped together in and out of their dances, their comfortable routines of talk. Hester told her that they planned to have children as soon as they were married because she'd be too old if they left it much longer. She'd like to start some layettes now but she thought that might send out the wrong signals to people, so she'd just have to wait. All the same, she and Owen talked about the names of the children they might have. She had a little booklet hidden in her sewing box called *3500 Names for Baby*, with a cover that showed a couple facing each other pointing over each other's shoulders in different directions, but looking all the while into each other's eyes. The woman had a sweetly curved belly beneath a turquoise sweater. Leila, said Hester. Too fancy, said Owen. Kenneth, said Owen. Too plain, too old-fashioned, Hester responded. Stephen. Yes perhaps, perhaps Stephen, but maybe with a 'v' instead of a 'ph'. Oh darling, *darling,* they cried to each other, and laughed. As if they were making love, Jessie thought, too private for her to witness.

'Don't let the old trout make you too tired,' Owen said tenderly.

'Owen.' Hester put her fingers to her lips, her eyes belatedly making signals in Jessie's direction.

But no, he was not referring to Ruth. 'Sometimes Mrs Trench takes you for granted,' he said, his face looking hot.

'We owe her, darling,' Hester said in a mysterious grown-up voice that meant enough is enough.

It was only when she had been in their company two or three times that Jessie learnt of the one problem that lay unresolved between them. She knew when Hester was expecting her, and had developed the habit of simply going straight in the unlocked back door. This time, she knew straight away that she should have knocked. Hester and Owen sat staring at each other across the dining-room table, their faces red.

'I'm not changing my mind,' Owen said. 'It's the one thing.'

'I know,' Hester was saying miserably. 'I just haven't got round to it.'

'Well then,' Owen said, 'you'll just have to tell her. The invitations are going out next week.' Then they saw Jessie, and Owen stood up, pushing the velvet-padded chair out behind him. 'I'll see you.'

'Owen,' said Hester, 'I will. I promise. It's bad enough, Susan not coming for her fitting. I don't know what's wrong with her, she's had months to get here.'

'Please don't go,' Jessie said to Owen. 'I was just, you know, just dropping in for a minute.'

'I have to, or I'll be late for milking,' Owen said. He hesitated, before stooping and kissing Hester's cheek. 'It'll be all right.'

When he was gone, and Hester was still trying to take charge of her wobbly voice, she told Jessie what was bothering them. 'It's the best man. I'm just going to have to stand up to my mother about him.'

'What's wrong with him?'

'Nothing. It's just that he's, well, he's Chinese.'

'Is it Harry?'

'Yes,' Hester said, appearing taken aback that Jessie already knew this. Hadn't Owen told her about their first encounter on Lou's boat? And why would he have held back on that?

Hester explained that although Harry was an older man, he and Owen had become friends. When Owen was just out of school he'd worked in the market garden.

'Well, do you mind about him being best man?'

'Of course not,' Hester said, her eyes pained. 'It's just that my mother's my mother, you know what I mean?'

Sooner or later, summer turns and then it's over. Something was bound to happen with all this stuff floating just under the surface. The restaurant was full the night the police came. Jessie looked up from a pork grill and saw two policemen standing framed in the entrance to the Violet Café.

'This is a raid,' said the taller of the two, a beanpole of a fellow with red hair showing beneath his helmet. 'Everyone out.'

'You can't do this to me,' said Violet.

'Yes, we can.'

'On what grounds?'

'On suggestion that liquor is sold illegally at this establishment.'

'Well, you go right ahead,' said Violet, tilting her chin in the air. 'You search the premises.'

'I can vouch for the place,' said Lou. 'Nobody's been drinking in here tonight. Ask the chap who just went out — he's got the pricker because there wasn't any booze here.'

'Thanks, Mr Messenger. If you wouldn't mind just removing yourself from the premises, we'll check this out for ourselves.'

'Go on then, everyone,' Violet said, 'you go outside. I'm staying here — you'll have to arrest me if you want me out. But I'm telling you, if you find everything in order and my girls have been humiliated in this way, I'll sue the lot of you.'

'Well.' The redhead scratched his head. 'Perhaps you could all just stand here at the front of the shop. Tell your kitchen staff to come out too. It's just a recce really.'

'Oh, not a real raid. I see. Well, come on then, you lot. Hester and Belle, get yourselves out here,' Violet said, standing at the kitchen door. The two women emerged, Hester wiping her face with the back of her hand, looking as if she was about to cry.

'What will Owen say, if he hears about this?'

'Oh stop it, Hester,' said Violet. 'This is a farce if ever I saw one.' The police were going around the tables inspecting glasses and cups and sniffing them.

Belle didn't look concerned at all. Her big blue eyes were dancing, as she pulled her pony-tail a shade higher, making herself look pert and pretty. Lou Messenger turned and looked at her as she came out of the kitchen, his eyes lighting up as if he had just seen an apparition or a blessed happening.

'Who's this?' he asked.

'I'm the dish-washer,' said Belle. 'Taken,' she said, slipping her engagement ring out of her pocket, where she kept it while she was working, and slipping it on her finger.

'That's my father you're talking to, Belle,' Evelyn said, in a dangerous mean voice.

'Well, I know that,' Belle said.

'We only let her out for special events like police raids,' said Marianne, seeming to take Evelyn's part. Evelyn shot her a grateful look.

The policemen had gone into the kitchen, followed by Violet. 'Crime down in the town, is it?' she said. 'Nothing much to do?'

'Just stay where you are, ma'am.'

'And nobody will get hurt, you mean,' Violet said, parodying their tone of voice. David raised his hands above the piano's keyboard.

'I said, don't move,' said the red-haired policeman.

'I'm just the piano player,' David said.

He played 'Little Brown Jug', a fixed glee in his smile, as if outwitting the police was the most entertaining thing he'd ever done. *Ha ha ha, you and me, little brown jug, how I love thee.*

The door behind them opened very softly while the two policemen were rifling through the kitchen, and John appeared soundlessly behind them. Only Jessie saw him come in. He winked at her. She thought then he'd left by the back door and come back, just like in the movies, and she wanted to laugh. John put his fingers up to his lips.

The police came out, the redhead in charge of the operation looking flustered.

'Everything seems to be in order here. Your diners can resume their seats if they wish.'

'Oh, thank you very much. And just whose idea was it to come down here and have some fun at my expense tonight?'

'Just routine, Mrs Trench.'

'I might just come down to the station in the morning and see the sergeant.'

'I wouldn't do that, ma'am. We're going to recommend that no further inspections of these premises are required.'

The remnants of the restaurant's guests were collecting up their belongings and queuing up to pay at the desk, wanting to get out of the place as fast as possible, except Lou, who kept staring at the place where Belle had stood. She had flitted back into the kitchen, without a backward glance.

Belle had a dream. In her dream Jesus had spoken to her, and told her that her life was about to change. She saw His face quite clearly, close to hers. He was not gentle and bearded, the way Wallace described Him. He was swarthy and stocky with muscular arms and a deep chest. Mary Magdalene was in the dream too. When He talked to Mary Magdalene, He was a bit cocky, a bit sure of Himself, as if He knew He could sweep her off her feet if He wanted to. When He spoke to Belle, He said, 'You're going to come along with me. Never mind the hangers-on and the holy rollers who wouldn't know a good time if they saw one.'

In her dream, she said, 'Whither thou goest, I will go,' like Ruth in the Bible, and she could never get it through her head that this was a woman talking to her mother-in-law about following her family, because it's what she felt love might be about, and she had never experienced this feeling: that out there, there was someone who she would follow to the ends of the earth if she could. Up until now, she had done what she must. Jesus didn't seem impressed with her response, so she said, 'Let the good times roll,' hoping to perk things up a bit. She saw how pleased He looked about this. When she woke up, she had the salt taste of tears round her mouth, as if she has been crying in her sleep. Wallace was very still beside her, his mouth slightly open, snoring in small grunts every now and then.

Belle sat up in bed, winding her hair round her fingers. It was nearly morning and pale threads of light were edging their way around the bedroom. She thought of waking Wallace because already this seemed like a bad dream, not a good one, and perhaps if they got together for half an hour she would forget it. Besides, she liked the habit of sex, but looking at him lying there beside him with his mouth like a fly trap, she thought that it was the act she wanted, not the man himself, not the stale routine of what happened in this room. She had had better sex, but she'd tried to close her mind off to that part of her life, the breaking in that prepared her for him, the handing over of her body like a parcel, and the torment of good behaviour until Wallace was allowed to have his way with her. Sex, Belle thought was what she did well, her private talent. It might surprise some of those girls at the café how much she knew about such a lot of things.

Perhaps she should just wake Wallace to tell him that her life was going to change. Like the signs of the zodiac which she sneakily read in the newspaper. He wouldn't like it though; he had almost won the battle to stop her going to work at the Violet Café. Soon he would win by the sheer force of marriage. She thought of Hester, who was anticipating her wedding with such certainty, and wished she could be the same. If she were to tell Wallace about her dream, he might see it as an even more urgent incentive for her to leave work. Very quietly, so as not to disturb her sleeping fiancé, Belle slipped out of bed, opened the bedroom door and then, when nothing moved behind her, went to the front door of the house, making sure the snib on the lock was up so she could get back in. Outside, a heavy dew lay on the snapdragons and geums that filled the front garden. The dawn promised a clear bright day to follow. Later the smell of the hydrogen sulphide that curled up from the ground would rise with the heat, but right then, she could smell the fresh astringent scent of the gardens all along the street. It was irresistible, the path that lay ahead of her, the silence broken only by waking birds. Belle walked barefoot in her white nightdress, gathered with blue ribbon at the throat, her hair floating over her shoulders.

She was so lost in this moment of total freedom that she didn't hear a car coming behind her. It was a red and white Chrysler Valiant, cruising down the street at low speed, its motor so soft she might be forgiven for not noticing it until it was almost upon her, as she crossed the road, intent on a neighbour's roses, their heads floating above a wall. The car screeched to a halt, and for a moment there was nowhere to run. She looked up, saw a face she recognised and was frozen to the spot, her cold white milkmaid feet unable to take a step backwards or forwards. She knew the man driving the car, and he looked just about as stunned as she was.

Belle stepped back onto the kerb, wondering if the driver would unroll the window and speak to her, but he gave her a small wave, as if insisting that everything was normal, and the car slid off into the gathering sunlight.

'Jesus is sweet,' Belle murmured to herself, as she turned and ran down the street, down the path of her father's house, slipped through the door and along the passage to the bathroom. She heard, as she passed the chiming clock on the wall, that it was seven o'clock already. When she found she was bleeding, that was the best thing that could start her day, because she'd been a week overdue, and her whole life had felt as if it was closing in.

'Sweet Jesus,' Lou Messenger said, too, under his breath, as he drove on through the town towards the shop. Only a few days ago, Violet Trench had cornered him when he was paying his bill. Leave my girls alone, she had told him. As if he didn't know plenty about her and more.

'Sweet Jesus, that was close.' He had enough trouble on his hands. He flicked on his car radio.

Out there in the world, late in November of 1963, something had happened, and one by one they were waking up to news of the stupendous event, and, for all the rest of their lives, they would ask each other what they were doing when they heard. They would remember the feeling, that nothing they knew would ever be the same.

It was eight o'clock the same morning. Jessie, cleaning the room, came across a yellow packet of photographs. She'd asked Marianne about the pictures that she was modelling for, but Marianne was vague about them. Soon she would get a whole pile of them when the man had had time, but right now he was busy on other work. That's what she said, but lately Jessie had been wondering if there were any photos at all. She had begun to think that Marianne really did go to a cleaning job. Jessie couldn't stop herself from opening the packet. She lifted the black-and-white prints gingerly. Marianne was revealed in various stages of undress amid a setting of fern fronds. The earth and mossy surfaces looked like Marianne's pubic hair, a silky blackened pelt. Like a small animal waiting to pounce from between the pale columns of her spread legs. A bar of sunlight fell across her face so that it was not immediately discernible as Marianne's.

'Interesting, are they?' Marianne said, from the doorway.

'Marianne, I thought you wouldn't be back for a long time.'

'Well, there you are, life's full of little surprises.'

'Marianne, the man who takes these photographs ...'

'Yes,' Marianne said, immediately on her guard.

'Is he the man? The married man you see?'

For a moment, Marianne looked afraid. 'Of course not. Whatever made you think that, stupid?' She snatched the photographs out of Jessie's hands, and pushed them back in the envelope. 'These are just snapshots, a bit of a joke.' Soon afterwards, she went out again, taking the envelope with her. David Finke came down the hall, looking as white and transparent as ice cubes. 'Have you heard the news?' he said.

Belle was overcome with uncontrollable shivering when she returned to the bedroom. Wallace was awake, and she saw how she'd startled him.

'It's nothing,' she said. 'You know, it's just the usual.'

But her teeth wouldn't stop chattering, and her whole body was locked in a spasm that went on and on, so that she appeared to Wallace to be curving and arcing before she fell across the bed. 'My little love,' he said. 'Darling Belle, darling, I'll get your mum. She'll know what to do.'

Lorraine came at his call, taking in the scene, running her hands over Belle's rigid body, stopping for a moment with a puzzled expression as she touched the wet ends of the night dress. Belle's lips were drawn back over her bared teeth. Her feet were freezing.

'Get a basin of hot water,' Lorraine told Wallace.

While he was out of the room, Lorraine propped Belle on the chair beside the bed, and covered her decently.

As he'd been instructed, Wallace brought back a wide white enamel basin with a thin blue rim, filled with steaming water. Lorraine placed it in front of Belle and guided her feet into it.

'I've seen,' Belle began, then stopped.

'Yes?' Wallace encouraged her.

She shook her head, mute.

'A vision? Did you see God? A miracle?'

Belle was still and unmoving.

'I think we should pray,' said Wallace. While he was out of the room he had summoned Hal, who now joined them.

'We should get the doctor, more like it,' Lorraine said. This was not exactly what she believed, because she suspected that whatever had provoked Belle's fit might not be medical. She didn't know exactly why.

Nobody was listening to her anyway, which was hardly new. Hal called on the Lord to hear their prayers, and so they did, calling on Him to save Belle, Lorraine all the while splashing the water over her daughter's feet and ankles, while Wallace clutched the hand of his pale white maid, imploring her to recover. After a while, Belle yawned and sighed. 'Thanks,' she said, 'I'm fine now.' Her toes were pink and shiny.

The crisis over, they left her to sleep. Wallace went out to collect the morning paper and found, to his puzzlement, that it was not there, but lying inside the front door, as if it had been dropped there by someone. But he had more stupendous news, just told him by one of the neighbours. 'President Kennedy's been shot,' he said. 'He's dead.'

'Praise the Lord,' Hal said. 'You could see the whites of that man's eyes all the way round.'

SEASONAL RITES

Dear Jessie,

I'm glad you're having such a great time, but I hope you'll think about starting for home before long. I have to have some tests at the doctor's next week, and I need someone to keep an eye on the children. I can always ask Jock's sister, I suppose, but it would be good if you could be here.

Mum

Jessie was totally distracted when this letter arrived, later the same day. Kennedy had been shot; she worked in the Violet Café; she had briefly been held in the embrace of a young man she thought about nearly all the time, every day.

Later, before they left for work, she and Marianne watched the news on Kevin's television, which he'd had installed in the sitting room. For once, they were allowed through the door. The pictures of the blood preoccupied them all.

Hester held a length of polished cotton in front of Jessie's waist and let it drop so that she could see the fall of the skirt. Jessie could smell her apple skin and breath. 'Hmmm,' Hester said, and walked away considering. 'That's about right. So what are you going to do about Christmas then?'

'I'd better go home and see my mother.'

'Have you talked about that to Mrs Trench?'

'Do you think she'd mind?'

'You'd have to ask her,' Hester said. 'She's not keen on time off, you know.'

'My mother's not very well. Well, that's what she says.'

'You can try asking,' Hester said, but she looked doubtful.

Jessie kept putting off asking. Christmas drew nearer, and Violet said that they were heading for the busiest time of the year. There was the annual carnival at the waterfront — not that she encouraged people like that in the café but still it did bring in the patrons — and then there was the New Year parade, and the whole town would be packed with visitors. Finally, when Jessie did ask, Violet turned on her, furious.

'Didn't you know when you took on this job that it was full-time? What's the matter with you? I treat you well enough, don't I?'

Jessie had to agree that she did.

'Look, Jessie,' Hester said, the next time she went around to her house, 'Violet's the boss. Perhaps you should just go.'

'You mean the only way I can go home for Christmas is to leave?'

'I shouldn't be saying this,' Hester said unhappily, her loyalties torn, 'but you don't want to upset your family.'

'You don't know my family.'

'Do you need to be one of Violet's girls? You don't seem the type.'

'I don't know what you mean,' Jessie said slowly.

'Well, you know, they've all got problems,' Hester said, almost absent-mindedly, biting off a thread, because Jessie was using the scissors to cut out a bodice. 'You're special, you tried to save Hugo. She was bound to be kind. But in the end, everyone has to toe the line.'

'So what are your problems?' Jessie asked.

Hester's throat flooded with colour, the way it always did when she was agitated. 'I don't have any. Well, not now.' She gestured helplessly around the room. 'I found it hard to get away from my mother. She thought I should stay home and look after her. But then I met Violet and all that changed.'

'So Violet solved everything?'

'Not exactly.' Hester was still choosing her words with care. She put her sewing down in her lap. 'I didn't want to be one of those women who never tried things, that's all. Who makes excuses for not living.'

'I know what you mean,' Jessie said, her mind made up. 'I like the café. I'm going to stay on.'

On Christmas Day, the café had to close. Violet said that, instead of paying guests, she would invite her staff for the best meal they'd ever had, unless of course, they were spending the day at home, in which case she wouldn't dream of asking them to change their arrangements. Evelyn did stay home with Freda and Lou, and Belle said that of course she would be sharing God's Word with His people and her parents and Wallace, and her sisters and their husbands and children.

'Have a wonderful time, Belle,' Violet said, with a thin smile.

In the end, there were Violet and Jessie and Marianne and David Finke, who couldn't get leave from the radio station to go home to Hamilton, and Hester and Owen accompanied (to everyone's surprise) by Ruth, looking subdued, and John. Afterwards, John would go to one of his brothers' houses. They all still lived in the town, in big houses made of brick and tile, with wide concrete drives and wrought-iron gates, spread around the new subdivision near the bay. They worked in the market garden. Harry clung more to the old ways than Sam although his wife was a modern woman who kept the accounts for the company, and was impatient with backward ways. Joe could neither read nor write, but had a wife all the same.

Violet had given each of the girls little phials of rich perfume. Jessie's was orange blossom, the perfume so strong and provocative it took her breath away. The square bottle, half the length of a fountain pen, was something she would keep with her for years and even when its tiny rubber stopper perished, and the last drops of perfume evaporated, she would still be able to unscrew the lid and catch a whiff of that haunting long-ago fragrance.

It was John and Violet who prepared the meal for the guests, placing simple Christmas food, roast lamb and new potatoes, on beautiful brightly coloured platters. John poured wine for them all, a fragrant chianti, from a bottle not a teapot, into stemmed glasses. They opened the doors out towards the lake. The water was so close, they could hear it lapping, while the island shimmered beyond them in a heat haze.

'Absent friends,' Violet said, raising her glass.

They raised their glasses obediently. Absent friends, they echoed.

'Hugo,' she said, raising it again. 'We miss you.'

'Hugo,' they chorused, except for John who said 'to my dad'. To my mother, Jessie thought, with a stab of guilt.

'To Kennedy,' Violet said, 'bless his wicked ways.' Not everyone drank to that; Ruth folded her lips and put her hands in her lap.

'This is poetry,' Violet said, dreamily surveying the feast, 'the poetry of good food. I wish my customers could see this.'

'I gather your customers are pleased with what you have on offer anyway,' Ruth said, intending to flatter, but somehow falling short of the mark. Her blue-veined hands trembled slightly as she lifted forkfuls of meat to her mouth.

'Well, there's good food and there's excellent food,' Violet said, resting her chin on her hand. 'I serve good food day after day, but it's a performance. When people come they want some drama, if I'm to continue this literary metaphor. It's like peeling clothes off at a play — if you just brought the players on naked the patrons would think they'd been cheated.'

'That sounds remarkably like sex you're talking about,' said Owen lazily. Jessie thought again what an appealing and pleasant man Owen was, and more complex than he seemed on the surface, not all raw meat and rough hands.

'Well, yes,' Violet agreed, 'sex does come into it. People do often come to a restaurant before a seduction — or that's what it was like when I lived in France. It's a little different in a town like this, although sex on an empty stomach is always a bit of a chore, even if it's just fish and chips, wouldn't you agree?'

Hester had blushed again. Owen put his hand on his fiancée's shoulder and said in a kind way that saved her: 'Hester will tell you that after she's married.'

Jessie saw the way Ruth quivered and subsided. There was some change in the air around Ruth — you could read this from the way she was being ignored. Jessie guessed that something had been resolved, a stand taken.

'Quite so,' said Violet, as if she was pleased with Owen. 'But you see, when it comes down to it, good food is about elementary things, like fresh eggs, and onions and parsley, oranges and bread and tomatoes.' She was passing round raspberries, settled in a dark green glass bowl.

'And truffles?' asks Marianne, who had only picked at her food, glancing out of the window at the lake from time to time, as if there was something or someone she hoped to see. Jessie wondered if she was looking for Lou in his white boat, with the scarlet letters on its side. There had been an uncomfortable conversation at the beginning of the meal, when Marianne said: 'I did think Evelyn might come. Well, what do the three of them do, sitting round looking at each other, just because it's Christmas Day?'

Violet had turned a long steady look on her. 'I don't think

it's any of your business, Marianne,' she had said.

'They did used to invite me to their place, some Christmases.'

'Well, this year, they didn't,' Violet had replied, looking exasperated. Now Marianne was trying to re-enter the conversation and Violet was ready to forgive her. 'Ah, truffles,' she said. 'Well, they're the dark heart of the poem of course, that which turns simplicity on its head, as any good poem should. The most elusive metaphor, in life as in art. I'm talking about the everyday things that we don't recognise for what they are. One year in England, after the war started, and Europe became off limits, as it were, I spent a summer in the countryside. I was still quite young then, and,' she hesitated for just a moment, 'very much in love at the time. Well, everything was rationed and people had long faces, talking about going without things, and yet everything we needed, with the exception of enough flour to make bread, was all around us out there in the countryside. And sugar, of course. But I never went without because I knew where to look for food. How to forage.'

Beside her, Jessie felt the pressure of John's thigh pressing against hers, and without thinking, found herself pressing back. David Finke had a rapturous gaze in his eyes, and kept looking at John. She felt herself going red, the way Hester did; how could he know what was going on under the table?

'But that's not the answer to the truffles,' Marianne said.

'You can't explain them,' Violet said impatiently, as if she was losing interest in the conversation. 'You simply remember them.'

'We need some carols,' Ruth said plaintively. 'Shouldn't we have some carols?'

'Tell me, Ruth,' Violet asked, at last offering Ruth some attention, 'have you been busy at the shop? I saw you were having a sale.'

'Not a sale,' said Ruth, 'just some Christmas specials.'

'Well, that's a comfort,' Violet commented. 'I thought you might have been closing down.'

There was a quick sense of malice in the air. Hester's eyes filled with a rush of tears as she looked from one woman to the other. Choices, Violet was always insisting on choices. At this point, David got up and went to the piano. He began to play 'Silent Night' and 'We Three Kings of Orient Are' and when they had sung themselves hoarse on *star of wonder, star of light,* he played some honky-tonk tunes that made them sing some more — *When you're near me, so help me dear, chills run up my spine/when I'm in your arms you give my heart a treat/everything about you is so doggone sweet* — and his white face seemed lost in itself. John's fingers strummed lightly on the edge of the table and the pressure of his leg increased against Jessie's. He hooked a foot around hers, where nobody could see, except David, if he happened to look up from the piano. The table in the middle of the otherwise empty café made them marooned, apart from anywhere else in the world. Violet rested her elbows on the table, her face damp from the wine, listening to the piano, and perhaps remembering other things. Then she stood up suddenly and walked over to the piano, gesturing to David to make way for her. He glanced up, saw something in the room that made his face white and hard again, and stood up. Violet sat down, her hands straying up and down the keys, searching for something, a thread of sound that would connect her with whatever was on her mind. She began to play a sweet haunting melody, running like water in the room, as if the lake was coming in, might enfold them; a blue woman with blue hair and eyes and a way of playing that made them want to weep and sing at the same time.

Only John was able to say, 'Delius.' He had withdrawn his

leg from Jessie's thigh, unhooked his foot, and was sitting as if he was totally alone in the room, except perhaps for Violet herself.

'Yes,' Violet said.

'My father's favourite. Music to be sung over water.'

'Well,' she said, and put the lid down firmly in its place, 'that's that.' As if Hugo had been finally put to rest.

The party was over. When all the dishes were washed and put away, Marianne and Jessie walked along the broad avenue leading back to the boarding house. David seemed to have disappeared. Jessie felt abandoned, wondering why John had touched her that way and then left her. The street was deserted, not a car or person in sight. The sky changed and clouds gathered. Behind them, as they walked away from the shore, the lake had turned mauve. A thick strange wind tumbled rubbish towards them down the street.

'You'd think my mother might send me a Christmas card at least,' Marianne said, her mood souring.

'Did you send her one?'

'Don't be silly.'

'Nothing from Derek?' Immediately, she regretted the question; she hadn't seen any Christmas cards come for Marianne.

'I've heard about him,' Marianne replied, looking more cheerful. 'I wrote to the bank and told them he was having it off with my mother and they sent him packing. He's left town.'

'Marianne, you didn't.'

'Why shouldn't I fix the little bastard?'

At the boarding house, the landlady who had just come in from Christmas dinner at her daughter's place told Jessie there had been a phone call from her mother the night before.

'I'm sorry, I forgot to mention it,' she said. 'Christmas, such a busy time.' Her tone reflected the extravagance of toll calls. And no, just in case Jessie was thinking of asking, she cannot ring her back, not even collect, because you just never knew with the Post Office. The next thing she'd be getting a huge bill and it would be up to her to get the money out of Jessie.

Marianne wondered if perhaps they might look at Kevin's television in the lounge, seeing that he had gone home for Christmas, but the landlady said that the assassination was one thing, but she might have known that once she gave Marianne an inch she'd take a mile.

Later, Marianne said she had to go out for a while. She came back sooner than Jessie expected, with a face like thunder, and lay on her side with her back to Jessie without speaking. Jessie saw how her shoulders shook.

Lou was eating chicken, which was on the dry side, cooked by Freda, and paid for by her, as she'd reminded him because he was short again for the housekeeping. He knew what she was on about. That gas-guzzling boat. The three of them opened the presents they had bought each other. Evelyn's gift to her mother was a silk scarf, tan and patterned with smudgy gold roses; for Lou there was a box of chocolates, the half-pound size. 'I couldn't afford a pound,' Evelyn said, fixing him with a level gaze. Since she was old enough to buy her first ice cream, she had always calculated costs with care. Freda had chosen Evelyn's gift, a beautiful leather satchel with her initials engraved on it, a way of saying 'here you are, all our dreams go with you' — or hers anyway, because it was hard for Lou to remember what dreams he was supposed to have about Evelyn. For him, there was a cashmere sweater so fine the wool seemed to melt through his fingers when he held it up. He had bought each of them a book recommended by the old woman at the bookshop. She had gift-wrapped them for him. Thank you, they said. Thank you dear. Thank you, Dad.

Lou had promised himself to do better by his family. He did not think he was a bad man. His father had often talked about the vileness of mankind, in the grave and serious way of a man whose life has been committed to stamping it out. A lawyer's son must be beyond reproach. Even though it grieved him at the time, his son would go off to war, because that was what one did, served King and country. It was just that it was all so bloody lonely, and at the time, Lou felt scared and young. When Freda's mother held a services' afternoon tea for boys going abroad, there was nothing else to do the weekend before he sailed, so he went. Freda had been there handing out cakes made with lard, and afterwards favours in the gardening shed, an older girl with a tight cunt. It hadn't seemed wicked, just something for which he would be forgiven, as he was for other girls he'd been with.

The first tour of duty, up in the Pacific, had been short. Freda had written to him, and he'd written back once or twice. When he sailed back into port, he saw what she hadn't told him in her letters — she was up the duff.

Duty. Responsibility. Other words in his father's ample vocabulary. He had wept, on the day of the wedding. 'Please Dad, don't make me.'

And still, when he was on his own, quick tears came to his eyes. He felt as if he was on his own now, and he could have blubbed, right here in front of them. Nobody seemed especially pleased that he was here at the Christmas table, in spite of the preparations. His daughter was going out with a nancy boy. She'd wanted to invite him for Christmas dinner, and Freda had agreed, but he'd said over my dead body, and nobody was speaking to him because of that. David is a nice boy, Freda had said, I don't know what you've got against

167

him. He couldn't answer that — it was just a hunch he had. He couldn't trust that white face and those pale eyes; he wasn't a boy he wanted his daughter to take up with. But nobody listened to him.

The girl looked at him from under her heavy eyebrows. He wondered if she could see into his heart. There she would see, written large, you are the person who ruined my life.

'I'm going out,' he said. 'Just for a little while.'

'Where?' Freda demanded.

'There's a wonky window at the back of the shop that we didn't have time to fix before we closed. I just need to check it out. Unless you want me to clear up.'

'We'll do it,' Evelyn said, wanting him to go, for the sake of peace.

Marianne sat huddled on the passenger side of the car, her eyes like big bruises. She's a pretty enough kid, he thought, but not worth all the trouble he was courting. None of this was ever meant to get serious. A bit of fooling around, a few cuddles with her best friend's old man. He saw it for what it was — a grown man playing around with a girl — and was ashamed. He had always thought her profile beautiful, had seen that she would be gorgeous even when she wore a gym slip, and sat in his kitchen drinking cocoa with his daughter. But God's honour, if he were asked to swear on it, he'd never planned this, and she didn't do anything for him, didn't turn him on at all.

'I thought you loved me,' she said miserably.

'You're a sweet kid.'

'When we got together it was fantastic.'

'It was just the once, you know that. I'm sorry, I shouldn't have done that.' Remembering it as quick café kitchen sex. Hard and fast when the girl was oily and hot and scummy from cleaning up, her night to stay late and the others had gone home. He had been ambushed by her longing.

'Sorry, is that all you can say?'

'Yes,' he said, steeling himself. 'I was sorry for you.'

'Thanks a lot. Sorry. Were you sorry when you gave my mother the clap?'

'You're crazy,' he said, trying to sound steady and even, but his pulse points were throbbing.

'I'm not,' said Marianne. 'I used to sleep in the same room as my mother. She couldn't keep her secrets from me.'

'I know she gave you a hard time.'

'She slept with my boyfriend.'

'D'you want to sleep with all the men your mother slept with?' he said softly. 'Jesus, is that it?'

'I thought I did.' Marianne had begun to tremble violently. 'But then when it happened between you and me, I thought this is it. It doesn't matter about her or any of the others, it's just us.' She laid her hot cheek on the car window. 'Anyway, your family don't talk to me any more, thanks to my mother.'

'Freda doesn't know for sure.' He said this and regretted it, because now there was an admission between them, that he had slept with Sybil Linley. He didn't know how he got into situations like this. 'I told you when you broke up with Derek, you should leave town. Start again. What's here for you? You're working two jobs, it's killing you.'

'You're here.'

'You need a father,' he said angrily. 'That's all.'

'So you don't, you know, feel anything?'

He sat in silence for a while. 'I have to get back. I said I wouldn't be long,' he said at last.

'So we're finished?'

'We were never started.'

'Will you kiss me goodbye?'

169

'Come here,' he said, and put his arms around her. She clung to him, sliding her hand into one of his pockets, as if for safe-keeping. Loosening himself from her embrace, he started the car's ignition. He felt tired and broken up.

David Finke had come home alone. He stayed in his room and played records. Dark palmy music. Music to sweat by. The wind had brought dull heat with it.

He would take the dark-eyed white-skinned girl out again. He would. He could do it. For a moment, at lunchtime, he thought he had glimpsed another kind of happiness. But he could see it was unattainable. He could take the girl out.

If he willed himself strongly enough.

Violet Trench's flat was very small, very white, with wrought-iron bars covering the windows. They reminded her of France, and when she looked through them, especially if the tree on the verge outside was moving and making shadow patterns on her wall, she thought of the years she spent there before the war. But that was a long time ago. There had been an inevitability about her coming to live in this place, rather than staying abroad. On the whole, she was happier here than she thought she would be anywhere else. Besides, love had arrived on her doorstep, not exactly uninvited.

On this Christmas Day, the dinner for her staff over, she climbed into bed in the late afternoon, listening to the wind that had risen outside. She lived in an ordered chaos — clothes stored close together, recipe books stacked high beside the bed with its soft fat pink eiderdown and silky feminine sheets, flowers in not one, but several vases, a tangle of pretty beads hanging from the back of a chair. There were few dishes to be found in the apartment, because Violet rarely ate here, except for an early morning snack, but there were bone china cups in the tiny galley kitchen, and glasses for wine. The phone book was under a pile of her freshly laundered lingerie but she didn't need to consult it for the number she gave the operator.

'I'm so sorry to bother the doctor, Pauline,' she said, when the phone was answered, 'but I'm so unwell, I wonder if Felix could visit me. I'm not far from the centre of town, well, you know where I am. No, no, I'm sure I'll be all right here on my own. I don't feel on my own, even though it's Christmas, because I've spent time with friends this afternoon. No, you didn't need to think of asking me round, you've got your own family to think about at Christmas. I don't know what's come over me — the most awful sick headache, sort of like a migraine, although I'm not given to them as a rule.'

Of course, Felix had been there before, he was by now a regular visitor. Her call had caught him off his guard, but he forgave her when he arrived because being with Violet was like being in a perfumed tent harbouring only delight, her blue hair floating around her shoulders in a hyacinth swathe. Even if he could stay for only half an hour.

LOVE, LOVE

Frottage. A word like French cheese. Jessie would come across it when she was older. Her erotic life would be represented for years by the desire for her body to be pressed against that of another who was clothed. She would laugh when she read that it is an abnormality, to desire people in this way, but it is what she and John did, pressing themselves against each other through their clothes. A dry root. How a woman drives a man crazy and keeps her virginity. Or a woman is driven crazy. It was what people did then, to keep themselves chaste, and you could see it any Saturday night at one of the local ballrooms, the young men and women with their bodies glued to each other as they danced. After the last waltz was over, would they, wouldn't they, go one step further and touch naked flesh? Not that the girls from the Violet Café went to many dances, except for Hester, who had some Saturday nights off to go dancing with Owen, the way she did when she first knew him. That was the thing about waitresses and dish-washers and cooks — their lives were the reverse of everyone else's. They slept late in the mornings and got up puffy-eyed at lunchtime, and their working day was just coming to life when other people were retiring for the evening, or going out to party and dance if they were young and free. It was what set them apart from others in town.

Instead of dances or visits to the movies, they went for walks or drives in the afternoon, or occasionally for trips on Lou Messenger's boat. These outings were organised by Evelyn, whose father seemed to be making special efforts to be nice to her. Nobody really wanted to go any more, except for Evelyn herself and Marianne. But at least these two seemed, for the moment, to be friends. Sitting between Marianne and David, each cocooned in their private selves, Evelyn looked more content, less inclined towards sharpness. All the same, Jessie felt out of it, even when John was there. There was no more skinny-dipping in hot pools.

'I don't want to go,' Jessie said one afternoon, when they were about to cast off.

'Why not?' John wanted to know.

'I just don't want to go. Sorry.'

As she climbed back onto land, John said, 'I'll come with you.'

The boat pulled away, trailing a wake through the slight algal bloom that had infected the water since summer began. 'Are you angry with someone?' John asked.

It was on the tip of her tongue to say you, of course, acting one minute as if you fancy me and the next as if I didn't exist.

'Stop,' John said. 'Calm down. I don't know what's got into you.' She was walking so fast he had to stride to keep up with her.

'Stop following me,' she said.

He looked as if he were about to do exactly that, then he changed his mind. They had arrived back at the café.

'Can you ride a bike?' he asked.

'Of course.'

'Well some girls can't. I've got mine out the back and there's a spare one that my brother left. He's been supposed to pick it up for ages. If you can ride a boy's bike, we could go off somewhere.'

This was how they came to ride together to the old place, where John had lived with Hugo and Ming and his brothers.

Because it was the weekend, there was nobody about, although someone had been there earlier in the day and watered the market gardens that lay all around them. Jessie's first impression was rows of ripening tomatoes, staked in long ripples as they reddened under the sun.

The house was bleached of paint, but neatly kept, as if it had just been left for the day. John unlatched the door, ushering her into a dim room, with a bench running down one side of it, woks and cooking utensils suspended from hooks on the wall. Beyond this room, she saw, as her eyes became unaccustomed to the low light, a bedroom, lined with bunks.

'Crazy,' John said, as Jessie took in her surroundings, 'they could have had whatever they wanted in the end. My mother would never change anything, and then my father became as stubborn as she was. They put their money into my brothers' businesses. I might open a restaurant of my own, when I've finished my apprenticeship with Mrs Trench.'

He had begun making her a cup of tea, first sniffing the leaves for freshness. 'My brothers have their lunch here when they're working in the gardens, I don't think there's any milk.'

'It doesn't matter.' She was sitting at the table, watching him, itching to look at the records in yellowed sleeves beside a wind-up gramophone. But she sensed that she was meant only to look, not investigate.

'Why wouldn't you go on the lake today?' he asked, handing her her tea. It looked more like dark scented water.

'I don't know,' Jessie said. 'I'm just fed up.'

'With Marianne?'

'With everyone, I guess. I have to think about going home. Back to Wellington.'

'Are you serious?'

'I should go and see my mother.'

'I thought you were mad with her.'

'Not really. My mother isn't the kind of person you get mad with. She's just inefficient.'

'Inefficient. You're a laugh. What can you do about that?'

'That's not what I mean. I can't explain.' Irene's odd irrelevance was impossible to describe, the way she could never see what was coming round the next corner, the hectic choices she'd made. All the books she had read.

'Tell me about the truffles,' she said, wanting to lead him away from the topic of her mother because she didn't really want to think about her. 'Why are they such a big deal?'

'They're called the black magic apple of love.'

'Is this where they grow?'

'Don't be silly,' he said, as if she was trespassing. 'They only grow in France.'

'But you said they grew round here, that first night I came to the café.'

'You imagined it. Anyway, women aren't allowed on the truffle beds.'

'Why not?'

'They're impure.'

'Women? What rubbish,' she said, and laughed, breaking the tension that was still simmering between them.

'I'll tell you a story, okay?'

'Okay.'

'There was an old woman who was tired and hungry and lost in the bush,' he began. 'She came to the house of an old man who was poor. Still, he asked her to come in and share his meal. All he had was some shrivelled potatoes, cooked on the hearth. As the old woman began to peel the skins off the potatoes, she turned into a fairy. "Don't be alarmed," she said. "I'm the fairy of the woods, and you're a kind man, and I'm going to give you a gift. These poor potatoes you've so humbly shared with me will bring the end to all your troubles." And in front of him, the potatoes turned into truffles, full of the scent that drives people crazy. Overpowering, mysterious truffles. So the old man got rich, but he kept on being kind and generous, and everyone still liked him. Which is unusual when people who have been poor suddenly become rich, like someone who's won the lottery. His children weren't such good people. They grew up lazy and selfish. Years later, the good fairy came back in disguise, dressed again like the old woman. The children refused to give her food and hospitality. So the fairy buried the truffles underground, round the roots of oak trees, and turned the selfish children into pigs to root them out.'

'A fairy story. Is that all there is?'

'Don't you like it?'

'Yes, of course I do,' she said, amused. 'Who told you that?'

'I made it up.'

'Was it Hugo?'

John had begun clearing up. 'He was just a father.'

Yes, she might have said, and I was the last person to kiss him, but she didn't.

The following weekend, Jessie thought they might go to the house again, but John said perhaps it would rain later in the day, and suggested, instead, a short walk near the lake. It had been decided, without actually being discussed, that they wouldn't go out with Lou and the others. Neither of them had told the rest about their trip to the house.

Together, John and Jessie wandered along the shoreline, arriving at a straggling bush area that stretched down the cobalt and yellow rocks and the pale turquoise shallows of a sulphurous bay. A notice board close to the lake edge described the way the acidic water could dissolve the webbing between the feet of ducks. John sat close to her, and let his hand fall awkwardly on her thigh. When she didn't push him away, he pressed down on her crotch. She felt a flare in the centre of her thighs, and turned towards him. She was wearing a yellow and navy striped cotton dress, for which Hester had chosen the fabric, because she thought the colours suited her. Jessie had wondered if she might look like a bumble bee, but she liked the soft satiny finish of the material. John rubbed the fabric in a circular fashion. She closed her eyes, waiting for him to lift her skirt and find the place between her legs. It's all right, she told him, but he didn't seem to hear her, as his tongue licked the inside of her ear. His hand moved to the bodice of her dress, travelling over the saucer shapes of her breasts. He hoisted himself into the valley between her legs, pressing himself to the cotton skirt, so that she could feel the softly curved outline of his penis, not what she expected. All the same, her own licking fire hadn't subsided, so that she heard herself calling out his name in a strange high-pitched voice.

He rolled off her, his face pleased and dreamy.

She wondered why this hadn't happened the weekend before, at the house, and supposed it must have been out of respect for the memory of his parents. And she wondered whether anything more would come of it.

Violet was holding forth again about the chemical properties of food and how it was cooked.

'Air is almost as important as heat, when you cook,' she told Jessie.

'Hot air?' Jessie asked.

Violet raised her eyebrows. 'Well, it depends,' she said. 'Food's full of all kinds of volatile properties that air can spoil. Or in some cases, air is just what you need. That's the secret, knowing when you need air and when you don't. If you boil water for a long time before you make tea, you drive out the air and make tea like dishwater.'

'Or vegetables?' *Cabbage, cabbage, never mind the da-mage.* The smell of it haunting every cranny of the house. 'Why are you telling me all this?'

'Oh well, Jessie, food's a journey you can't avoid. You might as well do it as best you can.'

Violet was measuring her up and down. The way she did. 'Hester will be leaving soon. I'd like you to take her place.'

'Do the cooking?'

'Hester and John can teach you.'

'I need to think about it,' Jessie said. But she could feel in her bones that she would say yes. She saw the way she and John would stand alongside each other of an evening, and how that could go on for a long time. The future stretched away before her in an infinity of bubbling pots. How to cook a steak and how to flamber. The knowledge that a sauce was ready when it reached the consistency of cream. The value of heat and air. How to read shadows. These were things Jessie had already learnt from Violet. When she looks back she will think that Violet knew she was planning to leave, that she placed temptation in her way.

As if to confirm that Jessie would not leave, Susan pulled out from being bridesmaid at Hester's wedding, and Hester asked Jessie if she would stand in for her. Hester's face was very red, hot with anger. 'I feel really stupid,' she said.

'I'm sure she would have come if she could.'

'No, she wouldn't. She didn't even have an excuse. Just sorry I can't make it. It's not even as if she had to pay for her dress. She never meant to be my bridesmaid.'

'Well, I'm really honoured that you should ask me,' Jessie said, wanting to make it all right. She could see it was now blindingly obvious to Hester that Susan was not the friend she had believed her to be, and that asking her seemed like an embarrassing afterthought, especially as she and Jessie hadn't known each other very long. And perhaps Hester didn't know very many other young women, no one else she could call her best friend. But then, Jessie decided, there were other girls at the café who could have been chosen ahead of her, and she did like Hester. And she couldn't think of anyone else who would ever be likely to ask her to be a bridesmaid. She would be too tall, or too plain, too angular altogether for frills and flounces. Although, as it turned out, it was nothing frilly that Hester wanted her to wear, but rather an elegant emerald-green satin gown that fell in a straight soft line to her ankles. When she caught her reflection in the glass, during the final fitting, she couldn't believe she was the girl in the mirror. Her hair was caught up in a knot; she had to lean down for Hester to place a circlet of green leaves and white flowers on her head.

Hester surveyed her, as if Jessie were her own personal creation. And so she was. No matter that Marianne had stopped speaking to her since news of her bridesmaid's duties had leaked out at the café, or that she must meet Harry and learn to walk down the aisle on his arm, for the bridal march, none of this mattered.

Or, that she had had another letter from her mother, written in a faltering hand:

Dear Jessie,

I'll certainly look forward to seeing some photographs of you in your outfit. I can't imagine you being a bridesmaid. I never had a white wedding, not for either of them — perhaps you remember my marriage to Jock? You were such a wee thing but you were as still as a mouse, as if you knew what a serious moment it was, though afterwards you ran a temperature. Well dear, I've got a bit

*of a temp myself right now. I had a little operation the other day,
nothing much, just a bit of a look see the dr said, you'll remember
I mentioned that I was having some tests. Nothing much to
worry about, I'm sure, things will settle down. I'm pleased you've
got nice friends, dear. But I still think you might be a writer, you
have a way with words, you know I've always told you that. Not
long until university starts now, so I expect you'll be home before
long. Can't wait to see you.*

  Much love, Mum x

Jessie didn't see how she could possibly get away, not even
for a little while. Hester was relying on her for every little
thing, including the throwing of a shower party that would
take place at her house. Jessie discovered how much time it
took to ensure that the invited guests didn't all bring flour
sifters or lemon squeezers, and that someone did have tea
towels on their list. Besides that, all of a sudden she and John
were responsible for feeding Violet's customers, and it was all
they could do that warm summer to keep ahead of the salad
preparation — and business just kept coming the way of the
Violet Café.

On the morning of the wedding, Wallace had such a bad
bout of influenza, which had been coming on all week, that
he couldn't get out of bed. Belle, who hadn't caught the bug,
said it was a shame but she could manage on her own. She
dressed herself with care, in a dusky pink dress with horizontal
pleats across the breast, usually kept for special occasions in
the church, a matching hat with a rolled brim that framed
her face, and white gloves that reached her elbows. She
dabbed something out of a mysterious bottle, which she kept
in her top drawer, around her throat and in the crooks of
her elbows. Wallace, watching these preparations from the
bed, was vaguely aware that he should be doing something

to stop her, but his temperature was a hundred and three. He supposed that she must have cleared it with her father to go on her own, but his throat was so raw he couldn't frame the words to ask her.

Perhaps it was because she'd been ill, as her mother and Wallace saw it, that she was allowed to accept the invitation to Hester's wedding. A date had been set for her to leave the café and begin the preparations for her own marriage. It had been agreed that Hester would make her wedding dress and even her father considered Hester a virtuous woman. Belle's family had treated her kindly since the day of her seizure, Wallace handling her as if she were porcelain, and might suddenly break if he was not careful. We should have got the doctor in, her mother said at the time. A passing fit, her father said. He, of all of them, looked at her in a different way, as if trying to measure some change in her. Belle was scared when he looked at her like this, because he knew her better than anyone.

In the church, Belle felt alien. All the stained-glass windows and dark panelled wood seemed ostentatious, as if she was one step away from the dreaded portals of Rome, even though it was the Church of England. The music began traditionally enough with 'Here Comes the Bride', which reassured her, because that was exactly the music she intended to have at her own wedding, but then Hester walked up the aisle, on the arm of a cousin on her father's side, who had flown all the way from England for just this duty, followed by Jessie Sandle, transformed into a stately Grecian-looking girl, and she was distracted by the gasps all around her. The train of Hester's wedding dress shimmered for yards down the aisle, encrusted with crystals and silver beads that shone under the lights of the church in a fiery incandescent glow. Thousands and thousands of them, perhaps hundreds of thousands, the newspaper reported in its wedding pages, and when Hester stepped up to meet Owen at the altar, the train collapsed over the step in a bright waterfall. Hester's face shone pinkly under the cloud of veil that obscured her face, and Belle thought that perhaps she would look like this when she married Wallace, though the dress was unattainable, unrepeatable, a miracle of devotion.

As Belle looked up, she saw Lou Messenger standing at the end of the opposite pew with his family, and she found she couldn't stop looking at him, nor he at her, so that all the lovely words of the service washed over them. She remembered the moment when she had seen him in his car and she couldn't have explained it, but a look of recognition had passed between them. Once or twice, Belle shook her head and tried to look away, but he was impossible to resist. She found herself shaping words she had never spoken to anyone. I love you. He nodded in agreement and for a moment she thought that he was going to cross the aisle there and then, but with an effort, he turned towards the ceremony, so that they both heard Hester saying 'I do', and watched her raise her shining rosy face to Owen's. The Chinese man, Harry, standing to Owen's right, presented the ring to be slipped on Hester's finger, and Ruth Hagley, between the wife of the cousin from England and Violet Trench, sat up straighter and put her chin in the air. Marianne Linley sat in the pew behind them, alongside John Wing Lee, and his brother's wife. Marianne wore a cream hat with a tiny veil shading her eyes.

The wedding reception was held upstairs in the tearooms at the swimming baths in the public gardens. Violet Trench had offered the café, but the venue had been booked for nearly a year and the deposit paid. This was back when Violet and Ruth were still not talking to each other. Besides, it was agreed, Hester should have her wedding where there was enough space for everyone to dance. The café had a dance floor only the size of a postage stamp, not enough room for

Hester to show off her fine train. She and Owen had hired a group of musicians who'd played at the Ballroom on Saturday nights for years, and they'd got to know them.

Belle ate tiny cucumber sandwiches and drank a glass of fizzy wine before the meal began. Between the main course and desserts, and before the speeches began, she slipped out of the room, down the stairs and out into the late afternoon air. She walked past the bath houses, to where Lou's red and white car was parked. He followed, not far behind, as if it really didn't matter that they were seen, catching up with her at the car, and opening the door for her. Belle found herself almost sobbing with the relief.

'It's all right,' he said. 'I'm here now.'

He drove with one hand on the steering wheel, the other pulling her close to him so that she was almost in his lap. They drove through the streets of the town, past the geysers, and out towards the open road that led to the forests, without either of them speaking. He kept driving south until they came to a dirt road that led off the highway, one of the logging roads going into the heart of the pines, and when that ran out they kept on going until there was just a path into the beech forests. They got out and walked between the trees, the branches forming a high canopy above them. Beneath them lay a soft carpet of dry leaves.

She leant into him.

'You're not ever going to leave me, are you?' he said.

'I don't know,' she said. Because already something told her that he would become her past, the best thing that ever happened to her.

Marianne left the reception early too. She saw Lou leave, and waited ten minutes or so, so as not to seem as if she was following him. But he had vanished into thin air. She walked disconsolately down to the lakefront, her needle-point shoes pinching her toes. The boat was anchored in its usual spot, too far away from the shore for her to go aboard. She called his name once or twice.

Harry made a speech. He said: 'Owen and Hester, I am wishing you in this year of 1964, good health and good appetite. Now you are married, I wish you to love each other more and more and have a smart little baby. Enjoy your life.'

Violet Trench raised her glass to propose a toast to Owen and Hester, 'the best worker I've ever had'.

To Hester and Owen, they all chorused. Below the tearooms the pale silky blue water in the baths trembled in the heat of the February afternoon. Hester's glowing eyes never left Owen, her glance travelling wherever he went in the room, even when she was greeting people. Jessie walked around distributing cake from a silver plate, small rich oblong slices, frosted with white icing and knobbly lemon-coloured letters that had read 'Happily Ever After', until they were shattered by a knife with a white ribbon tied around its handle.

'Save the last dance for me,' said John, when she delivered him his slice. He was hanging out with his brother Harry, who seemed uncomfortable and sweaty in his trim grey suit that matched Owen's, although his wife, Ann, was working the room as if it were her own wedding. Harry looked Jessie up and down and uttered a grunt, shaking his head.

'Take no notice,' John said.

Evelyn and Freda and David sat at a table talking to Patrick Trimble, the bookseller, who filled Freda's glass several times when she was not looking with sweet white wine. Ruth had decided that it would reflect badly on her if she didn't invite the opposition. Freda wore a strawberry hat with a brim, and

Evelyn a straw boater which Jessie thought suited her better than anything she'd seen her wearing before.

'I'm sure I don't know why Hester didn't ask you to be her bridesmaid,' Freda said to Evelyn, in her clear broadcasting tones, when she thought (or did she?) that Jessie was out of earshot. 'I am supposed to be a friend of her mother's.'

'It doesn't matter,' said Evelyn.

'Although I don't know that I'd want you in tow with that Chinaman they've lined up.'

'Mum, don't.'

'Where's your father?' Freda said, appearing to notice his absence for the first time.

'How should I know? Perhaps he just wanted a breath of fresh air.'

And it was scorching in the room, in spite of the fans.

John's suit fitted against the green satin dress so tightly that people turned to give him and Jessie knowing looks, and the older women pursed their lips. He was exactly the same height as Jessie, his cheek against hers, they were dancing so close that they simply put their arms around each other and swayed. John hummed in her ear. 'You're the girl for me,' he said.

'Why?' she said. 'Why me?' Evening had fallen, and they all looked different and beautiful, Jessie thought, as if their unscripted lives were becoming more connected. Although, she saw uneasily, that some of them were missing.

Violet gave John and Jessie a long look, as she danced with the butcher, Shorty Toft, whom Ruth had felt compelled to invite because his shop was just down the road from hers, so they'd been neighbours of a sort for decades. Violet looked beyond Shorty's shoulder and gave a little grimace in the direction of Felix Adam on the other side of the room. She rested two fingers of her left hand on Shorty's right shoulder and let her other hand balance like a hovering insect, so that he couldn't grasp it properly. All the same, she laughed as if she was enjoying a joke; her feet were light and so, surprisingly, were his, big man though he was. David was dancing with Evelyn, who had taken off her straw hat. Her straight dress was a trifle narrow, and David was not skilful on his feet. Still, they persevered, waltzing in a strict one two three at the edges of the parquet floor, so that they didn't bump into each other, apologising now and then for battered toes. In a pause in the music, David reminded Evelyn that he was on late shift at the radio station, and that he had to leave her now. When he walked her back to the side of the room, Patrick Trimble offered to walk downtown with him, almost as if he were a girl needing an escort, but David said no, thanks very much, it was okay. He'd see them all later. He looked over at John and Jessie and they smiled and waved to him, releasing each other from their embrace. David blinked, his thin white face more red-eyed than usual, and disappeared into the early evening.

Hester and Owen whirled around the room once more, faster and faster, in a dream-like trance, until it was time for all of them to stop.

THE GATHERING UP OF THE DAY

Wallace had decided to walk down to the café and meet Belle. He had been feeling lately that he was not giving her enough time and attention, and he wanted to reassure her that he did love her and that being married to each other would be as blissful as they had always imagined. She had appeared restless. He put it down to the culmination of patient years of praying and preparation, and reminded himself that she was still a young girl with a great deal of responsibility to face. He was proud of the way money was accumulating in their savings account. Between them, they had enough money for their furniture as well as the deposit on their house, and it would only be a matter of months now before everything changed and it would be just the two of them except when they entertained the parishioners of the Church of Twenty, or her family. Belle would be a grown-up matron, rather than a girl in her father's house. Wallace heard music and laughter coming from the café, and it sounded like the brazen revelry of infidels.

As he neared the corner by the lake, a couple walked towards him, away from the street lights, although a dim light still illuminated their shadowy embrace. The man had pressed the woman towards him, one hand cupping her bottom and drawing it in to him, the other her head, so that his fingers were spread across her skull, holding it while he kissed her on the lips. The woman allowed him to do this, putting her arms round him so that they appeared to be melting together.

He thought he recognised the man as Louis Messenger. The woman he knew — it was Belle.

Wallace stood still under the tree and watched to see what happened next. The couple eventually broke their mesmerised embrace and walked a few steps towards a car parked further along the road. Lou opened the door for Belle and she got in beside him, and in a moment the car started up and drove away.

At first Wallace thought he must have imagined it, hoped that he might wake from this nightmare, but when he moved his feet and legs they were real, and he had control over them, even though they trembled.

He walked home, got into his empty bed and waited. An hour passed and then two. At last she came in, quietly closing the door behind her, as she always did. There was no sound of a car to be heard, so he guessed she had been dropped off some little way away, so that she could walk home as she had on other nights, although how many other times she had practised this deception he was only beginning to consider.

When she was in the room, he reached out and put the light on. She looked at him with her big round blue eyes, suddenly afraid.

But he smiled at her, a big welcoming smile that she didn't trust. 'Take your clothes off,' he said. 'All of them. For me.'

That was the night before.

Violet's day started well or, at least, in a way that delivered her unexpected amusement. She parked the blue Volkswagen outside the butcher's shop, checking her make-up in the rear-vision mirror, and smoothing a velvet eyebrow with her finger tip before she alighted. The sky was such a radiant astonishing blue that for a moment she stood absorbed as if magically a part of it. It was still early in the morning, and she knew that it would soon be hot. A day for fans in every corner of the café, and the windows open towards the water.

'A right scorcher coming up,' said Shorty, by way of greeting. Already he had shavings of bone and fat speckled along the hairs on his thick forearms. 'What are we doing working on a day like this?'

'Well, some of us have to make a living, Shorty.'

'I don't know about that, Mrs Trench. I'm just about ready to hang up my apron. Thirty-five years in the trade seems long enough.'

'You're joking,' she said. 'What would I do without you?'

'That's what I reckon, Mrs Trench. You'd be lost without me. I've got a special present for you this morning.'

'A present?'

He slapped a tray down in front of her containing a large ox heart that looked as if it had barely stopped beating. A vein of fat ran along its left ventricle.

'A heart. What would I do with that?'

'Ah, now that's a good question. You never see recipes for heart meat, d'you?'

'I don't think my patrons would like finding heart on their menu. It's strange the way a heart is viewed.'

'Exactly.' He scratched his short stubbly hair with a bloodied finger and grinned at her. 'We don't eat hearts, Mrs Trench, unless we're cats. We give them.' He pulled the tray back towards him and looked at it proudly, his joke to start the morning off. 'Just remember, I'm offering you a heart that big.'

She laughed, with a touch of uncertainty, and smiled at him. He smiled back, his expression seemingly easy and amicable, his eyes more difficult to read. She started her task of choosing the day's meat.

When she got in the car, she held onto the steering wheel

for a few moments, before moving off, knowing he was still watching her from behind the plate-glass window of the red shop.

Ever since Hester had asked Jessie to be her bridesmaid, and Violet had invited her to be her apprentice, Marianne had hardly spoken to Jessie, except to tell her that it was time to put out the light, when Jessie wanted to read at nights (she had found an old pile of Zane Grey westerns and some discarded *Woman's Weekly*s in the laundry), and that she was moving at the end of the month. If she was still seeing her married man, Jessie couldn't tell. She and Marianne hadn't been anywhere together for a month or more. Jessie was working longer hours than Marianne, because now she was cooking for Violet Trench there was food preparation to be done before the café opened. Marianne didn't go out early any more, and slept a lot, as if she was exhausted all the time. John told Jessie that Sybil Linley had left town, trailing debts like confetti. Gone after a man, he'd heard, a young man at that.

'Was it Derek?' Jessie asked.

He looked at her curiously. 'I don't know,' he said, 'perhaps she just got a taste for young guys. I've heard some women are like that.'

If Marianne knew any of this, she gave no hint. Soon after John told Jessie about Sybil, Jessie saw Marianne's back huddled against her beneath the bedclothes again, and decided that her own days had become empty except for the time she spent at the café. There was nothing she could do in the room while Marianne slept.

Jessie dressed quietly, tucked a small pad in her white canvas shoulder bag, and let herself out. The day was light and fresh, full of promise. She walked through the town, down towards the gardens where canna lilies stood like bright flags, and planned how she would sit on the library's balcony, and write a letter to her mother.

The library had french doors that led outside to the balcony and another long garden, filled with rose bushes. Morning sun flooded the area and illuminated the spines of books on the shelves behind her. When she tried to write her letter, she found it harder than she expected, as if there was nothing much she could tell her mother any more, nothing her mother would understand.

Sometimes, Mum, I feel as if I'm living in a cell, I can see so much beyond where I am now, but I can't reach it, and I don't know whether it's what I want anyway. Other times I'm so overwhelmed with happiness and being here in the moment of what's happening to me that it's unbearable. You'll have worked out that I'm in love and you'll be saying that I'm too young and if you met him I'm not sure that you'd approve. I'm not sure whether my life's here or not.

When she read through what she had written, she folded the page over in the pad. The heat on the balcony was becoming intense, so she moved to the shade inside. The neat rows of books seemed like a reproach. It was months since she had opened one that mattered, as if she had become some other person from the diligent student she had been. On an impulse, she asked at the desk if she might join the library.

'Are you a visitor, or a permanent resident here?' asked the girl behind the desk.

'What's the difference?'

'You have to pay a deposit if you're a visitor. We return it when you leave, provided all your books are back. It's ten shillings,' the girl added, as if she had already decided Jessie's status. 'And you can only take four books, not six, like the permanents.'

Jessie explained that she lived at the boarding house.

'That's not a permanent address,' the girl said. 'Sorry.'

'All right then,' said Jessie, pulling out a ten-shilling note, all the money she had to last her the week. Suddenly she craved to read again, and already she had chosen a pile of books: Sholokov's *And Quiet Flows the Don*, a book of poems by T. S. Eliot, *A Beginner's Guide to Classical Mythology*. She would finish the letter to her mother when she got back to the boarding house. Or the next morning, because she had decided that tonight she really would tackle Violet about going home one long weekend. Violet must let her have some time off sooner or later. When she got back to her room, Marianne was packing her bags.

'You're leaving now?' she said.

Marianne hesitated. 'Kevin's been transferred,' she said. 'I'm taking his room.'

'Marianne, you said you were going to be an actress.'

'What's it to you? You've got a room to yourself, isn't that enough?'

'I don't see how you can go on the way you are, that's all.'

'So you're the expert on how one goes on. I heard how you and John had all your vital organs glued to each other at the wedding. That's not fucking, Jessie, that's making an exhibition of yourself.'

'Where were you that night?' said Jessie, flushing. 'With Lou Messenger? Was it him who took your photographs?'

'You snooping bitch.'

Marianne looked so angry, Jessie thought she might hit her. She put the books on her bed and edged towards the door. Marianne slumped down on her bed, her fingers knotting a small embroidered handkerchief.

'He's your married man, isn't he?' Jessie said.

'He was.' Marianne's voice was miserable and small. 'I see him all the time and he's driving me crazy, or I don't see him and that's driving me crazier still. You don't know what it's like. I go and visit Evelyn because she still expects me to, asks me why I don't come, and I make excuses, then I do go there and he's not there. We sit round and make small talk, the three of us, Evelyn's mother looking as miserable as sin, and me wanting to say, me too, I want to know where he is too, and Evelyn with that long face of hers, and her head that's already left home. Evelyn wants me to go flatting with her in Auckland — she's supposed to go and live in a women's hostel but she's not that keen. You know what she's like, she can't stand people near her, although she tries. She'd never have got through sharing a room like you and I have this summer. Besides, I can't do that — it's just another way of getting close to him. It would make me feel ashamed.'

'It's him that should be ashamed.'

'Ashamed. Oh, Jessie, you don't know half of it. He was one of my mother's boyfriends, before she got her hooks into Derek.'

'Marianne.'

'There you go, shocked again. There's nothing really shocking about sex, it's just the way it messes up your head. You'll find out sooner or later.'

'I know that already.'

'You're kidding yourself. Still, I guess it's nice to keep oneself for marriage, as Hester would say.'

'I miss Hester. Do you think she's all right?'

'Hester? Of course she is. She's got her heart's desire. Lucky old Hester.'

'I'll miss you too.'

'Like bloomers. I'll just be along the passage.'

'I still think you should leave.'

'What about you? Do you really want to live at the Violet Café for the rest of your life?' Marianne indicated the pile of books on the bed.

Jessie shrugged. 'Perhaps.'

'Oh well, Violet's got you earmarked for John. Do you mind that he's Chinese?'

'It's part of the attraction, I guess. He's different. Anyway, it's got nothing to do with Violet. I'm in love with him.'

Marianne sighed. 'Sure, you are. By the way, your stepfather rang. He sounds like a bit of an arsehole.'

'Jock? Are you sure?' A pit in the bottom of Jessie's stomach was opening up. 'What did he say?'

'Nothing much. You're to ring him. Just do it.'

'She'll kill me.' Meaning the landlady.

'She's out, she won't get the bill for a month.'

The phone rang and rang in the house at Island Bay in Wellington, but nobody answered. Jessie had a quick image of wild sea thrown high in the air above black rocks, and remembered the rush of cooling air that followed the waves. Later in the day, she went to the Post Office and rang again, but still there was no answer.

Outside, the street was full of blinding light, the heat so intense that the edges of the street bled tar.

'You need photographs, darling,' Freda said, 'you know, to put on your wall, to make you think of home.'

'I'm not going that far away, Mum,' said Evelyn, putting another pile of neatly folded cotton underwear in her suitcase. She was leaving the next day.

Freda slipped a pair of blue-strapped sandals in a paper bag and handed them to her daughter. 'Oh look,' cried Freda, pulling out a box of photographs. 'Here you are with Daddy when you were just a wee thing and he was home on leave. It was just before he sailed back up to the Pacific.'

The child in the picture had dark hollow eyes and tight black curls. The man holding her hand wore a sailor's cap tilted over his eyes. He had a cigarette in his mouth, a cavalier boyish stance. It was one of those matchbox-sized photographs, sharp and particular in its detail.

'Did you take the photograph?'

'I must have done, although there's another one here of the three of us together, so someone else must have taken that.' Freda handed Evelyn the second picture, and there she was at the end of the row, a woman wearing a hat like a porridge plate, white gloves and a tailored suit. She looked like the man's mother. The child was holding herself against the mother's skirt.

'Would you like that one, darling? The three of us.'

'I don't know that I want to put my baby photos up at the hostel,' Evelyn said, and then seeing the way her mother's eyes clouded, she added, 'Well, perhaps it would be nice. Thank you.' She slipped the photograph into her shoulder bag. 'I think I've done just about enough for now. There's not much left to do.'

'You're not working tonight, are you?'

'I said I would. It's extra money, you know. Did you have something planned?'

'Not really,' said Freda. 'I just thought. Oh well, never mind. I'll see you later.'

Thinking, of course, how she'd brought Evelyn this far, and how her life depended on her being there, and how this was the very hardest thing she had ever done, letting her go, sending her away. And it couldn't be soon enough, because there was nothing here for a girl like her. Her father was no help, and the girl Marianne had outlived her usefulness as

Evelyn's only friend, now that she drooped all over the place mooning about her broken engagement. And that was not all, of course, but she could hardly hold the mother's sins against the girl. Freda had thought that she and Evelyn would spend this last evening together, chatting and remembering, and looking forward. Somewhere, there lurked a small treacherous idea that one day when the moment was right, and Evelyn had become successful, she would slip out of town and join her, leaving all of this behind. 'Are you seeing David?' she asked, as Evelyn prepared to leave.

'I said I'd have a coffee with him at the café, just to say goodbye.'

Freda wanted to ask if it that meant goodbye for good, but decided to leave it. Part of her wanted Evelyn to have a reason to come back on a regular basis, but another voice reminded her firmly that David, with his light transparent eyes, was too much like Evelyn to be good for her, and she had a suspicion that he might not be good for any woman.

Freda sighed as she picked up the photographs and began stacking them in the box again. She paused over one she hadn't seen before, a recent picture, judging by the newness of the paper it was printed on. Her hands trembled as she sat and studied it.

Freda was not the only mother worrying about her daughter. Across town the chill shiver of loneliness was scurrying around Ruth Hagley's empty house. She hadn't long come in from her day at the shop, and now she stood in the hallway, her hand poised above the phone. Why not ring Hester? She was her only daughter after all, and they had shared a home for twenty-nine years until that man took her away. This house would belong to Hester some day when she was gone. She pictured Hester in her white farm cottage with its silly small rooms, the old-fashioned coal range which, however Hester cleaned and shone it, it was still just a coal range, an instrument of inconvenience. The way Hester had all the curtains and shades pulled up, it was a bit hard to miss its imperfections. And didn't she know that the new couch she'd bought would soon fade if it was left exposed to light? She had things to learn, that daughter of hers. Not that there was anything she wanted to be told. The last time Ruth rang, just that morning, she had heard a sigh of exasperation when she reminded Hester to boil all the drinking water out there on the farm. It was one thing to run a house in town, another for an innocent creature like Hester to look after a place in the country. Ruth thought of it as a dump, a rural slum, with hens pecking round the dusty backyard, and horse droppings along the fenceline that made her think of zoos. If she rang now, Owen would still be cleaning the shed, mucking out he called it, which filled her with distaste. He made excuses when Ruth rang. Just yesterday, he'd had the effrontery to tell her that Hester was lying down, and couldn't come to the phone. You know how it is, he'd said, in quite an insolent way. Ruth supposed Hester was having one of her bad periods. Well, for that she was thankful, the worst thing she could think of, next to Hester leaving home, and her being all alone, was that that man, the uncouth fellow who was now her son-in-law, would impregnate her daughter at the very first go. The first go. Oh. The thought made her dizzy. All the arms and legs and bits that went into it, her poor child pinned down in those absurd rituals and embraces. No wonder she had to lie down.

Ruth's hand hovered over the phone uncertainly and then she allowed it to fall on the receiver while she turned the handle and asked for Hester's number.

Hester had actually had to lie down after a fit of weeping

because, more than a month after the wedding, she had still not been totally deflowered by Owen. There was much sweating and straining on his part, and attempts at stoicism and not screaming on hers, but they had been unable to make all the parts fit together. A visit to Dr Adam was scheduled for the end of the week.

When Ruth rang, she said in a dispirited voice: 'What do you want, Mother?'

'Just thought I'd see how your day went, dear.'

'It was fine thanks, Mother.'

'I guess it takes a bit of getting used to, out there.'

'It does.'

'What are you having for dinner?'

'I've made a chicken casserole.'

'That sounds lovely. The one with cider and apple in it?'

'That's the one.'

'My favourite.'

'I know, Mother. What are you having?'

'Oh, I might open a little can of sardines.'

'You need more than that. Have you got some salad greens?'

'I didn't think to get any.'

'Bread?'

'There's some of that bread you brought in last week that's still in the cupboard.'

'Mother, I can't feed you now. You have to do it for yourself.'

Ruth gave a small wail. 'It's all right, dear, you don't have to worry about me now,' she said. This was her moment to put the phone down firmly in its cradle.

A northbound bus passed Hester and Owen's gate every evening around six. Hester had begun driving lessons in Owen's pick-up truck, but what with one thing and another, they hadn't been going well. Perhaps if she asked him when he came in from the shed, he would take her to town. If she pleaded with him, she knew he would, but she didn't really want to ask anything of him. She hadn't fallen out of love with him, not yet anyway, but she felt indebted to him in a way she couldn't explain. Besides, he'd already taken her to town on three rescue missions since their wedding day, such a few weeks ago. She took off her apron and filled a bag with groceries. Outside, the stifling air crackled with sheet lightning. When she hailed the bus, it stopped for her. It was nearly empty and with relief she eased herself into a seat near the front. She remembered, too late, that she hadn't left a note for Owen.

Wallace said Belle was a fallen woman and he didn't know whether praying together would do any good at all. First, Hal came in and beat her with his belt until she was black and blue. Then Wallace put her across his knee and spanked her, but it didn't make any difference. She had another man's smell all over her and even Hal wouldn't try to persuade Wallace to marry her, now that she'd been unfaithful, although it was clear that he'd like him to get her off his hands. Wallace realised now that there was something about Belle that had made him suspicious from the beginning; flirting was what came to mind. It felt now as if he'd been betrayed from the start.

Banks of cumulus cloud were building over the lake, each a collapsing catastrophe of swirling air and vapour. The water had turned purple and sullen as evening fell. It seemed dark, even for a late summer evening. Jessie had phoned again from the Post Office, got through to the house and spoken to her half-sister Belinda. The children were alone on the house. Why? Jessie had demanded. Where's Mum?

And then Belinda had started to cry and said that their mother was at the hospital and Dad was there too.

'Listen, Belinda,' Jessie said, 'you must listen to what I say. Get a pencil and paper, all right? Now this is the number that Dad's to ring when he comes home.' She gave Belinda the number at the Violet Café and made Belinda read it back to her twice. 'You have to give it to Dad,' she said. 'You have to tell him to ring me there.'

Evening at the Violet Café. The tables were full. The soup of the day was tomato, the fish terakihi and the special Steak Flambé, served straight from a sizzling pan and set alight with hot brandy at the table. Marianne and Evelyn were trying to teach the menu to Debbie, who would replace Evelyn as a waitress. Debbie was a sultry girl with astonishing ripe lips, the third of four daughters who lived with their father out in the western suburbs. Not a first choice for Violet but there seemed to be plenty of work going for young women that year — filing clerks, shop assistants, stenographers for those who had 'done commercial' at school, meter maids, veterinary office jobs (the young women loved those), library staff (for those who'd 'done academic'), tourist guides, boat hands, forestry research workers (for those who'd 'done science') — so who could blame the young women of the town for taking jobs that offered more regular hours of freedom? Violet had a feeling Debbie might be lazy and would have to be shown that she was not allowed an idle moment in her employment.

All the same, when the café opened, Violet's mood was still light, following her encounter with the butcher that morning. By way of entertainment she would have liked to tell John and Jessie that she was being courted because now she viewed them as a couple in whom she could confide, established senior partners in her enterprise. But while she was still turning over the wisdom of such intimacy, Jessie told her that she was expecting a phone call.

'You can't take calls here,' Violet said. 'You know that, Jessie.'

'I have to. Please. My mother's in hospital and I don't know what's wrong with her.'

'You should have attended to the problem during the day.'

'I couldn't. I've tried.'

'Really, Jessie, I thought I could depend on you.'

'But you'll let me speak to my stepfather when he rings? You must.'

'Well, I'll have to see.'

Belle had come in, off song and out of sorts as well. Violet could see it was going to take all her will to manage this evening.

Earlier, Belle had met Louis Messenger in the pergola by the bowling pavilion in the gardens. She rang him at work — twelve-thirty, please come. She knew that Wallace was supposed to help his future brother-in-law out in his menswear shop over the lunch hour, because he was short-staffed too. She counted down the hours until lunchtime, worrying that Wallace might not go, because she was being watched. But some sort of calm, a sense of resignation, seemed to have settled over the house, as if something had been decided. At twelve, he nodded briefly to her and closed the door behind him.

'I can't see you any more,' she told Lou, when they stood squeezed in the pergola behind a screen of leaves. 'He'll kill me. You don't know what he's like.'

'Then come away with me,' Lou said. 'You're the first girl I've ever really fancied. I'm in love with you, honest.'

'Lou, you've been with lots of girls.'

'Of course I have, that's how I know. I've never told a girl I

201

loved her. Not until this minute, I swear. Look, my daughter's leaving home tomorrow, so I can go now, I don't have to stay with Freda, I never meant to.'

'They'd find me, Lou,' she said, trying to keep her voice low because a group of bowlers were going into the pavilion for lunch.

'Who, who would find you?'

'My father. Wallace. The Church of Twenty.'

'You don't believe any of that? It's rubbish, they talk rubbish, they make up their own rules.'

'Maybe, Lou, but if they got me … I can't tell you. Can't take the risk.'

'You don't know what you're missing, how our lives could be. You've never had anyone else but that weird guy you're with. Mad Wallace.'

'Yes, I have,' she said, 'yes I have.'

'I don't believe it. Who?'

'I can't tell you.' Her face on fire. And then, because he really didn't believe her, she whispered a name in his ear. He shuddered and cried out in the hot summer afternoon.

'No,' he said, 'not that. Jesus, Belle. I've got to take you away. You have to come away with me. Save you from all this.'

'Oh, don't talk about saving me,' said Belle. 'I'm sick of being saved.'

'I'll die without you. I can't live without you, Belle. For Chrissake, my life depends on this. I swear my life's not worth living if you don't believe this. Don't do this to yourself. Get out of it now.'

On and on, until half past one, two o'clock, and she was running away up the street, and he was standing in the pergola in the gardens howling like a kid, his head leaning against his arm, the scent of roses in the air, and women in white dresses walking past and wondering about him. The weather had begun to turn, the sky was turning streaky and dark and the first shower of the day fell, so that he was wet when he got into his car and drove back to work. Wet and crying. He wouldn't take no for an answer. Later, he would see her again, make her see reason.

Leaving. It was in all their minds.

The special of the day was Steak Flambé but Felix Adam said he'd just settle for a good bit of fillet, thank you very much, with some of that nice gravy or whatever it was. If his wife wanted to indulge herself, by all means order food with fire.

John had shown Jessie how to make sauce Béarnaise. She had already made it twice on her own and each time he and Violet had assured her that she had the touch of a master. You understand the poetry of a good sauce, Violet had enthused. But tonight, at the moment when the consistency of the sauce should have been turning to that of light cream, something had gone wrong. The sauce looked curdled.

'What's the matter with you?' John demanded. 'You're away with the fairies.'

'I'll start over again,' Jessie said.

'There isn't time,' he said crossly, lifting the pot onto his side of the stove. 'Give it to me and I'll see if I can fix it.'

'What's the point? It's ruined.'

'So if you know all about it, how come it's such a mess?' It was not like them to quarrel when they worked; as a rule the rhythm of their almost wordless routine was so harmonious that it felt effortless. Touching and brushing, as they passed each other, brushing and touching. Like Hester and Owen dancing.

'Look,' he said, 'you take another egg yolk, and beat it in a fresh bowl. The sauce has to be added to it, a drip at a time. It would be a help if you trickled it in for me while I stirred it.'

Jessie stood so close that she could feel him breathing against her.

'John,' Jessie said, 'I have to go home.'

Owen came into the café, his face pale. 'Where's Hester?' he said. 'I need to see her.'

'She's not here,' said Violet. 'What *is* the trouble, Owen?'

When he turned away without answering, she said very kindly: 'Sit down, Owen. I'm sure it will be all right. The girls will get you a coffee, something to eat. You haven't eaten tonight, have you? No, I can see that.'

David, sitting at the piano and playing a medley of this and that in a soft and melancholy way, watched Evelyn as she laid a place for Owen at a recently vacated table. Tomorrow it would be over. The girl would be gone, and perhaps before long, he would go too. He'd given his best in this town, and over the summer he had tried to become one of those men he was expected to grow into, but it hadn't worked, and staying here would bring only heartache. David watched covertly for glimpses of John when the door into the kitchen swung open, and his face darkened. He looked back to Evelyn, wondered what he and the girl might say to each other, how they might say goodbye. He was sorry for her. Her father was there again, the way he so often was. This evening he had managed to attach himself to Dr Adam and his wife, lending an attentive ear to Pauline, but really he was watching the girls, the way he always did. If David had loved Evelyn, the way he might have, he believed he would have killed Louis Messenger by now.

Violet said, 'Marriage can take time, Owen.'

'That's what I tell her,' Owen said. 'But how can it not be

all right so soon? When we've never had a cross word in all those years we were courting?'

'I don't know all the answers,' Violet said, answering him slowly. 'I made mistakes of my own. I was careless and impatient and didn't always weigh up what was best for others.'

'I can't believe that,' Owen said, gesturing round the café. 'You always seem to be thinking of others.'

'Do I?' Violet lifted one shoulder and let it drop. 'That's very flattering. Do you know, Owen, I'm being courted?'

Owen wasn't listening. 'I do love Hester, you know. I'll wait for as long as it takes.'

Debbie, the new waitress, struck a match and held it under a silver spoonful of brandy, as Marianne produced a steak on a hot pan, straight from the kitchen. She placed it in front of Pauline Adam, as Debbie poured the brandy and set it alight with a fresh match. And it was in the ensuing rush of flames that lit up the faces of Dr Adam and his eager greedy wife that Freda Messenger threw open the door of the Violet Café. Pauline was bending forward, so that her waxy complexion looked as if it might melt in the merry racing firelight, when Freda lunged towards Marianne, almost causing a much bigger conflagration.

'Slut,' shouted Freda, in front of everyone, the guests, the staff, her own daughter, suddenly alarmed, at the far end of the café. Before anyone could stop her, Freda had pounced on Marianne, flailing her round the head with one hand, while in the other she brandished a small black-and-white photograph. 'This is you, you with your clothes off, you filth, you dirty little tramp. You're just like your mother.'

Marianne saw the photograph, and understood, as she raised her hands to protect her face. The flames had subsided; nobody noticed Pauline flapping her hands over her sizzling hair as everyone sat mesmerised by the spectacle unfolding in front of them. Violet stood up at the desk, and moved to intervene, but Freda was not having that. She threw herself at Marianne's blouse, grasping it at the throat, and tore the whole thing from her, so that she stood in her snow-white brassiere, the tops of her breasts exposed.

'My husband, and you,' Freda gasped. She turned to Evelyn. 'Your friend, this girl I've had in my house, all these years I've looked after her when her mother wouldn't, she's been at it with your father.'

In the kitchen, John said, 'Leave it, Jessie.'

Belle was standing very still at the sink.

'Let them sort out their own problems,' John said.

'I have to go,' Jessie said. 'John, let go of me.' Because he was holding her by her arms, his fingers in her flesh, in a way she had never felt before, hurting her. She was embarrassed that this was happening in front of Belle, but Belle showed no sign of noticing them.

'I don't want you to go,' John said.

Jessie pulled herself free and walked into the café.

Evelyn's mouth was pulled back in a snarl. Lou gaped at her across the room while Debbie, the new girl, hid behind a chair. There was an unpleasant smell of burning in the room.

'Freda,' Violet said, 'I'm calling the police. I'm warning you, one more step and you'll spend the night in the cells.' She was whipping the handle of the phone round, as she called the operator. 'Emergency,' she said.

'Oh, you're no better,' Freda hissed at Violet. 'No wonder the tarts all come to you. To think I let my own daughter come here.' Freda's breath was on Marianne's face. A weal was springing up on her cheek where Freda had scratched her. Lou stepped forward at last, grabbing Freda's wrists and bending them back, before she attacked again.

This was the moment Belle chose to emerge from the kitchen, wiping her hands on her apron. She went over and stood beside Lou and his struggling wife.

'It's not Marianne's fault,' she said. 'It's not Marianne he's with. It's me.'

Evelyn collapsed on a chair, looking as if she was about to be sick. 'Get that girl out of here,' Violet said. 'Somebody, take Evelyn away.'

Lou threw Freda's hands to her sides. Violet placed herself between the group and the diners, who for the most part were picking up their knives and forks, pretending they were not interested, although the place was as quiet as the inside of a church. Lou pulled a bundle of keys from his pocket and tossed one to Owen. 'The boat,' he said.

'Where will I take her?' Owen asked.

'You can take her to my old place,' said John. He stepped forward. 'I'll come with you and open up.' His voice held a bitter resigned note.

In a few minutes, Marianne and Jessie found themselves standing outside the café. In a separate group, Owen and John and David, who had got up from the piano without speaking and followed the others, accompanied Evelyn down towards the lake. Nobody called out or said goodnight or goodbye. Inside the café the phone was ringing but nobody answered it.

'Where are we going?' Marianne asked. She buttoned up the jacket she had pulled on as she was leaving the café.

'I don't know where you're going, but I'm going home,' said Jessie. 'As far away from here as possible. You should too.'

'I don't have a home. Just the room.'

'You've got your stuff packed. Go, Marianne.'

'Can I come with you?'

'I've got nowhere to take you. My mother's sick. You'll have to do this on your own.'

'When are you going?'

'Now. I'm hitching.'

'You can't. Feel the weather.' Rain spat in their faces and wind was raising the hair on the backs of their necks.

'Pretend it's morning and you're lying on a wet bank.'

They were standing in the gathering storm, beneath a street lamp. 'Bitch.' Marianne's voice held the vestige of a chuckle, despite the dark shadows under her eyes. The rain flattening her hair against her head making her look skinned and more naked than she already was. 'What about your stuff, Jessie? You have to pack up if you're going.'

'It's not worth taking. Return my library books if you're still here, would you?'

They found themselves awkwardly embracing. 'You'll be all right,' Jessie said. 'Think of Columbine.'

'I'll be fine. By the way, it wasn't Lou who took the pictures. It was Kevin.'

Part Five

Ways to Leave

1964

BOATING

The boat bearing Evelyn and David, John and Owen, headed out to open water, trailing a swollen wake. John's old house lay to starboard, although he couldn't make out its dark shape on the horizon. Rain and mist had closed in, obscuring the details of land. He remembered that the electricity at the house had lately been turned off, but they could light candles, make up a fire.

Even as John was thinking this, the first hard blast hit them. The stormy wind that had been sitting in the hills all evening descended to lake level. The sky was leached of all light. The rain turned fat and cold, driving into their faces, drenching them in seconds. Suddenly the boat pitched, riding high out of the water and throwing them all sideways.

'Go down below,' Owen ordered Evelyn and David.

But Evelyn, who had been in the boat more times than any of them, and had steered it across the lake, even when she was a child, wouldn't go down. Perhaps, knowing the boat and the lake as well as she did, she was more quickly afraid.

'Give it to me,' she cried, trying to snatch the wheel from Owen.

The surface of the lake had turned into a series of sharp chopping waves. It wasn't deep, not a big enough body of water to absorb the shock of sudden violent weather. When the waves came, they were like serried rows, leaving no gaps for the boat to squeeze through, no swell they could ride out, as they might have done at sea. Others had been caught on

211

the lake. Once John had helped rake out a body, so bloated that it fragmented when touched and had to be gathered up in pieces.

The curtain of rain had become driving and slanted, blurring in the wind and dashing spots in their eyes. Then, as a flash of lightning illuminated their path, he saw Evelyn and Owen struggling at the wheel. Owen pushed Evelyn away, his actions panicky, as the *The Wench* reared up, and turned sideways in what seemed like one long agonising motion. Then the deck rolled into the water.

John, Owen and Evelyn were thrown into the water. In a split second while wildfire raced across the sky, John saw the white shape of David's face in the space leading to the galley and he seemed to be laughing. How could he have seen this flash of joy? Yet he did see it, he knew it. The clouds parted, and a thin band of white moon emerged above the three figures struggling in the water. The boat was riding upside down, the hull above the waterline. Evelyn reached the hull and clung, her knuckles straining. Beside John, Owen was gasping in great ragged breaths of air.

'Not much …' he said. 'Not much of a swimmer.'

'Hold on, mate,' John said, grabbing his shoulders from behind. He began paddling towards the boat. Surely, such a big vessel wouldn't sink, might even touch ground if it drifted. Owen was heavy as well as frightened. He reached behind him, trying to climb up on John but succeeded only in dragging his head under. John hit him in the mouth then, as hard as he could.

'I've got to get home,' Owen said. 'I've got to get home to Hester.'

'Then don't fight me, mate.'

They had reached the hull. Inside it, John heard banging, the trapped animal that was David, wanting to be alive after all. He pushed Owen hard up against the boat, willing him to grab it. But Owen raised his arms in a supplicating gesture and collapsed.

'Come on, man, you've got to hold the fucking boat,' John screamed. He grabbed the other man's hand and found it floppy and limp and, quite suddenly, Owen dropped like a stone beneath him.

The boat settled further in the water. Evelyn had managed to climb out onto it and was scratching and clawing the timber. 'David's in there,' she cried.

'I know but we can't do anything. We'll have to wait till help comes.'

The two of them began shouting then, trying to tell David to stay still, to conserve his oxygen, but there was no sign he'd heard them. The pounding inside was persistent but growing more feeble. The clearing in the sky widened, and John thought he saw lights coming towards them.

'Who'd come looking for us?' Evelyn said in a weak pale voice. She was all skin and bone, he thought, skinny inside and out. But she deserved better than what she'd been handed, a jerk like her father. His brothers said Lou wasn't a jerk, he was an okay man who'd been unlucky in his life, but John wasn't so sure. One way or another, they were all in the drink, and Owen was already at the bottom. Still, Lou knew they were out here on the lake. Someone would come looking for them soon. He realised that the lights that he had seen came, after all, from a sprinkling of houses at the point. They were farther out than he thought, perhaps being carried towards the island. They might make land soon. Beneath them, the boat began to make a new ominous sucking sound.

'Come back,' he said, trying to pull Evelyn off. 'She's going down.'

'I'm not leaving David,' she screamed.

A wall of water appeared in front of John. In an instant, the boat, the dark flag of Evelyn's hair and the white cameo of her face disappeared beneath the surface. One moment he was swimming away from the boat while Evelyn hung on, and then it appeared that it was just him alone, and he was very tired and cold, and the wind, seesawing this way and that, was pushing him away from the island. John called out to Evelyn once or twice, but there was no answer. His voice was nothing more than an absurd whisper.

He lay on his back, too exhausted to swim. The smell of sulphur filled his nostrils, blown across the water in erratic gusts. Then the rain stopped and the lake began to calm. An incandescent moon was now sailing in and out between the piled cumulus. He remembered the way his father, Hugo, had taught him the names of clouds — cumulus, cirrus, stratus, nimbus — and then the refrains of their combinations and variations. There were so many things his father had wanted him to do, always urging him to try harder, as if looking for something special in him. One day he would want him to go away to university; on another day he would try to interest him in music.

And there were the visits to the woman Violet; sometimes he wondered if his father preferred her to his mother. Certainly they talked a great deal, but it was mostly to do with what planting should be done at the gardens and what markets Hugo and his sons should be searching out. Violet had been connected with the world of market produce since she was a girl, and after her travels abroad she had new ideas about what would sell. These visits had begun on her return from overseas, when he was still at school and before she opened the café. They had visited her in her tiny womanly flat, drinking dark coffee out of small cups, as plans were made. It was all very intense. Yet John had found himself drawn to

Violet too, and nothing that Hugo suggested appealed once she had offered him a job in the café. Perhaps he wasn't clever enough. Or disciplined enough, his father had hinted. He saw the way Hugo frowned when he said he wanted some fun out of life. You can work and have some fun too, if you work for me, Violet said. Not that I shan't keep you in order. Hugo said that he could do worse than learn to cook. But he wore a worried frown, as if some small chime of discord was sounding an alarm.

It had fallen to Hugo to bring up his son John. Now that he was going to die, John tried to summon his mother's face, but she had been a long time dead, and she had not mothered him as she had her other sons. He wanted to be a boy who was hard and strong like his brothers, or at least like Harry and Sam, for the brother above him was strong but in a way that made him afraid. John wished, too, that his mother had spoken to him in Mandarin, as she did to all the other boys when they were home. But his mother never talked to him in her native language. There are some things best forgotten, she had said, or words to that effect. As if forgetting was a job that you could get up in the morning and do. Besides, he saw that she had forgotten none of it, and her silence stood between them as some kind of reproach he couldn't understand. Hugo was the one who looked after him, and he treated him with a gentleness that had set him apart for as long as he could recall.

Ming didn't say goodbye to him when she died. Take me to the window, she had said to Hugo, on the day of her death. Let me look out on the lake. That was where she had sat, while the other boys, who had been called, sat with her and watched the light going down on a winter's afternoon. John had stayed late at school on library duty that day, and she hadn't waited. That was unfair, he believed, a sign that she had less regard for him than his brothers.

When he thought about who would mourn him, it occurred to him that Violet would, more than anyone. Jessie would be relieved, glad that she had gone when she did. He closed his eyes and thought about the homely girl with the lovely creamy neck whose body he pressed to his, and thought it was better like this. What was between them was all a lie, even though he liked her enormously, and wouldn't have wanted to hurt her for the world. But she would have gone anyway; she was ready to leave that night and what could he possibly have offered her that would have brought her back? He didn't understand why Violet had tried to set up their partnership, like an arrangement, or a marriage in the offing. As if she wanted to hold him there, keep her eye on him with someone safe. Well, it didn't matter now. All that was past.

The water round him seemed to be turning warm and turquoise, as if he had been overtaken by the silky sinuous blueness of the best days of his childhood by the lake. He held one of his hands up above his face; in the moonlight, it was a cold curled claw that he could no longer feel. Then it seemed impossible to think about anything any more except that he hoped they would find him all in one piece, that his fingers wouldn't have floated away, that the giant eels said to congregate at the river's mouth wouldn't make short work of him.

THE BEAUTIFUL GIRL

Lou had been in the forest for three days. Sometimes he whistled to himself; at other times he whittled pieces of wood and bark with an ivory-handled pocket-knife that his father, the lawyer, had given him for his twelfth birthday. Each gift he bestowed was presented with a ceremonial clearing of the throat, a small speech about the responsibilities of accepting the present, and of getting older.

Lou's first attempt at killing himself had failed. He had taken a piece of garden hose with him as he left home. When he'd come to the clearing in the forest, he tried it out, attaching the hose to the exhaust and leading it inside the car. Then he drank a bottle of whisky, in order to stupefy himself. He would just drift away into unconsciousness. All very painless. Nobody would think to look for him here at the end of this almost abandoned track, familiar only to him. Months might pass, years even. And still he would be in this secret place. Above him stretched a canopy of beech trees, their light leafy crowns almost meeting overhead. At the edges of the clearing was a stand of mingi-mingi and tightly gathered ferns. A tree fall, perhaps the result of wind throw, or of age, marked off the boundary on the south side. Lou sat on this fallen tree and contemplated the uselessness of that failed first attempt, the comic ineptness of it. The hose had been full of holes. He could hear Freda telling him that if only he had paid more attention to things around the home, he would have discovered this.

It took a day for him to wake up and find out what had caused the problem. He used his pocket-knife to trim the hose back, hoping to get rid of the offending gaps, but then it was too short. Besides he'd run out of petrol while the engine purred away on his fruitless bid. He had calculated the bare minimum of fuel needed to bring him here, so that he wouldn't be tempted to drive off. He wouldn't be going anywhere.

He could always hang himself. But if he failed? If he did a bad job at that too? Slow death, the full punishment. He was appalled that he was so afraid, but ashamed that perhaps he didn't want to die as much as he should.

Because, really, there was nothing to live for. LAKE CLAIMS LIVES — YOUNG PEOPLE DROWN. The headlines ran in a never-ending ribbon in front of him. The quarrel with his family. His boat. His girlfriends, their lives in tatters. Children, a voice in his head reminded him, a voice that again sounded remarkably like Freda's. They were not children, he found himself arguing. They were over the age of consent.

They were children when you met them. Her relentless voice had followed him, transporting him back in to some place in time, when girls with gap-toothed smiles, wearing frilly dresses with flat-chested bodices gathered at his house and sang 'Happy Birthday', and clapped for Evelyn, the child willed on to him.

But Belle wasn't a child. Belle had never been to the parties, never left his house bound for a school dance, as Marianne had done. Belle had come to him fully formed, an adult with a history as mysterious and ugly as his own. He was her first choice, the first man she had picked on her own. What would they have done to her by now?

'I looked at you and God brought me a vision of evil,' Wallace said, the night of the fight. As others were fleeing,

218

Wallace had appeared in the restaurant, soft-soled and fat-faced with a look of satisfaction, so that Lou knew he had been watched and followed.

The forest floor was littered with leaves and the raw spoils of partly formed humus, and carpets of mosses and liverworts, making every footfall soundless. He studied the leaves for what seemed like the thousandth time, their serrated edges and various colours, brown, darkly red, some transparent except for their skeletal veins, gathered in drifts. Already, the car was becoming concealed.

Once, or twice, he heard helicopters overhead and, later, a sweep of light aircraft. He sat very still until they had passed over. The day before he had eaten a mushroom, a fungus that looked like an exposed brain, with a long smooth pale stalk pushing its grotesque load above the leaves. Once, when he'd been hunting, he remembered being told by a companion that it was called a brain fungus, and that it was deadly poison. But if it was, all it did was make him vomit.

Running his hands over the stubble on his face, he felt the hollowness of his cheeks, knowing he was getting weaker and light-headed. On each of the three nights he had been in the forest, he had slept in the car, either passed out as on the first night, or slipping in and out of a restless sleep crowded with dreams. First his mother, the daughter of a grocer, who thought that marrying into the professions would be a good thing for her, even though his father was a man of colour. She never learnt French, but otherwise she had tried to live up to his father's expectations, the good life and the summers by the lake. Oddly, having provided her with all this, he spent the summers reading in remote corners of the house. She'd simply died after a while, as if the effort of pleasing him was too much. When Lou dreamt of his mother, he found himself asking her what to do, how she had got out of it. At what point, he wondered, had she simply been able to stop being alive?

They all filled these dreams then. Owen, so newly and perfectly married. The brothers at the shack by the lake who had been his mates, who had helped him build that first little boat that he had loved. Hugo's youngest son posted as missing along with the others. His daughter's sad-looking boyfriend, if that's what he was. And Evelyn. What of Evelyn? His own flesh and blood.

Evelyn was alive, that was the miracle. The searchers on the shoreline had found her, more dead than alive, washed up at the river's mouth.

He had gone to the hospital the second day after she had been found, parking close to the hospital door, so that he could slip in without drawing attention to himself. She was in a room on her own at the end of the corridor, in a high bed. As much as he could see her from the doorway, behind the oxygen tubes and ventilators that fed her rasping airways, her face was hard-edged and remote. She had pneumonia, the nurse who met him had said, but he couldn't go in. She was very sorry but Dr Adam had left strict instructions that only her mother could visit Evelyn.

And then Freda had arrived, bearing down on him from the opposite end of the corridor. A plump, moist-faced woman, swollen around the eyes, hung onto Freda's elbow with one hand, stumbling as she walked. In the other hand she held a bunch of flowers.

'That's Mrs Finke,' the nurse said uncomfortably.

David Finke's mother. Behind the two women, holding back, stood a man clutching the brim of his hat in both hands, not wanting to go forward with them. It occurred to Lou, then, that the prime purpose of Mrs Finke's trip from Hamilton was not to visit his daughter, but to retrieve the body of her son. And that this would be David's father.

Freda looked at him with narrowed eyes.

'Murderer,' she said. That was all. The two women entered the sickroom and the door was closed behind them. The man stood in the corridor, snot oozing over his upper lip, not wanting to raise his arm and wipe it away while he was being watched. Lou had turned away. The funerals would start happening soon, already that of Hester Hagley's husband had been announced in the paper. Strange how he thought of her by her maiden name already. As if she had never been married. And then, he supposed, his friends Harry and Sam and Joe would find the body of their brother, and it would be his turn too. As he left the hospital, Lou had tried not to break into a run.

That was all. He thought, with bitterness, that if she could have just waited another day to make her scene, Evelyn would have been gone, and everyone would have been saved. It was Freda's fault.

No it wasn't. It was his.

The girl, Belle. The beautiful girl.

And Violet, the woman with blue hair whom he'd known since he was a boy.

Violet had brought them all together.

Violet had first appeared in his life more than twenty years earlier, although they had only come to know each other since she set up the restaurant. When they met, just once before that, he had something she needed.

The day at the lake house had begun more or less as usual. Since his mother died, there had been fewer holidays. When he and his father did come south, the rooms felt cold and damp even in summer. Mildew touched the linings of the curtains, and there was no food in the cupboards, only baskets of bread and fruit that been prepared by the housekeeper in Auckland, and carried with them in the back of the car. Lou's memories of that time were of always going to bed hungry the first night, and of feeling as if he was lying between two sheets of ice when he climbed into bed. In the morning, he would bring in firewood, watched by his tiny father, almost hidden behind the timber. On these trips to the south, the lawyer wore a peaked cap and tweedy clothes, with shoes bought in London, a pipe clenched between his purplish lips. When a fire was laid, his father would take up a book and sit in silence, just as he had done when Lou's mother was alive.

That was a signal for Lou to leave if he wished, and entertain himself for the day. A little further round the bay, near enough to be neighbours, his friends Harry and Sam lived with their family. They were about his age. Sometimes he helped in their garden, and sometimes they went fishing or hunting in the bush. They were growing into rugged men, self-sufficient and, it seemed to Lou, wise in their ways. At a given time, he would reappear and his father would nod, as if satisfied.

But that morning when he first met Violet was different.

Lou was seventeen and about to leave school. If he had been anyone but his father's son, he would have left Auckland Grammar by then, because he appeared unable to apply himself to study. He didn't see the point. The lawyer would countenance nothing less than him following in his footsteps, but that was not what Lou wanted. Of course he could have left. He smoked cigarettes and had made love to several girls, and getting a job would have been easy. But the call-up hung over his head and nobody knew when the war would end, so he stayed on, marking time until he was eighteen, waiting to see what would happen next. He went less often to the house by the lake, choosing to stay alone in Auckland while the judge went south. But this time his father had prevailed on him to come, and straight away he saw that something had changed. A local woman had opened up the house. A fire was already set, a meal prepared. Soon after, the doorbell by the stained-glass door rang and, when his father opened the door, a blond-haired woman was standing there. She was at least half a head taller than his father.

'*Oh mon ami, j'ai arrivé,*' she cried in execrable schoolgirl French.

'*Enchanté,*' Lou's father said with a gallantry that horrified Lou, it seemed so artificial and absurd.

'You can tell, can't you, that I've been practising. Oh, you'll be so proud of me, I promise you.'

'I'm sure,' said his father.

'*Est que ce votre* …? Is this the boy? Your son. Oh, he's so handsome, so like you, so dark.'

'Louis speaks French well,' Lou's father said, suddenly stiff.

'How do you *do,* Louis?' she said, but he could see she was blushing.

The woman was voluble. She talked rapidly about all sorts of trivia, as if she had a list of topics in her head to work through. About a trip to the races where, it seemed, she had won some money. About books she had read — a travel guide and a collection of speeches by a politician. His father listened approvingly, nodding now and then. Occasionally the woman, whose name was Raewyn, would glance at Lou, her eyes narrowing. She likes my father, the boy thought, but she doesn't like me.

'Early to bed, young man,' his father said. 'Our guest and I have some talking to do.' As if he was still a child.

Raewyn had gone in the morning but his father was in no mood for Lou to stay indoors. He had brought some work with him, and piles of judgments lay on the sideboard waiting to be opened. 'Young men should be able to find things to do. You've got friends, haven't you?'

Lou went down to the shore and contemplated his boat. He considered going over for a visit, but the place was quiet, except for the youngest child playing noisily in the garden. In the distance, he saw the old man, Hugo, hoeing a sparse patch of garden near the lake. It was Hugo who had done the most to help him with the boat, shown him how to measure timber, how to set up a frame and how to use tools. He didn't know how the old man knew all these things because until then he had spent his life tuning pianos. Perhaps he had simply had a childhood of his own and was willing to share what he knew. But Hugo was deaf and they would stand there shouting at each other, with nothing much to say. Lou had developed a boy's habit of impatience. In the end, he decided to row to the township.

The broad tree-lined streets had always appealed to him, as did the spa baths and tourists, who made the town more cosmopolitan than the city where he lived. Not that there were many tourists around at that time. The streets were filled, instead, with soldiers on leave; dotted among them were war wounded who were being treated at the local military hospital. He met a one-legged man struggling with crutches and offered him his arm.

'Would you like a drink, mate?' the older man asked him.

'Suit yourself,' he said.

'You'd better hop it if the coppers call,' said the soldier, destroying Lou's illusion that he looked old enough to be in a public bar.

For an hour or so he drank beer with the soldier.

'If this war carries on, you'll soon be on your way. You ready for an adventure?' the man said.

'Yeah,' Lou muttered, looking at the place where the

soldier's leg should have been. 'I'd better push off.' He had remembered the boat tied to the jetty, the oars stacked in place.

At the waterfront, he found a woman with a child seated in his boat; she was about to cast off. 'Stop, that's my boat,' he shouted.

The woman looked up at him with intensely blue eyes. 'You shouldn't leave things lying around.' Despite the coolness of her gaze, he thought she was not as bold as she was making out. There was a tremor in her hands, and he saw the way she bit her lower lip. The child, a boy perhaps two years old, looked delicate and afraid, pushing himself into the woman's side at the sound of raised voices.

'You can't do that,' Lou said, putting his foot on the bow.

'I'll pay you,' she said.

'I don't need the money.'

'Most young men need money.'

Lou thought then, that perhaps he did. He was almost grown up and his father gave him a child's allowance. He had two shillings in his pocket, not enough to have contributed to the drinks he had had in the hotel with the soldier. 'How much?'

The woman produced a five-pound note. A fortune. 'I need this boat,' she said. 'I can't get transport and I have to get to the bays today, while it's still light. This is urgent.'

Lou folded his hand around the money. He realised he was slightly drunk, and it was hard to know what to do for the best. 'When would you come back?'

'In a couple of hours.'

'Tell me which way you're heading. I don't want it dumped just anywhere.'

'Over to the bays.' Pleading with him now. 'There's a market garden over there.'

'Hugo and Ming's?'

225

'You know them?'

'Sure,' he said, shrugging. She was already in the boat and the fiver was in his pocket.

When it got dark and she still hadn't come back, he thought he should go up town and call the police. Several hours had passed. What would his father say if he found Lou had allowed a woman and child to go out on the lake, and they hadn't returned? Would he be held responsible? Then, at last, as he stood straining his eyes in the dark, he saw a flare lighting the way, and two boats, like a tiny flotilla, approaching the shore. When they were nearly there, the leading craft peeled away and began to head back across the lake. He could see Harry was rowing the boat, and called out to him, but his friend didn't hear.

Lou saw then that the woman was alone.

She threw him the rope, pulling herself on to the jetty while he held the boat steady. He turned to speak to her, but she had already disappeared into the night.

Cloud cover had descended and obscured the moon. The whole business had given him the creeps and he found himself not wanting to row back across the water in the dark. At a hotel near the lake, he paid for a room, using the receptionist's phone to ring his father and say that he would be late. 'I've been delayed by my friends, and now it's too dark to row home. I'm sorry.' His father didn't sound as troubled as he might have expected.

In the morning, he rowed back while it was still early. From the outside, the house seemed very still. Lou opened the door carefully, not wanting to disturb his father, an early riser who liked to work from the moment he was out of bed. Walking down the passage, he heard small cries from the main bedroom, looked in and saw the tangle of blond hair, white and brown flesh on the bed. 'Whoo,' his father hollered.

'Whoo-up.' And the woman, her feet knotted firmly together behind his back, laughed. 'Keep going, oh yes,' she cried.

This was his stepmother, who saw him off when he went away on his second and last tour of duty. Raewyn, wearing a big hat and flat heels to diminish her height, stood between his father and his own new wife, Freda. When he came back, his father had died, and Raewyn had all his money. She had sold the house by the lake.

Later, Lou went to live in the town with his wife and their baby. Sometimes, people asked him if the child was his little sister. He stayed looking much the same as he had in his teens until he entered his thirties, when a hollow developed in his left cheek, and a small pouch of flesh gathered beneath his chin. His daughter was not a bad little kid, he supposed. She tried hard. That was the best and the worst he could say about her.

The sorrows of childhood. He'd had them, and so had Evelyn. A wave of anguish overtook him. In the past, when he thought of limbs entwined, the way he had seen his father and Raewyn, he'd thought of the pleasures of voyeurism. Now he could see only the tangle of bodies that lay somewhere in the lake.

He wished suddenly that he could speak to Violet Trench, who had never talked to him about grief, and yet he understood that she had experienced it. Perhaps she could help him sort out this whole mess; he would not be entirely misunderstood by her.

The first time he entered Violet Trench's café, she had looked up at him, startled.

'Do we know each other?' she said. His wife, who by then earned her living at the radio station, had told him about the new venture by the lake. He was as surprised to see Violet as she was to see him, but not as disconcerted. Immediately, he thought what a fool she was to have acknowledged him, because he might not have recognised her, nearly twenty years after that day by the lake. Then again he'd always had a good memory, and hers were not eyes to forget.

'Almost certainly,' he had said, smiling and holding her eye. So that he had a power over her. He knew that she would have given a lot to have turned the moment back and held her tongue, but it was too late.

Strange the way things began, because that power that he wielded over Violet Trench was the beginning of all of this trouble. She would have kept him in check as she did everyone else, were it not for what he knew.

'I have not committed a crime,' he said to himself, or did he say it aloud? For a moment he thought that he could go back and face them all.

But he couldn't.

It was a crime. Worse, his father would have said, a sin, a mortal sin, although the perfect gentleman was no better than the rest. All the same he would have passed judgement, and he would have been right.

Lou studied the leaves beneath the trees. He could walk into them as far as he could go, and he would be gone without trace. He would lie down in them somewhere and his life would forsake him. Someone, sooner or later, would come across his car; it would be locked and he would be gone. They would shake their heads. The pigs got him, they would say, the wild pigs. It might even be true.

There was a strange persistent smell in the air, like garlic. He was so light-headed he didn't know exactly what he was doing, but it seemed to him that he should set forth as unencumbered as possible. He took off his shoes and socks and placed them in a row, rolling the socks out flat into their original shapes before setting them beside the shoes. Then he pulled off his shirt, and laid it down flat too, with the arms stretched wide. Barefoot and bare-chested, he set off into the trees. Soon he was swallowed up by the filmy ferns. Far overhead in the linked branches of the beech trees, he saw the receding sky.

Part Six

Jessie Sandle

1980–

PHNOM PENH

The Foreign Correspondents' Club in Phnom Penh is a worn and battered-looking building from the outside. It faces the confluence of the Mekong and Tonlé Sap Rivers, the second of which is fed from a vast lake to the north of Cambodia. Inside, a flight of stairs leads to the accommodation level, and above that is the FCC itself, its walls open to the sky, with bamboo curtains rolled up above them, ready to be dropped to the balcony floors if a heavy monsoon rain passes by. Quivering chandeliers are suspended from the ceiling; often the electricity fails, and there is simply darkness. Everywhere, the surfaces crawl with pale green lizards. The place fills up from breakfast time, and stays full all day, and into the night, with journalists smoking long French cigarettes, or coarse tobacco rolled in Rizla Reds. They drink Dirty Mothers and gin tonics or shoot B52s — a mixture of Baileys, Kahlua and Grand Marnier — or Kamikazes, vodka and triple sec with a beguiling hint of lime, almost harmless one might think until the third or fourth goes down. The journalists have laptops they can slip out of their satchels, but when Jessie Sandle started working out of the place she couldn't hear herself think for the rattle of old Remingtons, as rapid and noisy as artillery fire.

Jessie's room, one of three on the second level, seemed more or less like home in 1980. The big white tiled room was furnished with a dark-slatted wooden bed and a dressing table. A ceiling fan made slow waves in the humid air, while an occasional burst of electricity through the generators allowed Jessie light and some spurts of tepid water. She had learnt to write by candle and torchlight. She considered herself fortunate to have a room. In the old days, before Pol Pot's regime, journalists congregated in the old Hotel Le Royale, closer to the action in the city, with rooms for all. But now it was an empty shell, its swimming pool a breeding ground for mosquitoes. The trickle of journalists arriving from the West found beds where they could, and hung out here. In the middle of warfare, one didn't think about other more permanent bases, though Jessie had an apartment off London's Eccleston Square within walking distance of Victoria Station, for which she paid rent, but rarely saw. Not that Cambodia was officially at war any longer. Saloth Sar, also known as Pol Pot, had been airlifted from the capital in a helicopter, when the Vietnamese army toppled the Khmer Rouge. He had left in much the same manner as the departing American generals had left Saigon in '75, and Lon Nol, the previous general, had made his escape the same year from Phnom Penh — the fashionable retreat for oppressors. All the same, bursts of gunfire erupted from across the river, as prowling guerrillas roamed the periphery of the city and stole along the riverbanks.

By day, there was little to see but magnificent, empty boulevards lined with the ruined and beautiful houses left behind by the French colonists. In those few buildings, occupied by recently appointed government employees, buckets of water were hoisted through the empty lift shafts. Pigs and cows stayed indoors with their owners to keep them safe from thieves. It was more than a year since the Vietnamese tanks had entered the city, but there were few signs of freedom.

'This is the city of the dead,' Jessie wrote in her first

dispatch since her return to the Cambodian capital. 'It is not that people are absent from the streets. They are arriving, thousands by the day, to look for those who are missing. But what they find is the evidence of death.

'The people who lived here, up until the morning of 17 April 1975, have largely disappeared. On that morning, five and a half years ago, roughly the time of the Cambodian New Year, columns of Communist revolutionary troops, known as the Khmer Rouge, walked into the capital. They wore black peasant clothes or simple khaki uniforms. They walked in total silence, greeting nobody, and they carried guns. Many of them were under fifteen years old. This was their moment in history, or non-history as it turned out, for this was to be Year One, the beginning of recorded time when they overturned the oppression of foreigners — the Americans who had bombed them in the past — the colonial legacy of the French, and the "feudalism" of those who had worked for the bureaucracies which ran the country before. They believed the city belonged to them, and that the people who lived there must move out and do the same work as the people of the countryside. Two million people were siphoned out of the city, to toil in the rice fields, no matter how old, or young, or infirm they were. Those who looked like intellectuals of any kind, even those who simply wore glasses, were likely to be put to death, socially unredeemable and expendable. They were designated "new people", because the revolutionaries believed they had exorcised their history. Money, the markets, formal education, books, Buddhism, private property and freedom of movement were abolished. The revolutionary regime called itself Democratic Kampuchea.

'Today I witnessed a place of utter desolation, a former high school in the suburb of Tuol Sleng, which served as an interrogation centre during the revolution. The walls of the classrooms are lined row after row, thousand upon thousand, with passport-sized photographs of those men and women who were tortured before being put to death. They have been photographed moments before their execution, their terror etched on one dark wall after another. There are rooms still filled with instruments of torture, racks and whips, and handcuffs to hang people from the walls. Cells have been built into some rooms, just wide enough for a human being to stand, but not to sit or lie down. More than twenty thousand people died in Tuol Sleng, before being trucked out to Cheung Ek, the killing field, but nobody knows for sure how many there were. Mothers and fathers seek their children, children seek their parents, some simply come to learn what has happened. Outside, in the thick red dust of Phnom Penh's streets, survivors huddle under palm shelters and children chase cockroaches for sport, although these are cooked on open fires when they are caught.

'At night the dragonflies hover like helicopters in the navy-blue light over the Mekong, and sentries watch the tall reeds by the water for signs of movement. Pol Pot may be gone, but the followers of the Khmer Rouge have not put down their arms. They are all around, and the fields are filled with their landmines, so that the unwary loses a leg as easily and casually as a packet of cigarettes might be mislaid.'

Jessie had left New Zealand two weeks after her departure from the Violet Café. A hastily arranged passport, a cancellation berth on a ship going to London, and she was another of those people who stood on the bow while land receded and took on a dim shape and then there was nothing to see except the sea itself and flocks of gulls. While others on board held streamers stretched from the hands of tearful relatives on the shore, Jessie stood by herself and waved to nobody. Her half-sister Belinda, who now lived with Aunt

Agnes, had begged to be allowed to go down to the harbour to see the ship leave, but her aunt had said in a brisk no-nonsense voice that there was school tomorrow, and Jessie was a grown-up and wouldn't want children hanging around on her big day. She had repeated this to Jessie in a voice heavy with meaning, reminding her that she had made plenty of exits without any help from her family, and look at the trouble that had got her into. Aunt Agnes had not been impressed by the arrival of police at the door, looking for Jessie and asking questions about the disappearance of some man she was involved with up north. I wasn't involved with him, Jessie said, not that way, Lou Messenger was just someone I knew.

A right sordid mess by the sound of it, her aunt had replied, snorting. Not to mention all those people drowned. She'd read in the paper that they were still looking for some of the bodies. To think you were mixed up with a bunch like that. She didn't exactly wrap her skirts around the children, but she might as well have, as if contact with Jessie might contaminate them with whatever filth she carried. Only part of Jessie cared, even noticed. All of it too late. The coffin lid was already closed over her mother's face when she got back to Wellington and the undertaker said that no, he couldn't take it off. In fact he was under strict instructions to do nothing of the kind.

So that was it, a patch of raw earth where she'd watched the cheap pine coffin lowered into the ground, while Belinda and the other children sobbed, and her stepfather, Jock, stood as far away from her as possible, with a resigned look on his face as if he wasn't part of the proceedings. She was joined by two people the others didn't know, her grandparents who she had lived with when she was very small. They stood apart until it was time for the grave to be closed, then Jessie joined the family. Two of the girls she'd known at university had turned up too. They said, why didn't she come back, she was sure to be able to pick up some papers, even if she didn't do law. I can't stay here, Jessie said. You must see that. In the house at Brighton Street, all her mother's belongings were cleared away, so that nothing, not even a trace of her powder or a hair clip, could be found. Collect your stuff, Jock told her, though he and his sister had had a good clean-out in her room; to them, there wasn't much left that seemed worth keeping. The clothes her mother had gathered to send her stood in a suitcase in the hall.

'You're a selfish bitch,' Jock said. 'I thought you were trouble from the beginning. There's some money owing to you from your father. Your mother was keeping it for you.'

Three hundred pounds.

'You're nothing to me,' he said.

'It's mutual,' she said, her hand closing around the money. Enough to get away. She was becoming expert at that.

Jessie wore a dusty khaki shirt and trousers, and ankle boots to protect her from snakebite. Her face was bare of make-up, her frizzy hair pulled back and wound behind her head, so that, from a distance, she could pass for a man. That Hepburn woman, some men remarked, but she didn't see herself like that. What they did, out there in the East, wasn't glamorous.

At the end of each day a clean, ironed set of khakis would be waiting in her room, and changing into them was the extent of her preparation for dinner. When she had washed her face and hands, she felt cleaner and stronger, as if putting the grit and sorrow behind her for a few hours. This evening, she went out on to her balcony for a moment, trying to shelter in shadows. A huge moon was dangling in the sky, and she thought she saw an outline withdrawing near the shoreline of Sisowath Quay. So they were being watched, and closer than they had thought.

There were new faces at the bar, but then there always were. The population shifted and moved from day to day. The FCC was full of people who told their life stories over a few drinks to others who would be gone in the morning. They would make promises of eternal friendship to those they never expected to see again. Or might not see alive. Not everyone who went out in the morning came back. There were deals going down all the time — people trading trips into the countryside, a ride in a chopper, a seat on a plane leaving the country the next day, or going up north. Some crazy fools were going up the river towards Siem Reap where there were strongholds of guerrillas at every bend, and boatloads of pirates who boarded any floating object or, in some cases, shot it up in the water before they even reached it. Jessie was in the habit of weighing up the consequences of each operation. A great story wasn't worth following if she didn't survive to put it across the wires. At all times, she carried money inside her boots so she could buy her way out of trouble. So far, she had got through, but some day she might not.

A woman as tall as she was standing with her back to the crowd in the bar. She was dressed in a loose-flowing blouse made of pale aubergine silk, with sweeping sleeves and slits at the hips, and a sarong. Her dark hair was crisp and turning grey. The wife of visiting military, was Jessie's first uncharitable thought. The woman turned slightly, her eyes scanning the room and settling on Jessie.

Jessie was looking for a man called Paul Greaves, a publisher she'd met in London, who was interested in a book about the hunt for Pol Pot. He was supposed to be travelling out to Australia for a conference and said if he could get a visa he'd come through Phnom Penh and see how the story was coming along. They would sleep together too, which was what they did sometimes in London, when his wife took their children away to the country in the school holidays. Jessie, as often as not, had a war to go to, and that aroused her as much as sex. This frightened her, when she paused to think about it: the idea that her passion and her flights to violence were somehow inextricably linked. I hate bloody wars, she would say, if asked why she was always at the front. If nobody tells the truth, the world will never know. She thought Paul might not make it. You don't have the guts, she'd said, teasing him over a dinner she'd cooked for him at her apartment.

'I could if I tried,' he said.

'I don't think so. You'll get as far as Bangkok, and as you come into land you'll smell the heat and dust and shit that rises up to meet you before the wheels touch, and you'll think what an adventure, I'm brave to have got this far. And you'll remind yourself that you are, after all, a father. You'd be right to do that. You don't need to get mixed up in what I do.'

'What is it about you and Asia? It's as if you're in love with it,' he'd said, spooning an oyster into her mouth.

'I am.'

'Why?'

'I can't tell you that,' Jessie said, as if she truly hadn't considered the matter and didn't know. 'Just something that grows on you,' she added, as if that was all there was to it. But it wasn't, of course. She had set out for China, years ago, got stuck in Indochina and never left. Not really, even if she took breaks from it now and then. She could see her life going on, or not, because one day she thought she might die out there and that thought mattered less as time passed.

Tonight she wished Paul was with her, just for a few hours, here at the Foreign Correspondents' Club. When she was away working, she didn't often want to sleep with a man, but tonight, because of the slight possibility that he might appear, she felt a hungry ache, a desire to be touched, not by beggars' hands.

240

Instead, she found herself shaking hands with the woman at the bar.

'Annette Gerhardt,' she said. 'From Switzerland. I'm with the Red Cross.'

Jessie saw, now that she was close to her, that the woman was stronger-looking than she had assumed at first glance. She had broad cheekbones and a high aquiline nose. Her voice was heavily accented, a shade imperious.

'You're a doctor?'

'Yes. I'm planning to head north tomorrow. There's a group of children in an orphanage at Battambang that's been hit by guerrilla crossfire. Our convoy wants to get medical supplies there.'

'I know about them,' said Jessie. 'I don't think you'll find many of them left.'

'We've got enough supplies to set up a camp hospital for amputees.'

'You won't get through,' Jessie said.

'We've got protection from the Vietnamese. We are the Red Cross, you know.'

'I don't think that'll mean much to the Khmers if they come across you. Is this your first time out here?'

Dr Gerhardt hesitated. 'I need a driver, that's all. One of mine is down with malaria.'

'You could have mine,' Jessie said, 'but you'll have to wait another day. You need to start travelling at dawn but I'm not going to break curfew tonight to find him.'

'What's the catch? Why would you offer me your driver?'

'Because I could come with you.'

'Oh no,' said Annette Gerhardt. 'Not that. This is tough work.'

'Yeah,' said Jessie. 'I know about that. I spent two years in ambulance choppers in 'Nam. You might find me useful, I can use a tourniquet. And Kiem's a good driver. He was a long-distance bus driver before all the killing started and he can interpret as well.'

Annette tapped her fingers on the edge of the bar, before beckoning over a young man, thin and fair, with hollow blazing eyes. 'My assistant, Donald; he's an Australian. He carries mine-detection equipment. I need to talk to him before I make a decision.'

Donald had elbowed his way through the crowd at the bar. The women journos looked like stick insects, poking their cigarettes in the air and using their hands for expression. The men were resigned almost, detached as if they were already in danger and knew there was no escape. Jessie supposed that, to newcomers, she looked the same as her colleagues, and really she was little different. Hungrier for a story of her own, perhaps. Some of them got lazy, dined out on other people's work. Or there came a point when you had been under fire once too often, and you either did nothing or went over the top. She remembered a time like that in Da Nang. Instead of covering the defence of the air base, she had got carried away and made contact with a group of Viet Cong anxious to tell her their story. Suddenly, in the middle of it, she was fleeing into the jungle alongside them. That had been years before and, thinking herself lucky to be alive after she'd escaped, she had gone back to England and applied for a tutor's job at Sussex, where she had taken her degree. When she found herself in front of the students on the first morning of her new job, she had looked at them without speaking for a long time, then walked out of the room. Her nostrils remembered the smell of explosives and the scent of frangipani in the jungle air, and she felt less afraid of the East than she did of the classroom.

She saw, at a glance, that Donald was like her, scared but insatiably attracted to danger. It was written all over him. When they had been introduced, he said, 'So you're a Kiwi?'

'I was born there,' she said cautiously. 'It was a long time ago.'

'What does he mean?' Annette asked her.

'It means I grew up in New Zealand.'

'I wouldn't have picked it.'

Donald snorted. 'Spot it a mile off.'

'A good little country,' Annette said approvingly. Condescending, Jessie thought; could she be getting thin-skinned? 'Hard people. Perhaps we could wait another day. Your man will be coming in the morning for you?'

'Kiem? I gave him the day off, I plan to touch some bases I have here, before I go north. I was planning to go up the river towards Kampong Chhnang on Thursday, if the worst came to the worst, and then across to Battambang.'

'What are you looking for?' asked Donald.

'Everybody's looking for Pol Pot of course.' Trying to keep it light. 'Not that I think he's there — he's somewhere up in the mountains towards the border. But there are better scents the farther north you go.'

'Crazy Kiwi girl. You'd be better off with us,' Annette said. 'Can you find this man Kiem tomorrow?'

Jessie sighed. 'I can try. You've seen what this town's like. It's a real maze — so many shacks have sprung up on the edges of town, and they all look pretty much alike.'

'Do you trust Kiem?' asked Donald.

'He'll want to come back to Phnom Penh, if that's what you mean. He's got family.'

'It doesn't seem right,' Annette said. 'Risk their lives for a few dollars.'

'Then they'll do it for someone with fewer scruples than you,' Jessie said shortly.

Jessie rose soon after dawn, but not before the city was stirring. A man with a battered cyclo was at her elbow offering his services before she had had time to cross the street.

243

'I'll need you two, perhaps three hours. Very hot. Can you last that long?'

The man's hands trembled over the flare of a cigarette.

'Take me to the markets, then we eat. All right? Food, to make you strong. Go all day, perhaps. Many dollars.'

He held up his hands, five fingers.

'Two, okay?'

'Okay. We'll find Kiem and I'll give you three dollars. You know where I can find Kiem?'

'Maybe.' But she could see he was already formulating an idea of where he would take her. It would mean a long ride around the city, but she wouldn't necessarily find what she was looking for. The drivers talked to each other while they looked and waited for fares outside the club. A search would have to be seen to be done. The way the cyclo driver was pedalling gave her hope.

At the market, Jessie stopped the cyclo driver at a food stall and ordered noodles for them both. She squatted beside him on the pavement when the food came, picking it over and deciding it was a bad risk, thin and watery and probably floating with amoebae. If she was going to travel tomorrow, she could do without dysentery.

'How far?' she asked the man. 'Where is Kiem?'

'Perhaps far.' Now that he had eaten, the cyclo driver was more evasive. Bad move, she thought, and yet that was the very thing she sought to avoid — easy power over him. She had wanted the frail man simply to be comfortable, but she saw it was unlikely that he had the strength to take her much farther.

'Which way? Tell me which way, and I'll pay you two, maybe three dollars, and let you go home.'

'Four, ma'am, four dollars.'

'You tell me where to go, I'll give you four.' Because she

244

could see he was too ill to take her any further. Holding the money where he could see it, but tightly.

He drew a rough diagram in the dust beside them. She studied it, committing it to memory. 'Sure?'

When he nodded, she said softly, 'You'd better be right. Nobody at the FCC will go with you any more if you're making it up.'

'I'm not making it up, ma'am. That is where Kiem goes to be with wife. Okay.'

Jessie was knee-deep in dust before she had gone more than a hundred metres. People closed round her, imploring her to stop and feed them too. This was the year of famine in Cambodia. The year before there had been nobody left in the fields to plant rice. So many men had disappeared that women were banding together and calling themselves families, *krom samaki* or solidarity groups, gathering to plant rice. But then they went into the fields and their legs were blown off when they stepped on landmines. Aid had begun to trickle in from the outside world, as images appeared in newspapers and on television screens abroad, of starving and destitute Cambodians collapsing besides the roadsides or struggling across the borders. Perhaps things were better than a year ago, but when she looked round, Jessie wondered if, after all, she was on a futile mission. What was she really here for, to get a scoop, or to save the world? And she didn't know if she could do either. Somewhere around the end of the sixties she had seen a movie called *Medium Cool*, about a news photographer covering the riots at the Democratic convention in Chicago, who had got involved with his subject. It was one of those slightly grainy art-house movies that most people forgot but it stayed with her. The moral dimension. How far does one go? Jessie still asked herself this during long restless nights. Since she was a teenager, she had never slept easily. A young man, crouching beside the street, looked at her with beseeching eyes, his hand out, and her stomach lurched. He rubbed his stomach. 'Hungry,' he said. She slid him some riels, enough for a bowl of rice, knowing she would regret it. Within seconds, she was being mobbed, hands clutching her clothes, wrestling her to the ground.

'Get in here,' said a man's voice roughly. 'For Christ's sake, hurry up.'

She pulled herself free, throwing herself through a shop entrance. The words 'Lou's Lot' were painted in rough letters above the door. A man stood in the shadows, not moving to help her.

'You better shut the door, Jessie.' A familiar voice.

It was in a bar, too, that Jessie had last seen Belle Hunter.

She'd been under fire on and off for seven years and the editor on her desk said it was time she stopped; she really would go crazy if she didn't get some rest. 'Look at you,' he said, when he took her out to lunch in London. She had grabbed a fork like a weapon when a waiter dropped a plate.

'Nerves,' she said, apologising. One day not long before, outside Saigon under a white hot sky, a bomb had flipped the journo beside her into the air, landing him head down, flattened like a squashed pumpkin among a platoon of soldiers who had suffered similar fates. The ground was strewn with shattered helmets and the detritus of human remains. She had escaped with shrapnel wounds in her left calf muscle.

'Go home for a bit. I don't want you walking out on us again.' Because after the failed attempt at teaching she had gone back again and again, to Vientiane, Saigon again, Hanoi. Now she was due to go to Phnom Penh, the hill of Penh.

'This is home. I live here. Well, sort of.'

'Never think of New Zealand?'

'Oh shit, yes, of course. But I try not to.'

'Sometimes you talk like a New Zealander,' he said, and laughed.

Going back to New Zealand felt more alarming than shellfire in Vietnam, but she did it anyway.

At first Jessie hadn't known Belle, sitting on a high stool in the house bar of the hotel where she had stopped for the night. She remembered her as a pink and white girl with lashes so fair you would think she didn't have any and that skinned look from having her hair pulled back. But this Belle had a lemony yellow tint in her shoulder-length hair, dark fringed eyes and fingernails so long they curved. When Jessie saw her from the far side of the room, she was resting an elbow against the bar as she sipped a gin and tonic, silver bracelets tinkling when she raised her arm. The tip of her tongue flickered along her top lip. Flirting with the barman. She wore a tight shiny red suit with the skirt riding high on her thighs. With a little snort of recognition, she called out: 'Jessie *San*-dle.'

The barman looked disappointed when he saw Jessie, turned away.

'I don't believe it's you,' Jessie said. The hotel was an hour south of the town. Jessie, tired from driving, hadn't wanted to complete the journey there, not just yet. Several times during the course of her trip she had paused, pulling up to look across the desert at the mountains, as if in doing so she might recapture that first time she travelled north. As she stood by the road, watching, she thought she saw herself riding by in a bus. And as the memory returned of the night she had travelled back in the cab of a logging truck, through fog and darkness, away from the town, she shivered and moved on.

'Belle Hunter.'

'Clever old you. How did you know I'd gone back to my maiden name?'

'I didn't. So you got married then?'

'Yes, of course.'

'Not to Wallace?'

'For a while.'

A warning sounded in Jessie's head, reminding her that she was not a reporter now. 'That was brave of you,' she said, for want of anything better.

'Brave of him, I suppose. Poor Wallace. He'd have done anything for me.' The door wasn't completely shut.

'So what happened?'

'Oh well, you know, a couple of kids, pigeon pair, Shantelle and Wally Junior, but he gets called Junior. I've got some pics. Would you like to see them?'

'Love to,' Jessie said, peering in the dim light at a gawky pair of adolescents. The older of the two was a girl looking much like her mother, a darker version of the Belle of old, not the woman sitting before her, swinging her legs. There was a boldness in her smile. The boy was thickset, with a gap between his front teeth.

'I miss them,' Belle said, after an awkward silence. 'They went with Wallace after we split. We lasted five years, which I guess is a miracle. If you believe in miracles, which after a while I stopped doing.'

'Perhaps you'd already stopped when I met you,' Jessie said, surprised at knowing this, because she had hardly thought of Belle Hunter in years, just the consequences of what she'd done. Suddenly it seemed obvious.

'I don't know,' said Belle slowly, putting the photographs back in her wallet, with an air of embarrassment. 'Well, I did think I'd found a miracle once, but you know some things are too good to be true.'

'Lou?'

'Never mind. What are you up to anyway? Did you settle down?'

'Not exactly. I'm a war correspondent. I just travel around.'

'Like me,' exclaimed Belle. 'That's what I do. I'm in home appliances. I'm giving a demo here tomorrow — would you like to come?'

'I think I'll be gone by then, I'm heading north. But thanks anyway.'

'That's okay.' Belle looked resigned, as if she had expected Jessie to turn her down. 'Let me buy you a drink anyway.'

'Did they ever find Lou? I heard he went missing.'

Belle looked at her curiously, unable to absorb Jessie's long absence, and how little she knew of what had passed after she left the town where they met. 'I never heard much about that,' Belle said, after a pause.

'Do you think he's alive?'

'Oh, I shouldn't think so,' Belle said. 'Tell me about your wars, Jessie.'

'They never found a body.' Hester's mouth was pinched around a line of pins. She was making a wedding dress that had to be altered within forty-eight hours, because the bride was pregnant. Same old story — silly girl. Hester was sorry, but she really couldn't stop working, though if Jessie wanted to put the kettle on, she could make them both a cup of tea. When she opened the door her expression was unfriendly. 'You could have written,' was the first thing she said. 'About Owen.'

'My mother had died.'

'Everybody had died,' Hester said, relenting and letting her in. The old house hadn't changed since the last time Jessie was there. Only Ruth Hagley had gone.

'She's in a rest home,' Hester said briskly, when Jessie enquired. 'She's far better off.' Hester was in charge of the house now. She made wedding dresses, as a business. Weddings were the coming thing, and she was in on the ground floor. 'Things have changed you know, Jessie. People plan weddings like proper *e-vents*. They used to be so home-*made*.' It was odd the way people used emphasis, as if to convince themselves of the changes taking place. 'They use wedding consultants like me.'

'About the Messengers,' Jessie said, when the tea was poured.

'Well, you probably heard, Lou vanished after the accident. Freda and Evelyn are long gone. They went to California. I've heard that Evelyn did well. She's an economist. One of my clients saw her in *Time* magazine — she's working for Reagan now. Fancy him running for president.'

'Good God, tax cuts for the rich and all that.'

'I don't know anything about that. I don't have time for politics.'

'But I do. I'm interested in the way economies justify deficits in order to fund wars. Perhaps Evelyn could tell me how it's done.'

'Jessie,' said Hester firmly, 'I don't care if Mickey Mouse runs the world, Freda and Evelyn left town without saying goodbye, just like you did. Like most people for that matter. Besides, my client only *thought* it was Evelyn. Her name isn't Messenger now.'

'And Lou was never found?'

'Not that I've heard of. Well, his car was all fixed up for him to kill himself, but it seems that he didn't. But he never touched his bank accounts.'

'You'd have thought they'd have waited to hear what happened to him.'

'Why? Why would Freda stick around? People were pointing the finger at her too. I can tell you, Jessie, after that accident I pretty nearly went round the twist. Have you ever married? No, I thought not. Well, I'm a widow, remember? I had someone and I lost him when he was brand-new as husbands go. Thanks to Lou Messenger.'

'Did they look for him?'

'Of course they looked for him. The police were searching for weeks. What stupid questions you ask.' Hester's face was flushed an angry red.

'I'm sorry. I should go.'

'Perhaps you should. I don't know why you want to rake over old coals. You seem to have done all right for yourself, with all these trips of yours.'

'It's not exactly like that.'

'Isn't it? Well, I don't know about that. You and Violet Trench, you weren't people who stayed around.'

Jessie knew that Violet had left town years before with Felix Adam. She wanted to ask Hester about this, but she could see it might be one scandal too many. Jessie had written to Violet's lawyers long ago in an effort to trace her. Her father's money was not the only gift she had received. Soon after she arrived in England, a letter was forwarded to her. She supposed that Jock had sent it on because it had a lawyer's address on the back. Perhaps he thought it was trouble following her. But the letter bore the news that Violet Trench wished to give her a thousand pounds, following the sale of the Violet Café. She was going away soon, and Jessie was not to try to reach her. The money was sent to Jessie, the lawyer's letter said, with an expression of her profound regret about the events at the Violet Café, and the hope that Jessie would 'do something useful with her life, and follow her aspirations'. It did not say what it was that Violet so deeply regretted. At first, Jessie had thought she wouldn't reply, decided against claiming the money, and then changed her mind. She had aspired to very little up until then, except to please Violet and stay with John Wing Lee for the rest of her life.

'I lost John,' she said to Hester. 'I know it wasn't the same, but he was my boyfriend.'

'Well, he survived,' Hester said. 'What are you complaining about?'

'He did what?'

'He got ashore that night. His brothers took him home and didn't tell the police.'

'Where is he now?'

'Oh,' said Hester, smiling her strange bitter smile. 'Married. So I heard, not that I did the wedding. I'd leave that one well alone, if I were you.'

As the door closed against the steaming Phnom Penh street, Lou Messenger said, 'I thought you'd have given up on pretty Asian boys by now. They always did get you into trouble.' He was older, grey-haired, with a flabby gut and a cigarette burning down to his fingers. A drink stood on the fly-spotted table in front of him, though it was still only ten o'clock in the morning. The room was heavy with the smell of cooking and opium, wafting through the door behind the bar.

'You're supposed to be dead,' Jessie said to the man in the shadowy room.

'I heard you were in town,' he said. 'Call it the resurrection.'

'Don't tell me,' Jessie said. 'I've seen it all before. Some rats never do desert sinking ships. They keep hoping it'll re-float.'

'Not quite,' said Lou. 'Even I didn't stay around when Pol Pot's lot moved into the city.'

'But somebody told you they were coming, I'll bet.'

'Funny you should mention that.'

'So let me put it together. You ran a bar here until '75 and now you're back. Same bar?'

'Nobody else had moved in.'

'So who are your clients? There aren't many foreigners around.'

'I look just like the locals.' He grinned, the old lazy smile that had enchanted the girls she had known, back at the Violet Café. As if reading her thoughts, his smile faded. 'I wasn't to know,' he said.

'That people would die? I don't suppose you did. Evelyn could have killed herself that night.'

'That's a touch dramatic, isn't it?'

'But you don't know. The weather saved you from knowing what she'd do.'

'A freak accident. I sell food as well as booze. Have something.'

'I ate at the club.'

'No you didn't. They tell me you looked a bowl of noodles in the face less than ten minutes ago and couldn't handle them.' As he spoke, he turned to a wok on the fire behind him and scooped out two bowls of fried rice.

Beside her bowl he placed a thick glass of beer. 'To old times,' he said, raising his glass, as he settled on the other side of the table. '*Bon salut.*'

'I didn't know you spoke French,' she said, intending sarcasm.

'You wouldn't. I had a bigger past to bury than you'd ever guess.' Although he had served himself food, he didn't appear interested in eating it.

'Don't expect me to be sorry for you,' Jessie said.

'Oh, I don't, believe me. I've had some good times here. I took myself up to the temples at Siem Reap, in the mid-sixties, worked a bar up there for a bit.' He talked then about the massive temples at Angkor, and coming across a monk in saffron robes, cross-legged beside burning joss sticks in the gloom of the ancient stone walls, and of how the smoke from the incense had floated so far above him, straight up to a distant dot of blue sky, and the way he'd felt his spirits lifting with the possibility he might still be redeemed.

'Very Zen, Lou.'

'You've gone troppo yourself, Jessie.'

'Not likely. I've got a neat little flat in London near Victoria Station. I can go back any time I want.'

'You're kidding yourself. I recognise people like you. They get that dried-up-round-the-edges look. You want to keep out of the sun, Jessie.'

'Did you go back to Thailand during the occupation here?'

'There was a living there.'

'And you weren't a waiter, I'll bet. This isn't *Casablanca*, Lou.'

'You're eating my food, and drinking my booze, and you want to know where to find Kiem, so why don't you just shut up?' When she didn't answer, he said: 'Look, it's not as bad as it looks. There are some things I don't do.'

'Like what?'

'Children. Oh, don't purse your lips, you know bloody well kids are being sold in this city. What can people do? There's a ready market.'

'Perhaps the kids are better off out of here. If they go to the right homes.'

'Yeah, Jessie. That's one way of looking at it. The trouble is it's turning into a paedophiles' picnic spot.' He pulled his lower lip down and stroked a piece of tobacco from inside it, an old man's fumbling gesture. But he wasn't so old, still, she thought. Mid-fifties. 'Actually, I do buy kids. Some nuns came back and opened an orphanage a few months back. I give them some kids now and then, gives them something to do.'

She studied him, trying to work out if he was telling the truth. The way he sat with his arms folded, as though he didn't care whether she believed him, was convincing. A cold flatness had descended behind his eyes, so that he appeared indifferent to her. For an instant, she saw him standing by a blue lake, laughing, naked, his penis slightly erect, dark hair in his groin and on his chest. And yet she'd never known him, never had, never seen him care about anything or anyone, except the night when his wife, Freda, had come into the Violet Café, and the girl Belle had said that she loved him. 'Isn't that playing God? Perhaps they don't want to be Christians.'

'Ah crap, Jessie. What a load of bullshit they've taught you. Do you know what happens to little girls here? They get fattened up for the markets when they're two, three years old so men can stick their dicks in them. You got a better moral solution?'

'All right,' Jessie said. 'Okay. I don't know why people do what they do. I write what I see. This was a beautiful city once, and now it's a bloody hole and it needs all the help it can get. Will you let me do a story?'

'No thanks. I don't need anybody reading about me. I'll get someone to take you to Kiem's place when you've finished, and then you can forget you ever saw me. Is it a deal?'

'If that's what you want.'

'I do. Have you been back?'

'To New Zealand? Once. A few years ago now.'

'Who did you see?' He was engaged again, in spite of himself. A team of rats scurried across the floor towards a rice sack. His eyes travelled their wake. 'I'll bring the cats in when you've gone.'

'I saw Hester. She does weddings, and is generally in hate with the world. And Belle. She's selling home appliances these days.'

'Oh yeah.' As if he had to think who Belle was. 'John, did you see John?'

'I thought then he was dead. Like you.'

'You're really out of touch. Speaking of abandoned children, you know he was Violet Trench's son?'

'That's ridiculous.' She pinched herself under the table. But straight away she knew she was being offered a missing piece. 'How did you find out?'

'I lent her my boat one day when John was a little kid. It was the middle of wartime, and this woman turned up at the lakefront. I'd never seen her before — a real good-looking woman. She was beside herself, wanting to take the kid across the lake to Hugo's place. I used to go there a lot. Harry and Sam were mates of mine. Uppity of course, that was Violet, but she needed my boat.'

'Did she tell you she was John's mother?'

'Not exactly. Well, who knows, perhaps the kid wasn't hers, but if he wasn't, why had she carted him halfway around the world? I heard later from Harry that she'd brought him from London. Anyway, she got the boat off me, and then she didn't come back until late that night. It caused me a bit of trouble.'

'And then she went away again?'

'Disappeared, but the kid was left there. Then she comes back and opens the café. She knew I knew.' He drained the glass he had refilled twice since she arrived. 'You ever hear from my daughter?'

'I heard she was in America,' Jessie replied.

'Yeah, maybe. Her mother was as mad as a snake, you know.'

'Perhaps she was driven crazy.'

'You'll bake if you stick around much longer,' he said, inviting her to leave. 'It's hot enough to boil a monkey's bum out there. I'll get someone to show you the way.'

'Lou,' Jessie said, standing up, 'how did you get out of the forest?'

His expression went blank again. 'I walked,' he said.

'It was too far.'

'I got to Auckland and shipped out.'

'You never touched your money. Hester told me.'

'There was never enough to bother about.'

'I don't believe you.'

'Why don't you just fuck off, Jessie? Things can happen to people who ask too many questions round here. Do you know how many *bo dai* have gone missing in this country in the last ten years? Yeah, I can see that you do. Remember a man called Caldwell? You don't even have to go missing. Someone comes to your room at night and opens the door. Room service, they say, and you open up, just a crack, but it's enough. Or perhaps you don't even do that — but they have a key, and the next thing you're lying in a pool of your own brains.'

In the heat, Jessie shivered. Dead war correspondents. 'Malcolm Caldwell. Yes I do. He was an apologist for Pol Pot.'

'A Marxist. He thought the Anka would protect him. But they didn't.'

'You know who shot him?'

Lou picked up a cat that looked as much like a rat as the animals it was being sent to hunt. 'I don't exist. Don't look for me again.'

'Thank you,' she said. Sarcastic, but it was her best defence, and besides he would have her taken to Kiem. 'Thanks for everything, Lou. Especially the diversion that got me lost.'

But it was nearly the end of the day before she found Kiem, on the road that led to the killing fields of Cheung Ek. Her *krama*, the scarf that served as headgear, was wet with sweat, her clothes matted with red clay and dust. She was almost ready to give up, because if dark fell, she would be as good as dead, and just moving in the direction of the killing fields made her skin crawl. She had been there once, a place of total desolation. Recently exhumed skulls, some still wearing their blindfolds, and torn clothes poked through the earth. She had been surrounded by total silence. No birds sang near there. People didn't speak in that monstrous place. As she neared Cheung Ek, she found herself increasingly afraid. Now that she had been in the East all these years, she sensed some Buddhist force at work in her. It was said that the spirits of those who were not buried in the place that they came from would wander alone and restless, seeking help. But she had nothing to give them.

She was riding on the back of a motor-bike, saddle-sore and exhausted when the driver came across Kiem.

He was asleep in a hammock, beneath a thatched roof, fanned by a young wife who was close to giving birth. Suddenly, Jessie didn't want Kiem to go on this expedition.

Not that she could explain this to him, because once he saw her he became excited. Yes, he did want to come north with her. He wouldn't be put off. This way he would take care of his wife and babies. They negotiated a price, Jessie starting low, in the hope of putting him off. His face fell, and she offered him what the job was worth.

Back at the FCC, there was a change of plan. Reports had been coming in of guerrilla activity and such heavy retaliatory fire by the Vietnamese that the road to Battambang was virtually impassable. The Red Cross group's second target was a group of amputees in the Kampong Chhnang area, and now they had switched to that as a first option. If the road was good the Jeeps could get through in perhaps half a day, but much of it had been sucked away in the last monsoons, so that it could take days, skirting the washouts. During the day, in Jessie's absence, the group had been exploring the possibility of taking a boat along the river, but it was crawling with pirates, and the banks were full of snipers. Annette Gerhardt had decided to take her convoy by road to Kampong Chhnang.

'Is Kiem up to it?' she asked Jessie when she appeared, showered and changed, and settled opposite her.

'He'll go where I want him to.'

'Is there a but?' asked Annette, noting her hesitation.

'He has a wife and children, and another one due soon. If I had a choice, I wouldn't take him.'

'C'est la guerre. Oh, I know what you mean. What would our mothers say if they could see where we were?' Annette had shed her elegant clothes in favour of fatigues. She looked exhausted, as if she too had been out in the heat during the day.

'I don't know,' Jessie said. She had downed two bourbons in quick succession. 'My mother died when I was eighteen.'

'That's hard. Mine is still alive, an old woman, but strong in her mind and spirit, and her body not in such bad shape either. I'm lucky. What happened to your mother?'

'Cancer. I wasn't with her when she died. I should have been but I couldn't bear to tear myself away from a boy I was in love with at the time. A young Chinese man.' Jessie felt the drink, the heat, and the unexpected sight of Lou Messenger, risen from the dead, making her loquacious. She tried to remind herself that she was a self-contained woman who didn't need to tell garrulous stories to strangers. But why should she think of herself as different? This woman and she were going to face life and death together, and then, if they survived, they would go their separate ways. There had been a telephone message from Bangkok to say that Paul Greaves couldn't get a flight into Phnom Penh and he'd have to keep going to Sydney. 'You remind me of someone,' Jessie said. 'A strong woman I knew around about that time when my mother and so many people died.'

259

'So many people? This sounds like a complicated story.'

'Yes, that's true. I was with a group of people, the Chinese boy was among them. Well, he had one Chinese parent — after today, I'm confused. I knew his father too, or I thought I did, and it turns out neither of them was Chinese.'

'This is the one you were in love with?'

'Oh yes, very much in love. I thought John would marry me. I was such a plain girl and he was beautiful. I can't tell you … he had a heat about him. But, I don't know.' She had stopped to read the specials. The fish was always fresh. Today it was baked with tomatoes, olives, capers and anchovies, and a touch of French basil. Violet would have approved. Where did they get all this stuff from, while outside, beyond in the dark, there lay nothing but misery and starvation? She found herself settling for Peking duck, wrapped in Mandarin pancakes. A gesture to the past.

'He was in love with someone else?'

'I suppose so, though I didn't see it at the time. This woman I'm telling you about was called Violet, and it seems that she was his mother, though I didn't know that either. I've only found out today, and it's been something of a shock. Anyway, a group of us girls worked in her café. Violet was very self-centred, she named it after herself, and she liked to be in control. She thought she knew what was best for all of us. She wanted me to marry John, but all her plans backfired when several people who worked for her went out on a lake and drowned. The place fell apart after that. I wasn't with them, because I was on my way back to my mother, but I was too late, you see. She had already died. I'd waited too long.'

'So you lost your mother and your lover on the one night?' Annette said. 'That's a very tragic story.'

'I did lose my lover, if you could call him that, although he didn't drown. I found out years later.'

'The mother didn't tell you?'

'I think she decided that it had all been a mistake. But then, perhaps she felt herself surrounded by mistakes.'

'I don't think I'm like this woman you're talking about,' Annette remarked. 'I like to be sure I'm not making mistakes. I have other people's lives in my hands.'

'Well, I hope you're right. So did Violet, but she let go at the crucial moment. I left my country hurriedly, after all these disasters. I don't know where all the people went after that night. As it happens, I met one of them today. He runs a bar down by the markets, one of those seedy little shacks with bad food on the side, and a sack of *can sa* behind the counter, and God knows what else out the back. His name's Lou Messenger.'

'Messenger? I've heard of him.'

'Well, I've been out here a long time, and I hadn't.'

'He goes by different names. He's a bad man. Have nothing to do with him. He traffics in children.'

'There are often two sides to a story,' Jessie said evenly.

'Not with men like that.' Annette was stabbing the air with her lean brown fingers, making her point. 'I tell you, if you're a friend of his, I don't want you near this mission.'

'Look, I ran across him in the markets. I hadn't seen him for nearly twenty years. He told me he never wanted to see me again.'

'If you're sure.'

'Let's get some sleep,' Jessie said, folding her napkin. 'We're going to need all the rest we can get.'

That night she dreamt of the strange boy who had enchanted her in the town, and the way she had held him in her heart for so many years, cherishing his memory. And now he was alive. She woke to the sound of machine-gun fire in the distance, and lay wide-eyed, remembering the reality. On the

261

night of the accident she must have been worn out by desire for his pale body which, except for that one naked glimpse, had remained inaccessible beneath its clothes. The pressure of him against her, the shape of his thin chest and his penis which swelled and died away, had absorbed her so completely that she had lost the will to think for herself, overwhelmed by the need to stay near to him, night after night. Doing what was asked of her by Violet Trench.

After the deaths and disappearances, and her own flight from her past, Jessie stopped desiring John, as if her body had been brought to its senses. The week she went back to Wellington, she had lain down at the back of the bait shed with Antonio, the Italian boy she'd been to school with, and let him fuck her — got it over with, as it were, so that she could go on with her life, doing what other people did.

She had followed him to the shed reeking of fish, and when he'd said his usual hellos, and grinned at her, she had reached out and touched his throat with the tips of her fingers and stroked it, as if seduction came naturally, now that she'd seen so much of it in action. He had looked curiously at her arms when she took off her cardigan for them to lie on. 'Who gave you the bruises?' he asked. John's fingerprints were as blue as irises on her skin.

'They're nothing,' she said, giving herself up to the pain of the first time.

Afterwards, he said to her, like a shy girl, 'Jessie, I shouldn't have. I'm engaged now.'

'I'm sorry,' she said, though she wasn't because for the moment she felt languorous and full of sweetness, as if all the preparation she'd done with John had paid off at last. 'What must you think of me?' she went on, as she pulled her stockings on one after the other, and snapped on her suspenders.

'You were my *reading* coach,' he said with wonder and despair.

'I guess we're quits,' Jessie said.

On the way back up the hill she cried for what she hoped would be the first and last time, leaning against a lamp post leading up to Brighton Street, and sobbing until she thought she was going to be sick. The sea behind her was ravishing, honey-gold light spread across the waves, the black mound of the island perched in the bay, reminding her of that other place. John was gone now and her mother had abandoned her too. There was nobody to go home to. She thought it would go on like this, pleasure and goodbyes and what sense she could make of the spaces in between.

Another dawn. An unfurling of the light over the Tonlé Sap. The heavy white scent of frangipani, rice paddies dotted with ibises, bougainvillaea rioting in wild profusion over the remains of a shelled *wat*. Now they were in country. The trip had taken longer than any of them expected because the countryside festered with landmines and even the marked roads were dangerous. Jessie was spending her second night sleeping in a hammock, clear of snakes and scorpions. She felt gritty and gummy-eyed, dust clogging her nostrils and pores. The evening before, they had run a gauntlet of casual sniper fire that had missed its target, as if the guerrillas were half-hearted about their prey. A patrolling Vietnamese platoon, bristling with AK-47s, had taken them under their wing and formed an advance guard that had succeeded in keeping the mission safe up until now. They spent the first night in a small village close to an open plain that afforded their guards a view of marauding Khmer Rouge. None of them slept well.

They were not going directly to Kampong Chhnang, where Annette was taking medical supplies to the town, but first of all to a place a little to the south, where, they had been told, there was an encampment of wounded women and children. Looking at the spot on the map, Jessie couldn't see what features of the landscape would be likely to draw together a group of the injured. Kiem studied the map with her, and gave a surprised little snort of pain.

'You know where we're going?' she asked him.

'The aeroplanes,' he said. 'They make a landing place.'

'There aren't any planes coming in here.'

'He may be right,' Annette said, joining them. 'I've heard another story of this airstrip.'

What awaited them, further across the shimmering, humid plain, was a rolling aerodrome. It lay abandoned, except for a couple of guards in a makeshift sentry box inside a barbed-wire compound. Huddled in a makeshift shelter in scrub, at the far end of the runway, were four sick and wounded men. There was no sign of the women and children Annette had expected. Kiem spoke to the men. They said there had been more of them. They had come to see if an aeroplane would take them away, but they were fired on, and anyway, they now knew that planes didn't come here, in spite of the runway. Some had been able to escape; others had crawled away, because they believed nobody would come to help them, or someone would come and kill them. One of the wounded men knew more than the others. The airstrip had been built for Chinese to bring in military equipment to the Khmer Rouge. Now it was nothing, going nowhere.

Kiem had begun to weep as he listened to the men speak. 'They say that if all those who died building this strip had been lain side by side they would have stretched the length of the runway.'

'But that runway is at least three kilometres,' Jessie said. She was snapping pictures as they talked.

Kiem nodded. 'Put one man, and one man and one man, all the way up, still not all the people who died.'

'Perhaps three hundred thousand,' Donald said, hazarding a guess. He had had little to say for himself throughout the entire journey, and spent his evenings before nightfall searching out clean weed to smoke in the dark.

Kiem shook his head as if the numbers were meaningless. 'Many people.'

Donald shrugged. 'How many million lives did it take to build the temples at Angkor?'

'But this is not a temple,' Annette exclaimed, surveying the ugly rolling strip of tarmac.

'We have to get away from here,' Jessie said to Annette. 'If the Khmer Rouge get wind that we're here we're likely to be fired on.'

The doctor nodded, grim-faced. Donald began bundling the men into the front Jeep. One of them was protesting.

'He thinks his wife might come back to him if he waits here.'

'He'll be too dead to see her,' Annette said.

'I think he's waiting for her spirit to visit him,' said Jessie.

'Poor man. Tell him it is better that he comes with us,' Annette instructed Kiem.

The man did come with them, Jessie holding water to his pale lips as the Jeep lurched back the way it had come. His *krama,* which he wore as a loincloth, gaped open to show his reed-like limbs — what was left of them. He was so emaciated that she was afraid she might break him, as she sought to prop him up against the Jeep's interior. She had taken pictures of the airstrip, which she believed would be news on the outside. Clearly, the Vietnamese would know about it, but largely she believed it was a hidden thing, and the thousands of missing people a secret yet to be revealed.

Through Kiem, she continued to ask questions, but the men could tell her little more.

'You have a story?' Annette said.

'Perhaps. But I need more eye-witness accounts.'

Next it was Kampong Chhnang itself, a town by the river, where they were greeted by scores of thin and wasted citizens who tried to climb on the Jeeps as they rolled through. This was Annette's territory now. Jessie retreated to the riverbank to think. The Red Cross team would camp here for the night, while they set up a base and collected the injured. Annette and Donald would stay for a week to treat as many sick and wounded as they could, before returning to Phnom Penh for further supplies, and a second attempt at reaching Battambang to the north. One of the Jeeps, driven by Kiem, was heading back that night, and Jessie was expected to go back on it. Yet she needed more than pictures of an empty airstrip and the hearsay testimony of the four men.

Kiem had brought her food: a dish of deep-fried sparrows, another of steamed lotus stems, and some rice. Jessie crunched the crisp delicate bird bones and remembered how her mother used to feed sparrows on the back lawn at Island Bay. She had never had much stomach for sparrows.

Through Kiem, she tried to ask more questions of the people in Kampong Chhnang, but nobody would answer her. 'It's too close,' he said. 'They are afraid of what will happen if they tell. All their houses might get burnt down tonight.'

'But you knew about it. Somebody told you.'

'I heard word from my uncle and his friends who have gone back to Siem Reap, since Pol Pot has gone into hiding. I do not want to say more.'

'Where in Siem Reap? Near the temples? Angkor Wat?'

'No, in the city on the lake.'

Jessie had heard of it, a huge collection of houses built on stilts over the water, like a floating city, only it was known as the Vietnamese Fishing Village. 'I could take a letter to your uncle.'

'He won't talk to anyone.'

'Will you come with me, up the river?'

'Up the river, no.'

'Then find me a boat that will take me. Please, Kiem. Ten dollars. Many thousands of riels. Look after your wife.'

He gave her a long considered look. 'I think they will kill you. I think, Madame Sandle, that you are very brave and very mad.'

Jessie did nearly die on the boat upriver, when pirates boarded the flat-bottomed wooden craft. The river flows into Tonlé Sap Lake, a vast inland tract of water, so wide that land is not visible for mile after mile, where sky and lake meet. There were six men on board when the boat set off, as well as Jessie. It was night when the pirates came on board. Much later, she would attribute her survival to her acceptance of death, drained of the fear that might have encouraged her to fight back, rather than any particular cleverness. Instead, she lay still among stored sacks of rice and vegetables until morning. When she emerged at dawn, and the screams and shouting had died away, two of the six men were left. She supposed they must have been Pol Pot sympathisers or they would have been dead too. Nothing was said as they travelled on together up to the city on the lake.

As far as the eye could see, reed-thatched houses stretched across the lake, decorated with pots of bright marigolds, so that the surface of the water seemed to be trembling with orange fire. This might have been the fishing capital of the world, the water dense with carp that the villagers were allowed, once more, to catch for themselves. Baskets of the fish were carried away on the backs of bicycles. This is what Jessie ate in her days by the lake — fish, freshly cooked in pots over live coals, the smoke swirling round her face. At night she slept in a hammock in an abandoned house, listening to the water lapping around the poles that surrounded it. She slept in fitful catnaps, her camera tied to her waist. She thought about going inland to see the temples and check if the damage inflicted was as bad as rumour had it, but the journey on her own seemed too improbable, too likely to end in failure, or captivity. She reminded herself, like a mantra, a story is no good to anyone unless the reporter can deliver it. But finding Kiem's uncle was proving a next-to-impossible task. She had searched for him in a longboat with the people next door, who grudgingly agreed to take her with them. Nobody wanted to acknowledge her presence. On the third night she thought she felt a fever coming on, and sat up in the moonlight. The still air held a static crackle of menace. In the dark, she made out a man crawling on his belly towards her.

'Cannot find,' he said, in a whisper. 'Uncle is dead. You bring us bad trouble.'

A volley of shells erupted in the sky, raining fire. One landed and set a house on the lake alight.

The East. Gone troppo. On her own in a grass hut without a mosquito net, a Caucasian woman among a million Asians who didn't need her there, in an immense bright terrifying landscape. Of course the guerrilla fighters knew she was there, and would punish those who continued to harbour her. Or demand a ransom for her, back in Phnom Penh. And, if they didn't get it, or simply tired of having her around, they would lie her face down, her arms tied behind her back and slice her head off with the end of a hoe, a favoured method for killing foreigners. She had broken all the rules. If she disappeared, there would be an outcry in the world media, but it would be brief. Journalists often went missing. She could not think of one person who might care enough to pay her ransom, although several might feel obliged to make a gesture.

In a few hours there would be a ferry of sorts. If she was quick and careful, she could board and make her way south. Before it got light, Jessie crawled over a plank across the scum and sewage that the lake city spewed into the water, guided by the runner who had found her. She huddled again among sacks of strong-smelling fish and stacked bamboo poles until the ferry began to move. At first the lake felt empty, and very cold, in spite of great heat during the day. Scores of feet began to pass overhead, until the ferry filled. Soon the upper and lower decks were crammed with three times as many people as it could safely hold. The ferry, powered by an asthmatic diesel engine, shuddered and roared, causing the vessel to lurch from side to side. When they had been underway an hour or more, Jessie, fearing she might suffocate, crawled out of the hold into the light. In the stern, the coldest part of the boat, a group of women sat huddled in sarongs and *krama*. When she appeared, they looked at her curiously, uncomfortable and afraid. One of them, different from the rest, moved aside to let her sit down.

This woman was dressed in European clothes, of a kind. Well-creased slacks, a high-necked sweater and a checked coat and, on her head, a peaked cap. Sportin' Life, Jessie thought, a female version. She must have spent time with Americans. In her lap, Sportin' Life held a plump sleeping girl, perhaps two or three years old, her spread-eagled limbs appearing almost lifeless. An unnatural sleep, perhaps. Jessie looked more closely at the child. Although the woman was Khmer, the girl was not. The perfect slanted seams of her closed eyelids suggested Chinese Cambodian, and a strand of fairer hair made Jessie wonder if there had been a Caucasian parent — an American soldier, perhaps, or a French planter. A pink bow held the girl's hair in a topknot on her head. Someone had painted her fingernails and toenails bright red. Jessie gestured to the woman, offering to let the child lie across her knees. Looking down at the small face, and feeling her warm body against her own, she thought that the girl had been drugged.

'She's so pretty,' she remarked, not knowing whether she could make herself understood.

The woman in the peaked cap nodded in agreement, and pinched the girl's flesh. 'One hundred dollar,' she said.

'Oh my God,' Jessie said, to no one in particular.

'You have her. One hundred dollars. Very good price.'

'No,' said Jessie. 'No, I don't want to buy her. I'll take her picture.'

'No picture,' the woman said. A man appeared on the ladder leading from the upper deck. He waved his finger with an angry gesture at Jessie. The other women had pulled away, so that they were not connected with Sportin' Life, or the child. They knew what was going on here, and were powerless to stop it. The woman in the peaked cap must be a regular traveller on the ferry, stupefying the children she was taking to the markets and disposing of them in Phnom Penh. The man above threw a blanket over the woman and child, covering them from Jessie's view.

In her left sock, which she hadn't taken off for a week now, since she left Phnom Penh the week before, Jessie still had one hundred and fifty American dollars.

As the ferry pulled into the city, Jessie said to Sportin' Life: 'I will take the child. She'll be my child now.'

This was the girl whom Jessie would call Bopha, which means flower. She would be known to the nuns in Phnom Penh as Jessie's daughter.

BOPHA

In the beginning, the convent was built of thatch and mud. The floor was hard earth from which fine red dust emanated in small ceaseless eddies. The nuns swept it down before prayer. There were four sisters at the Home of Holy Rescue — Sisters Perpetua, Veronica, Therese and Mary Luke. They had come, they said, because God had called them to feed the destitute. They combed Phnom Penh's dusty streets, wearing their wimples and crosses, looking for the hungry, and found plenty. This was a favourite joke among them. Jessie could see how often they made it, passing it around in conversation like an incantation that made them laugh. Sister Veronica was the cook. When she discovered Jessie had once been a chef, she threw her arms around her and said that God had brought her to them. I've never been good at bread, she said, perhaps you could do bread for us. Jessie had never made bread, but she did then, in the weeks that she stayed at the convent. It was good bread, sweet-smelling loaves that sprang back at the touch. Her new family, as she had come to call the sisters, were delighted. You can stay with us a long time and get to know the little girl, they said. Sister Perpetua was the administrator, the person who ordered supplies and kept the records; Sister Therese took care of housekeeping, which included emptying the latrine buckets, something she did as if God's grace smiled on her every day; Sister Mary Luke ran the nursery, because they found not only hungry people but also abandoned children in the streets. There was just one, at

271

first, a little boy whose mother appeared to have died giving birth to him; her body lay beside him in a pile of rubbish near the markets. And then someone brought another baby who they said they'd found too, although they never did hear the real story, and suddenly Sister Mary Luke, who had found it hardest to adjust to the heat, and cried very easily, had discovered the meaning in her life that God had been just waiting for her to find. When there were six children, the sisters decided to call themselves an orphanage and sent home for funds to build an outpost mission dedicated to the care of lost children. This was where Jessie brought Bopha, the girl she had bought for a hundred dollars.

She had walked into the Foreign Correspondents' Club with the girl on her hip. Annette Gerhardt watched her as she came up the stairs. The child was barely awake, but she clung to Jessie with a grip like a frightened monkey, scrabbling up and trying to attach herself to her hair.

'Nice to see you're alive then. You've been on a mission of your own.'

'I'm sorry I left. You seemed to be managing.'

'Oh don't worry about it, we never expected a nurse. You've only got half the world's press banging down the door of this place looking for you. I reported you missing.'

'God, no. Please don't tell them I'm here. I don't want prying eyes.'

'So what are you going to do with her?'

'I don't know,' Jessie said. 'I haven't thought really.' She was struggling to hold the child, afraid she might fall from her arms. 'I'm not giving her away, if that's what you mean.'

'But you've paid for her, perhaps? Oh I can see it in your face. It's so obvious, or you would want to be out there in front of the cameras, telling your latest great adventure.'

'I didn't think you were a woman who judged others. I thought we were friends.'

'Friends. Pah. What you have done is a crime.'

'It was not like that,' Jessie cried.

'Like what? An impulsive moment. A rush of blood to the head. When we do good in the world, we have to be committed to it. We either leave it to others or we go on and on, even when it is difficult.'

'You're not modest, are you, Annette.'

'Look at you, look at the child. She needs food and clean clothes. That is what she needs in the next five minutes and you haven't an idea how you will provide even those necessities. She's not a puppy or a kitten. You can't put her in a basket, you know.'

'I have a friend who will help me.'

'Your Mr Messenger. Oh now you are going down a dark tunnel, Miss Sandle. I would take care if I was you.'

One day, in the nursery, when Jessie and Sister Mary Luke were bending over the babies changing their napkins, the nun said, 'Why don't you stay here? You've never married. You could become a bride of Christ, like us.'

'It's not that easy,' Jessie said, wiping hair out of her eyes with the back of her hand.

'What is harder than this?'

'I thought you were happy here, Sister.'

The nun crossed herself quickly. 'I am, but I have children now. Isn't that what you want too?'

'You need a better building,' said Jessie. 'You need money and equipment.'

'Bopha needs a mother.'

'She has several mothers,' Jessie said dryly. 'You'd soon get sick of supporting me. I think you need someone to help you keep the children in better conditions.'

The convent moved to a concrete building with tile floors,

and an open dormitory with fans on the top floor. Alongside the orphanage stood a small chapel, painted white and adorned with a plain cross, although it was difficult to see in the dust. The rooms in the orphanage were cooler than most in the city, with a sweet dimness that gave them a mysterious feeling. Whenever Jessie entered the convent, as she was to do many times, she was filled with a fulfilment of spirit she had never expected to possess. Sometimes she knelt in the chapel and put her hands together and prayed, even on days when she had gone to a *stupa* and placed incense before an image of Buddha. A slow unravelling had begun to take place within her, of how she had come to be part of this place, and the role she now played in shaping its future. For a long time she had held to the view that history needed witnesses, and that what she had done when she had lived in the heart of danger and war had a meaning and purpose, that it was more than just adventure. Now that she had given the world stories, it seemed not enough just to tell people what had happened in this uneasy and restless country, now she must be responsible for changing it too, or at least restoring it. She never saw Annette Gerhardt again, but what she had said left its impression — that one must stand by goodness of purpose, not leave it to others. But there was more to it than that. In this wilderness of inscrutable shifting morality, she had had to commit a crime in order to do right, and there was so much she had to learn about reconciling the values of one culture with another. Her own life had been overwhelmed by a tremendous change that had occurred one wet night in a small town halfway across the world. When she was younger, she had held herself responsible in some way for what had taken place at the Violet Café.

In the convent, she had begun to re-examine the events of that night, peeling away this guilt, slowly beginning to understand that it was not one, but several stories unfolding about her at the café, and that her own story was, in fact, that of her and her mother. Her mother's face, in dreamy repose, would sometimes float before her, eyes on some distant object or idea, finger marking the place in a book. And in this respect, Jessie believed, it was not what she had done that mattered, but what she had not done earlier that day. Or in the days before, when her mother had first asked her to come home. Action changed things, she concluded, not vague longings and indecision. Morality could not be defined in any tangible way unless someone took a stand and said, 'This is what I believe and this is what I will do.' Sometimes she wished that the old man Hugo had lived longer. Certainly, his death had changed the course of her own life, but she would like to have known him better, to have talked to him more. Now that she understood he was not John's father, she divined some quality of goodness that must have stretched his resources to the extreme. If he had been able to take a child, so casually delivered to him, so too could she.

This and other feelings — among them love for the child, Bopha — were what led Jessie Sandle to build a convent and support the women who ran it.

After a period of turbulent unrest in the city, the sisters were anxious for the children. In 1985, Mary Luke said to Jessie, 'I think you should take Bopha out of here. Things aren't getting any better.'

'You know I don't want to do that,' Jessie said. 'She may still have a mother and father alive. You don't know how she was passed over to the market woman. Besides, you know my situation, I can't claim her as my own.'

'You could adopt her.'

'I don't want to take her from her own country.'

'That's very admirable, but not realistic. There's nothing here for her. I wish it weren't the case.' Sister Mary Luke's voice had a soft Irish burr, but she had grown in authority since she had begun taking care of the children and spoke her mind more often. Her chin strap was pulled tight over a fold of flesh that quivered round her chin, giving her an air of solidity. 'What is the greater evil? Look at Bopha, she's at least eight years old now. This country is still struggling for a system of justice, still selling stamps off letters at the Post Office, so that children can be fed.'

'What's that got to do with Bopha? She's fed.'

'You know what it has to do with her. She's beautiful and clever, and things will take a long time to come right here. She might be too old to get an education by the time the schools are working properly again. What do you expect her to do with herself in the future? She'll grow up and marry perhaps, and live an unequal life.'

'She might rebuild the new Cambodia.'

'Or she might not. We might be overrun by bandits and the children taken away in the night.'

'Are you serious?'

'Of course I'm serious. You know there are so many of the people living abroad now, so many refugees. She'd find other Cambodians overseas, if you encouraged it. Or is it simply that, now you're famous, you don't like the idea of giving up your life in London to take care of a child?'

'I'd have to talk to the British authorities in Bangkok.' Jessie had dual British and New Zealand passports, but there was no diplomatic presence in Phnom Penh from whom she could seek help. 'I'd have to see what the procedure was about adopting her and taking her out of the country.'

'I'd do that,' the nun said. 'Perhaps you'll find, after all, that it's impossible. But I think you should try.'

*

The British Embassy in Bangkok was in a vast compound in Wireless Road, a magnificent piece of real estate in the heart of the city. A long drive led from the walls that lined it, through beds of orchids and other bright teeming flowers, both English and Oriental, past a flagpole flying the Union Jack. The whitewashed buildings with their shingle roofs were gathered together like a complete working town within a town, surrounded by long verandahs. They made an oasis of calm, a few steps removed from Bangkok's insane sound and pollution and the smell of durian, which was ripe and vile at that time of year. Inside the compound, the scent of frangipani was overpowering, reminding Jessie of Phnom Penh.

Other times when Jessie had come to the embassy, it was in an official capacity, flashing her press card to security. This was different, or so it seemed until she offered her name. The man at the desk in the Consular Section asked her if she was by any chance the well-known war correspondent, and when she agreed that she was, said that he would have to pass her on.

'My business is personal,' Jessie said. 'Just an enquiry.'

'All the same,' the man insisted, 'you need to see someone higher up than me.' As if she was not to be trusted, might be setting a trap for him.

She found herself sitting at a long table in a teak-lined room, and decided that her hunch was not wrong; there were two people in the interview room, as well as a secretary taking notes. A man called Trevor Smith, with bland pink features and light blue eyes, was asking the questions. 'Can you establish the parentage of this child?'

'She's an orphan who has been in the care of a non-governmental organisation in Phnom Penh for the past five years.' Jessie said. One of Trevor Smith's ears folded forward as if it was permanently cupped. 'The Sisters of Holy Rescue.'

'They'll vouch for this?'

'Yes.'

'Has any attempt been made to find her parents?'

'She was found on a southbound boat out of Siem Reap in 1980. The child is Eurasian,' she added. 'A child of war, perhaps.'

'Who found her?'

Jessie hesitated. 'I'm not sure of the circumstances in which the child was received. I first saw her at the Foreign Correspondents' Club when I was working in the area, soon after the Vietnamese took over. It was a pretty confusing time.'

'Who brought her to the FCC?'

'I can't tell you that,' Jessie said.

'There are rules governing the transfer of foreign nationals from one country to another. In what capacity are you seeking a passport for the child? As her guardian?'

'As her mother. I wish to adopt the child.'

'I see.' Smith's wild-card ear seemed to move of its own accord. 'A great many people wish to adopt children. You'd have to go through a process of assessment in London to see whether you were a suitable parent.'

'I understand that.'

'There'd be a great deal of paperwork, but I expect you're used to that.'

'I think that's the least of my concerns,' Jessie said, attempting a smile.

'Well, then, we should get started here. You realise it will take time.'

'There's no way I could take her with me on a visit?'

'Now? Oh come, Miss Sandle, there's no hope of that.

Well, I'm sorry of course.' He moved his pen carefully around his desk. 'I do have a dinner invitation for you, if you're free tonight. Our Third Secretary, Mr Atcheson, and his wife are giving a dinner party, and invite you to come. I was in Mr Atcheson's office when I received the message that you were here. He says his wife knows you, and as they had a cancellation for their party, he'd be delighted if you could make up the numbers.'

'I don't recall a Mrs Atcheson.'

'Mary. Oh, great gal — she says it was a while ago. I'm sure you'll catch up.'

As Jessie arrived back at the compound, later that evening, she learned that dinner was in honour of one of Margaret Thatcher's junior cabinet ministers, out on an official visit.

Brian Atcheson and his wife stood at the door receiving their dinner guests. Brian was a big man, perhaps six four in his socks, with wide but stooping shoulders, a large head with a grey prickle haircut. His wife, seeming tiny as she stood in his shadow, wore a cream silk dress with a Grecian flow that showed off her tanned arms. Her crisp iron-grey hair was swept back from a profile of such immaculate and flawless complexion that for a moment Jessie thought she must be much younger than her husband. And there was something so familiar about her raised chin, as if she was slightly scornful about receiving guests. Jessie was first in the row waiting to enter the room.

'Jessie,' the woman drawled, moving out of her husband's shadow and extending a cool hand. 'You're far too important these days to be arriving first at a party.'

Jessie glanced down, seeing how rough her own hands were from weeks of scrubbing soiled napkins and working in the convent kitchen, before looking into eyes she knew very well. Mary Atcheson was Marianne.

*

Marianne held sway at the table, the perfect hostess, turning from guest to guest, drawing each out to tell stories and jokes, between the main course and dessert. Somewhat to her surprise, she was seated next to the minister, a man with a satin-close shave and an inexhaustible line in stories about military engagement. 'My dear,' he said, leaning close to Jessie's shoulder, and wiping his mouth with his napkin, 'you should have been with us in the Falklands. We had a wonderful time when I was out there during the war. I was sitting taking tea one afternoon, and our boys were positioned all around the garden. Well, the Argies came jumping over the hedge and our boys just knocked them off, pop pop pop among the cabbages. Now that would have been one for you to write up.' He slapped his hand down on the table beside Jessie's plate, exploding with laughter.

'Now, we come to Jessie,' said Marianne, intervening smoothly. 'Let me tell you how I met Jessie. We've been friends for almost a lifetime. Well, a very long time. I was a *waitress*, would you believe? In a pretentious little caf at the ends of the earth, owned by a supercilious old hag who thought she could run all our lives. It was right before I went to drama school — all so Bohemian, darlings. I can tell you, I've done the lot, you could write a book about my life. And Jessie, well, our famous Jessie was a student from down south, who'd run away from home. Oh darling, don't look at me like that, you know perfectly well that you had. I was called Marianne in those days, God knows why my mother gave me a name like that — it's so very sixties now, isn't it — but seeing Jessie's here, I'm 'fessing up to my secret. Jessie was a star right away. Our Violet, that's the old girl who, by the way, had purple hair, moved her up the ranks very quickly. Jessie got to be a *chef*. Didn't you, Jessie?'

'Yes,' said Jessie, 'I was a cook at the Violet Café.'

'You see, we all have our secrets.' Marianne glided on, as if everything about their lives had been revealed.

When dinner was over, they drank brandy out of giant balloons in the sitting room, beneath soft shadowy lights, and the minister held forth. Under the layer of talk, Jessie said, 'I'm glad that things turned out well for you.'

'Thank you,' said Marianne, tilting her glass sideways. 'I started acting you know, bit parts in revues in Auckland, then Brian came along. He'd gone out to New Zealand on a trade mission when he first went into foreign affairs. I was his first and last foreign affair. It's turned out very well. I like the life. A hard life for the children in boarding school, but they're survivors. Like me.'

'I don't feel the same way about Violet as you do,' Jessie ventured. 'She didn't mean things to happen the way they did. She sent me a gift later on.'

'A gift.' Marianne snorted. 'She sent me one too. Shall I tell you what it was? A box of sticking plaster.'

'You're joking.'

'There was a note in it, telling me to put myself back together.'

'Marianne.' (She couldn't bring herself to call the woman Mary.) 'I've got something to tell you. Lou's alive. I saw him.'

'Oh, him.' Marianne feigned indifference, but her eyes flicked around the room to see whether anyone was listening to their conversation. When she was satisfied that they were not, she said, 'I know that. We know all the foreign nationals living in the territory. I could tell you things about yourself that even you don't know. Don't look so taken aback, why should I care about Lou Messenger? I've known for years that he was alive. Belle Hunter told me when I was buying shoes in Christchurch one day.'

'Belle sold home appliances. Well, that's what she was selling the last time I saw her.'

'Belle would sell anything that people would pay money for. Oh God, you've got so *moral*, Jessie. I didn't mean it. I don't know. It was shoes she was selling the day I saw her. I'd slipped back home for a few days to see my mother. She married a lovely chap. They farm down south. Well, of course they're too old for it now, they've got people working for them these days. Anyway, there was Belle, kneeling at my feet, shoving them into some very nice Italian leather jobs, and muttering away about Lou. She offered me a hundred dollars off.'

'The shoes?'

'Yes.'

'Did you take them?'

'Of course,' said Marianne, looking sideways. Then she laughed.

Jessie was stunned by the night, and the rich food, after her weeks in the convent, and by Marianne's smile, the way she glided through their history as if nothing untoward had ever happened to either of them. Argies. Popped them among the cabbages. *Cabb*-age, *cabb*-age, never mind the *da*-mage. A world of make-believe.

'Well, Lou left her a little present, didn't he?' Marianne was saying. 'I expect she showed you the pictures of the children. How I detest people who're always flashing their loved ones out of their wallets. Really hokey.'

Wallace junior. Perhaps. No, it was the girl who was older. Jessie was silent. Marianne said, 'This girl you've come about?'

'I thought that was supposed to be confidential.'

'Oh it is. You have to be careful, Jessie. People know about that convent. And the children Lou Messenger's taken there.'

'But …' Jessie began to say, feeling her face redden.

'That place is marked. Oh, I don't think anyone doubts your good intentions, Jessie. Life's full of moral contradictions out here in the East, but I'm sure you know that better than I do. We're really alike, you and I, we've learned to paper over the cracks. I decided not to suffer for mine, not to let them get in the way of the present. But every now and then they trip you up. The view is that anything Lou's touched is morally indefensible, and why should I argue with that? Perhaps you've forgotten, Evelyn Messenger was my very best friend. You might have trouble convincing the authorities that you'd never had anything to do with him. If you take my point.'

'You won't help me then?' Jessie had said.

Marianne gave her a long level stare. 'I won't get in your way.' She waved for a waiter to bring more brandy.

Jessie stood and felt her head spin. 'Goodnight, Marianne,' she said, moving swiftly to let herself out. Outside, the air was hugely overheated, the humidity as thick as linen, with traces of lightning illuminating the sky over the Chao Phraya River. The night had just begun in Bangkok.

Back in the hotel, she wrote a letter to Sister Mary Luke.

Dear Sister,

I do not believe that it will be possible for me to take Bopha back to London with me. I will never forsake her. As long as I live, I will think of her as my child. There may come a time when I am able to claim her as my own, to educate her in the way that she deserves, but that time has not come. Perhaps her country really does need her, but that is not an excuse; it is a hope for the future. I ask one favour, however difficult, that you will allow her to follow in the Buddhist faith if she chooses.

CAROLINE

Dear Jessie,

Perhaps by now you will have forgotten us people you used to know when you were young. It's a while since you looked me up, at least ten years. I must admit that I felt angry when you turned up on my doorstep without an appointment (ah, there I have you, Jessie, you didn't think someone like me would need appointments to be seen, but I can tell you I'm very booked up ahead these days). It wasn't so much that you were inconsiderate, it was thinking about how you had run off and how many years it had taken you to come back, walking in, as if nothing had changed. I can tell you, everything changed that night when Owen died. Each day has seemed like eternity. People used to say to me that I should shift away, go to some other place. But where would I have gone? And why should I? Instead of my mother looking at me with reproach because I had gone off and married Owen, I could bare my teeth at her, for not wanting more for me, for not understanding how my life could have been if I had been married younger, if I hadn't listened to her. You may think me a bitter woman, but that is not altogether true. I will be fifty next year, and I've come to terms with what I've got. This house, which is so eccentric and well preserved that now the historical society wants me to leave it to them for a museum. Hah! Plenty of life in me yet. They'll have to wait a while. I still have my brides.

Oh my brides, Jessie. You've never been one. Well, it's hardly surprising. You were an attractive enough woman, back to front, but a bride needs a bit of cleavage and a big smile. I can't remember you smiling much, Jessie. Perhaps that was your trouble, you were an inward sort of girl. Well, I love helping the girls here organise their weddings. I make their dresses and cut out their veils and help them choose the right colour to have their shoes dyed, and go to the florist with them, and talk to their mothers about how to do things with style. I'm very popular. People know if they don't get me the minute they're engaged then they'll miss out, and have to wait as long as I did. Hester's Wedding Treats — that's the name of my business. And fancy, I'm quite well off. I didn't have to sell Mother's house in order to put eggs in the nest.

Anyway, Mother's dead, and we won't dwell on that. Would you believe she had a letter from Freda Messenger before she died? No address, just a Washington postmark. She said Evelyn had a couple of sons when she was in her forties and she'd set Freda up in one of those little towns they have in America with security all around. Sounded to me like Evelyn had had her locked up, but what would I know about that? No mention of the economy.

You'll probably think I'm hard. That I'm looking for someone to blame. And there were so many I could have, but what's the point of that? Violet Trench was the one who felt the most remorse. I should have seen it coming she says to me some nights when she's in her cups. You can't bring them back, I tell her. Go to sleep.

Oh yes, I haven't told you, Violet lives with me. She's a widow now. Lord, how the years roll on by, and sweep people away. The good doctor died on her, when they were climbing in Argentina. Well, he was, although I suspect that Violet was close by in a swank hotel sipping very dry martinis. Heart, of course. The man was in his seventies. You'd wonder why the travel agents would allow a man of his age to go rabbiting up mountainsides, but then Violet tells me that these tour operators have got no scruples at all, they just take the money and leave their clients to it. Still, you might know more about things like that than I do, I've never travelled, wouldn't want to.

I was sorry for the old biddy when she came back to town. She had nowhere to go, and it was her that set me free in the first place. At least free enough to experience a little of what life is about, which I hope for your sake you've managed to do, although sex without marriage is promiscuity, I've always believed, not that some of the poor girls who come to me seem to have cottoned on to it. If they want alterations done, and the dresses letting out, they have to let me know a month in advance, which means of course that I often get to know before their own mothers. Not that I'd breathe a word.

I should have Violet put away, I suppose, but she can still get around, and she does like a tipple in the evenings which she wouldn't get in the rest home, so I let her stay on with me. I quite like the company, to tell you the truth. But just lately she's had a bee in her bonnet, and she thinks you might be able to help her. She wants to trace some relative of hers called Caroline. She thinks she might live in London, and says you might remember her kindly enough to be willing to help. (Did she give you some money? I never did think of Violet as a real business-woman.) So before we go into all the details, perhaps you could drop me a line and let me know if you've time in your schedule to do the old lady a favour.

Hester

London was crackling with October's early frost when Jessie read this letter, although it had been written in June. It was at the bottom of a pile of mail she had collected from her lawyer's office where correspondence was redirected on her trips away. The blue aerogramme had a homely look about it, stuck together off-square and addressed in round scribbled handwriting. Jessie studied the New Zealand postmark, for a moment not registering the sender's name written on the back. When she did, she placed the letter on the polished

286

mahogany hall table, and slowly took off the grey woollen coat that fell gracefully from her shoulders when she walked. It was lined with forest-green silk. For some years, she had been moving from place to place giving lectures and talks. Her first book, *Indochine, The Heart's Tragedy*, had been so favourably reviewed that she had been invited to tour in America, stopping first at Harvard, where she was a guest lecturer for six months, with a regular offer of a half-time place for the next three years. A whole series of appearances followed each of these teaching stints. They had taken her criss-crossing the States, up to Canada, over to Paris and Belgium, where she spoke through interpreters, and several times to Australia. The Australian trips were a convenient stopping-over place for her annual trips to Cambodia. She always tried to be there with Bopha for the New Year celebrations. She didn't consider going south to New Zealand these days. It was, she believed, a country she had now put behind her altogether. From time to time, she heard news of her half-sister Belinda, who had married young and had two daughters by the time she was twenty. They sent her cards and notes that started out in round childish hands with the words 'Dear Aunt Jessie, thank you for the money for my birthday.' Always much the same. Their handwriting was beginning to take shape, reflections of how their signatures would appear when they were adults, one of them tentative, the second one bold and flourishing. I think Sally might turn out like her Auntie Jessie, Belinda had written at the bottom of one of her notes, with an exclamation mark. The nearest she had come to expressing an opinion of Jessie.

Two of these letters from Belinda's children were in the waiting pile. These were the first she opened, making a mental resolution to do something about seeing these children. Not that she expected to soon. When she had poured herself a drink, she sat down by the gas fire and read Hester's letter, noting the date at the top.

The trees had grown so close to Hester's house that Jessie felt as if she was entering some dark domain. Branches of evergreens touched her face as she walked up the path. Little had changed, although the exterior had had a new coat of Spanish white paint. A sprinkle of snowdrops were scattered beneath a lemon tree, and some winter roses huddled on a patch of bare turned earth.

'You might have told us you were coming,' Hester said, flustered, when she opened the door. 'It's just like you — we don't hear from you in years, you don't answer our letters, and then you just turn up. Out of the blue. As it were.'

'I did ring,' said Jessie. 'May I come in?' Hester was dressed in loose black pants and a flowing red and green jacket that reached her knees. Her long white hair was bundled into a floating bun like a movie actress playing a nineteenth-century pioneer, and steel-rimmed glasses perched on the high bridge of her nose. She had thickened around the waist, and grown folds round her chin, but with a tape measure slung over one shoulder, she looked the part of the wedding planner, a woman to whom people turned.

'You've got a visitor, Vi,' Hester sang out ahead of her.

Violet was seated in a low chair beneath one of the tasselled lamp-shades in the darkened sitting room, where Jessie used to stand while Hester pinned up her dresses. She was sitting motionless, her back to the door, so that the first Jessie saw was her fine blue hair, dressed up exactly as it had been at the Violet Café, shining in a halo of pinkish light. Beside her chair stood a walking stick.

She turned as the two younger women came through the

door. Jessie was afraid she would see a ravaged travesty of the past, but Violet's face seemed little changed, and prettily made up, as if she was expecting visitors. The lines around her mouth had deepened, and a scarf obscured her throat, but her eyes were as blue as Jessie remembered, and as direct.

She said, 'I knew you'd come, Jessie.'

Hester was fidgeting in the background, offering tea or coffee, and regretting that she hadn't baked this morning — there were only bought ginger snaps. Did Jessie take milk these days, or did she only drink that Chinese stuff, now that she was an expert on the Orient? 'I do keep up with your doings, you know. Your name's in the papers. I cut out all the reviews. I expect you think this is too small a country to come and give your talks, but I can tell you people here are interested, and very interesting. They belong to book clubs, all sorts of things. This country has changed, you wouldn't believe it.'

'She does like to fuss,' Violet said indulgently. 'But she looks after me very well. She's still a great cook, even though she's got a medieval kitchen. You know, she could afford to upgrade it.'

'She likes spending money, don't you?' said Hester, arranging a fine cashmere rug around Violet's knees. 'Why would I need a new kitchen? That one's always done in the past.'

Jessie supposed, then, that they would tell her about the woman Violet was seeking. But Violet was intent on leading Jessie through a recital of her journeys, encouraging her to be outrageous, demanding that she describe what it was like to ride in a helicopter, to be under artillery fire, how to avoid snakebite in the jungle, and to tell her the best newspapers to order if she was travelling in the East. She steadied her cup in two hands; her joints were thick with arthritis.

'You're thinking of taking a trip then?' said Hester, in a lightly mocking tone.

'Well, I would if I could. Haven't you got a client coming soon?'

Hester slammed her cup down on an occasional table. 'Well,' she said to Jessie, 'if that's not an invitation to get lost, I don't know what is. Wouldn't you think?'

Jessie thought of offering to leave, but decided it was pointless to have travelled all the way from London just to invoke a quarrel, even if that was what Hester was looking for. 'I'll fit in,' she said.

'Jessie's come to talk to me about looking for Caroline. You know that, dear,' Violet said.

'Whoever Caroline is,' Hester said, her voice tight. 'I get to do the donkey work, track Jessie down, write the letters, but what happens next? I get thrown out of my own house.'

'Don't mind us,' Violet said, 'we're just two silly old widows.'

Jessie was tiring of the game of insults the two women were trading. Violet appeared to be paying a high price for a comfortable home, as a latter-day Ruth Hagley. 'I was thinking of staying a day or so,' she said. 'I can come back tomorrow if you'd rather.' This wasn't really true, but she thought why not, if she must. Sooner or later, she would go and see Belinda. Since she had found Bopha, she felt more strongly drawn towards the idea of seeing her mother's grandchildren. Perhaps she was not entirely immune to family. But she was booked to fly back to London in three days, so if she stayed here, Belinda and the children would be passed over again.

'No,' said Hester, suddenly quitting the argument. 'I've got someone coming, as it happens. A consultation with a pig-headed girl. She wants to wear the trashiest shoes and jewellery. Well, why should I care, but people will know she's one of mine. You just stay and take your time.'

When Hester was gone, Violet said, 'She blames herself, of course.'

'For what?'

'Owen dying. They'd had a quarrel, you know. He'd come to town to look for Hester.'

'That's dreadful,' said Jessie. 'I had no idea.'

'Well, they were normal, I suppose. I've tried to tell her that. People will go on punishing themselves.' Violet appeared to be gathering herself together. Was it Hester, Jessie wondered, who put the delicate blush of rouge on Violet's cheeks when she dressed at the beginning of each day? Violet must sit here day after day, pampered and made pretty by Hester. Perhaps, rather than being unkind, Hester was simply exhausted.

'You've probably worked out who Caroline is,' Violet said, at last. 'I expect Hester has too.'

'Another of your children?' Violet appeared to flinch. 'A daughter.'

'You heard that I had a child?'

'A son, I was told.'

'Who told you that?'

'Lou Messenger.'

'Aaah.' Violet expelled a long breath. 'Lou Messenger.'

'You knew he was alive?'

'There've been rumours, of course, for years.'

'I met him in a downtown bar in the middle of Phnom Penh, just after the Vietnamese drove Pol Pot out of the city. He exists. Well, he did then, though it's a fair while ago. He thought John Wing Lee was your son.'

'Well, what can I say about that?'

'That it's true?'

'Oh yes, it's true enough. I still feel badly I suppose, about trying to hold you back when I did. I took advantage of you,

291

your awkwardness and your neediness, of you wanting John as much as you did. I can say that, now that you've turned out so well. You're quite dashing, Jessie. Oh yes, I admire what you've become.'

'Please, don't make a speech,' Jessie said. 'You didn't ruin my life.'

'Well, it wasn't my son I asked you to come here and talk about. Or your ruination, which clearly never happened. Although it has to be said that the summer when you girls all worked for me at the Violet Café made great changes in people's lives, and some of them were intolerably damaged. Don't think I have no regrets. I've done enough damage to my own life. But I did see that it wouldn't have worked out for you and John. Your landlady brought in the library books you'd left behind. I don't know why she couldn't have returned them herself. But when I looked at them I understood that it wasn't just because of your mother that you'd gone that night. You would have tired of the life.

'What I'm leading to is the question of choice. You see, Jessie, I had to choose between one child and another. At least, that's how it seemed at the time. I took John to Hugo, who had been the first real love of my life, only at the time when I was in love with him, it didn't seem right. It seemed sinful even to think like that, because his wife was dying, in the room, between us, inch by inch. So I went away. I wasn't entirely without principles in those days. I met a man when I was a student at the music school in Versailles. I'd gone to Paris for the day. He was a soldier from England — when being in the military meant having a career — a well-off, fastidious, and rather arrogant man, but we had some good times together when it started. He gave me an excuse to drift away from music and follow what had come to interest me more, the pursuit of good food and good living. I decided to marry him, not that there was much choice — I was having his baby. But it did ease the longing I had for Hugo. Of course, my new husband had to take me home to meet his family. They didn't like me from the beginning. They thought of me as his little colonial, like Katherine Mansfield, you know, the bourgeois girl on the make. Not that I was any girl by then, of course. Oh, I'd lived you know, I expect they saw that. The halls in the house where they lived were lined with pictures in gilded frames, of all the relations who had gone before, not like those of a tin canner's daughter from New Zealand. But soon we had a girl. Caroline. She was picture-perfect, like one of those children in the advertisements for Pears soap — long blond curls tied back in a ribbon. She showed early signs of artistic talent, much greater than I imagine I ever had as a child. We doted on her, her father and I, but not on each other. His family's view of me soon made its mark.

'The war was a relief. My husband went away and I was free in a sense. Caroline had her grandparents, and I started to go to London more and more often, on the pretext of helping with the war effort. It's hard to explain what it was like, the nights in the shelters, and everyone close together while the bombs went off. Not romantic, like some people have painted it, but terrifying and bleak. I met a young man who was so different from my husband, and Hugo for that matter. Or perhaps I was influenced by the knowledge that Hugo had mended his heart quickly after I left New Zealand too, with Ming, the woman from China. I'd been intrigued by this news. Perhaps that's why I couldn't stop looking at this young man who had come to London from China to study, and hadn't been able to return when the war broke out. He was staying with relatives over a fruit shop in Clapham Common. His body had a smell about it that I find hard to describe. I think of lilies or lemons or truffles, although it was not any of those, but something tart and sweet and altogether mysterious.

'Of course, the inevitable happened. We made love — in bomb shelters, in the room that I had taken, close to where he lived, everywhere. We went off into the countryside when the summer came. I'm ashamed to say this, but it was as if Caroline didn't exist, perhaps because she was part of my husband's family, whom I'd come to detest.

'Had I forgotten Hugo? I suppose so. I can't really remember now, my mind's clouded about this. Hugo had set me on a path, and this was where it had taken me.'

'I can't help asking, but do you think you were really in love with Hugo?' asked Jessie curiously.

Violet stiffened opposite her. 'I beg your pardon. I loved Hugo all my life. What makes you ask?'

'I met him. It just seems surprising.'

'You met him the night he died.'

'All the same, there's a difference, isn't there,' Jessie persisted, 'between loving someone and being in love with them? Even though you can do both. I can see I've offended you. But you're a woman used to getting what you want. In some ways I've modelled my life on what I saw in you. Headstrong and independent. I think if you'd wanted him so badly, you would have stayed behind.'

'You're talking about you and John, aren't you?'

'I suppose I am. Perhaps I'd have come back. But I thought he was dead, that's the difference. Lots of us carry round romantic images of what might have been, but they're hardly ever true, don't you think?'

Violet plucked in an agitated way at the rug that covered her knees. 'You couldn't possibly have modelled your life on mine.'

'What did you expect when you began the job of changing

us? Whose image were you offering us?'

'I wanted you to look in the mirror and see yourselves, that's all. That wasn't so bad, was it?'

'No,' said Jessie truthfully. Because what Violet said did make sense. 'Why don't you just tell me what happened next?'

Violet sighed and fidgeted again. Jessie saw how exhausted she had become, as if age washed over her in waves.

'I became pregnant again. I wanted this. It's a gift, I suppose, that women seek from men who intoxicate their senses, as this one did to me. To have their children, to show the world how the man has possessed them. And then, of course, they don't want the child, don't need it, have to give it away because it was never theirs to have in the first place. I've heard stories about Belle Hunter. Well, I believe them. She got what was coming to her, and I don't hold it against her. She got what she wanted from Lou, the same as I took from my lover. She didn't need any presents from me.

'But I was in a fix, of course. This was a long time ago. The war was on, I had a husband, and a daughter who somehow I'd mislaid, everyone knew that I hadn't seen her father for a long time. Time went by and I started living over the shop in Clapham Common with the baby and his father. I wrote a letter to my mother-in-law. I said I'd had to go home to New Zealand because of an illness in my family. Or perhaps she suspected the truth. The last time I'd gone there I was already some months along the way with this pregnancy.

'I wanted my little girl again. I loved the boy, but I couldn't have them both, I'm sure you can see that. I took him to a children's home and left him there for a day or two to see whether it would work, but I couldn't do it.

'I formed a plan in my head, to hide him away somewhere where I could get him back later on. And that's what I did. I took him to Hugo. Perhaps you're right, it may have just been his constancy that drew me to him, but it's hard to let go of one's illusions at my age, Jessie. Anyway, that's one side of it, what happened to John. The other is that my husband's family made sure I never saw Caroline again. My husband had come back while I was away, years had passed, and he had begun divorce proceedings. A scandal for his family, but they had to act quickly, I understand that, punish me for my desertion. I went to the house. They must have seen me coming. They wouldn't let me in. Caroline's not here, they said, but I was sure that she was. They said they would call the police if I came back, and I believed them. I felt that I must vanish or this girl of mine would be caught up in an endless tug of war. I worked in the restaurant trade again, this time learning a few cooking skills, doing front-of-house in a smart little French place in Soho, and from there I went to Sydney and ran a place near King's Cross for a bit. Closing in on my boy, as it were, until the moment was right. Then I came back here, as I often did, and I met this remarkable girl, Hester, who knew it all, a self-taught original. She made it all so easy, she and Hugo. Extraordinary.'

'She's amazing all right,' said Jessie, privately reflecting on Hester's martyrdom. 'So where's John now?'

'Oh, John, he's around somewhere.' If Violet knew, she clearly wasn't going to tell Jessie. Perhaps, Jessie thought, she didn't want to admit that she didn't know.

'This isn't fair,' Jessie said.

Violet said then that she'd lost touch with John when she went to America with Felix Adam. She had thought of marrying Shorty Toft, but she was saved from herself. 'He cut off my account at the shop, you know, when I said I needed time to think about his proposal. It was just an excuse of course. Poor Shorty wasn't up to all the rumours flying round about the café.' For a moment, she almost smiled. It was strange, she said, the amount of malice that humorous men sometimes harboured. 'I was quite grateful to him for that bit of spite. It put some spine in me, when it came to Felix. I'd decided to go for nothing but the best.'

Jessie closed her eyes, trying to recall the laconic doctor and his waxy-faced wife, and found it hard to be convinced.

'John had his own family,' Violet said. 'They cared for him after the accident. I had thought of him as dead, like the others, but he wasn't. Nobody bothered to tell me for three weeks.' This was how she put it, that his family had closed around him, kept him hidden and maintained silence. She had supposed that the brothers were sending her a message — that he didn't belong to her. When asked why they did it, they had told the police that they couldn't read English and didn't know that John was missing. 'It was rubbish, of course. Perhaps I was wrong to try and lay claim to him again. Still, I'd had him for a little while. And now I want you to find Caroline for me. Eh, Jessie? How about it? I think you're the right person.'

'I don't know about that. I'm not a detective.'

'Oh, you can do it all right, you're good at asking questions these days. If you would do me that one favour.'

'John might still want to know about you. More than Caroline.' From where she was sitting, none of it seemed like a good idea.

Violet sighed, her eyes suddenly tired. 'John had a mother. It's best left. Caroline didn't. I want you to try and find her. You can't imagine what it's like to lose a child.'

'Well, yes I can,' said Jessie.

'Oh well, then you must tell me about it sometime.' Violet closed her eyes, her head fell forward and, in the space of a blink, she was gently snoring, her crooked hands clasped across her stomach.

Marianne rang Jessie one morning. She was back living in London. 'I've heard on the grapevine that Lou's dead.'

'Where was he?'

'Up in north Thailand.'

Jessie had known that Lou was long gone from Phnom Penh. He'd been robbed too many times to make it worth his staying. 'He wasn't all bad,' she said.

'Good riddance to bad rubbish. You should do something about Bopha.'

'Is that why you've rung me? To tell me the coast's clear.'

'Well, it was never not clear.'

'That's not what you told me.'

'I just think it will be easier. Anyway, Bopha's old enough to know what she wants, isn't she? Hey, I'm taking Alannah to the zoo, do you want to come with us? We could feed the monkeys.' Alannah was Marianne's first grandchild.

'I'm not mad about zoos,' said Jessie, who had had to leave restaurants in Cambodia because of caged sun bears, chained and grieving. Saving sun bears had become one of her causes.

'Well, they're interesting places. Never mind. So shall we do lunch? Go to a movie? Would you like to be a lady who does lunch with me, Jessie?'

'Sometimes,' said Jessie.

In the end, it was decided that Bopha would go to high school in London, and back to Phnom Penh during the holidays. This was less trouble to arrange than Jessie had expected. As if it might have always been a live possibility. At first, Jessie was designated her guardian. She had decided that the time for a more formal procedure had passed, that possession was not what Bopha would want.

One Sunday morning, Jessie sat in the apartment, surrounded by the morning's newspapers. Bopha came out of the shower, her head wrapped in a towel, her face shining with steam. Soon she would be seventeen. She had grown long-legged and slim, and moved with a slow, elegant grace. Like a dancer, Jessie thought. Or a nun. She was trying to decide whether to go back to Cambodia the following year, or to go to university. Privately, Jessie hoped university would win out, that perhaps she could go back later, if that was what she still wanted, but Bopha must decide for herself. I want you to make up your own mind, she had said more than once.

'What's that you're reading?' Bopha asked, coming to read over her shoulder.

Jessie folded the newspaper over. 'Nothing,' she said. 'Oh, never mind, it's some frightful story about a Russian adoption gone wrong. These kids who are adopted out of their own countries get into some dreadful difficulties. It's not as if they can go back.'

'You've got a thing about adoption, haven't you?' Bopha said.

'Well, I was adopted once myself, and it wasn't a great success.'

'Is that why you never adopted me?' Bopha asked.

Jessie glanced up at her, startled. 'Partly,' she said, slowly, 'and partly because you've been raised by the nuns.' There was another reason, of course, but she didn't want Bopha to know about Lou, and the way she had sought him out again to find the nuns. The way her knowledge of Lou had dogged her footsteps. 'Well, you know, I was a single woman too, not necessarily the ideal mother for you. Would you have wanted me to adopt you?'

Bopha's eyes were full of tears. 'I didn't think you wanted me enough.'

'Bopha, that's not true.' Seeing how upset the girl was, she said, 'It's not too late, I guess.'

'D'you mean that? Would you?'

'Are you planning to adopt me?' Jessie said.

When Bopha said, 'Yes, I want you to be my mother,' Jessie's heart lifted, as people's do when they are nearing the end of a journey.

Jessie looked for Caroline for a long time. After she had been to New Zealand to see Violet, she searched telephone books and electoral rolls, and placed an advertisement in *The Times* but nothing happened. All of this was intense and time-consuming. At some point, she decided that it was all too much. From then on, she put aside three days a year which she called her Find Caroline days. There had been an accumulation of these days, years and years of them.

She was shopping with Bopha in Harrods for a new evening bag, when something happened that made her stop looking. The Atchesons were holding a retirement party for Brian in their Hyde Park apartment that evening. Brian was taking an early retirement. Jessie sensed a disappointment that he had never made it to ambassador status. There would be more time for their grandchildren, they said gamely.

Bopha had wandered away from her side, interested in acquiring a new duvet. She was always cold in London at the beginning of each trip, even when it was summer. Jessie picked up a bag that took her eye, looking inside to check the compartments, and glanced up, seeking a saleswoman. Instead, she saw a woman standing beside her, checking the beadwork on another bag. For an instant, Jessie took her to be Violet, the Violet she had first known, or perhaps a little older. Only the hair was different, a stylish ragged bob; otherwise she could have passed for her, a trifle haggard and thin, but beautiful, the kind of woman who would attract attention anywhere. An artist of some kind, Jessie thought, for she wore a bright silky jacket, and her fingernails appeared to have a trace of paint beneath them. 'Caroline,' said Jessie. 'Is it you, Caroline?'

The woman straightened up, startled, and looked at Jessie with a cool stare in her blue eyes. 'I'm sorry,' she said. 'I don't think we've met.'

'Are you by any chance Caroline Trench?' Jessie asked. 'I mean, was that ever your name?'

The woman, who had seemed momentarily frozen to the spot, lifted one expressive eyebrow and her shoulder, in a half-shrug, much as Violet would have. 'I haven't the faintest idea what you're talking about.'

'But you're Caroline?'

'My name is Caroline May,' said the woman. 'Now if you'll excuse me.'

'I'd like to give you my card,' said Jessie. 'I've been looking for this person for years. Perhaps you could ring me if you ever hear of her.'

'Please go away,' the woman said, her tone flat and cold. 'If you don't, I'll call store security.' She walked away from Jessie without taking the card.

Your daughter is alive, Jessie wrote to Violet. She is an artist and a very beautiful woman, and I'm sure you would be proud of her.

She didn't think Violet would hear this letter when it was read to her. From what Hester wrote, Violet didn't give the impression of hearing anything much any more. Nobody really knows what she hears now, she had said in her last letter. Jessie thought that if she could hear this message, it would be enough.

Part Seven

The Truffle Gatherers

2002

It's hard to believe anyone could have lived that long. As if Violet Trench couldn't master the art of dying. Yet in the end she has done it, after ninety-five years of living. She went like a lady, the woman at the rest home tells Hester. No complaints. She wasn't one to complain. Hester says this at the funeral, her cheeks glowing with pride. She is the one who has seen Violet through it. More or less. Hester wishes she had been there when she died, but all of this has been going on a very long time. Goodness, it's twenty years since she first caught Violet putting washing powder in the peas instead of salt. And they all know how it is, you simply can't be in the right place every time. Hester is just glad she has been there for Violet. Bless her. She's been a wonderful woman, who's played her part in all their lives.

'Sanctimonious claptrap,' hisses Marianne, seated in the front row beside Jessie. They are in a small chapel attached to a funeral home. The casket in front of them is made of the best dark wood, decorated with a spray of Prince of Wales violets, the big strong variety.

Hester has rung everyone who she thinks 'ought to know' that Violet has died, not that she expects them to come of course, those who are too busy or too far away.

Jessie rings Marianne to cancel lunch because she is flying out to New Zealand that evening. Marianne is not one of the people Hester has contacted. 'You're crazy,' Marianne says, because it is only a week since Jessie flew home from Bopha's wedding in Cambodia. 'You're too old to be traipsing all round the world the way you do, you'll get blood clots.'

When Jessie says briskly that of course she is going, she might be old, but you're only as old as you let yourself be, Marianne says, 'All right, calm down. I'll meet you at the airport.'

'You'll do what?' says Jessie. 'I don't believe it. You haven't been there for nearly forty years.' Jessie is referring to the town, not the country, because she knows that from time to time Marianne visits Sybil in New Zealand. The whole subject of Sybil is closed to her. Marianne behaves as if she had a perfectly normal childhood; her mother is an engaging and elegant old woman, much loved by her grandchildren.

'I need to make sure the old witch is really buried,' Marianne says of Violet, 'besides it would be a bit of a gig, wouldn't it, you and me, just like old times. We are travelling business class, aren't we, Jessie? If you're doing any of that crazy economy stuff, I'll upgrade you when I book.'

So that, when they cross Asia, Jessie nearly forgets to look down, as if she might see Bopha on a dusty street, waving out to the planes going overhead, but then, over to the left of the flight path, not far from the Equator, lie the green paddy fields of Cambodia between stripes of red dust and the glint of a city, a flash on the horizon. Bopha has married a young man called Tan with a sweet melancholy face. His family had come to see Jessie and the nuns, on an earlier visit. It felt like an arrangement, but Bopha insisted that this was the man she loved, and nobody else would ever do. They had met teaching school in the countryside that lay between Phnom Penh and Ta Pao in the north. 'May my everlasting soul rest in peace, and may His Holiness never get to hear about this,' Sister Mary Luke had muttered when, in keeping with tradition, the bridegroom had led his friends and family, garlanded with frangipani buds and bearing brightly coloured gifts, in a procession down the street, to beat down the door of the convent and take Bopha in marriage. A fat, lazy rain had begun to fall, and the people in the procession had had to put up umbrellas, rejoicing that the rainy season was coming. A good sign. There would be no honeymoon for Bopha and Tan; in the morning they went back to work teaching school in the bridegroom's village.

In the end, everyone is at Violet's funeral who might be expected to come, except Evelyn, whom nobody has heard from, and the children of Felix Adam, who have never forgiven their father for marrying Violet. Once, long ago, the eldest daughter had sent a stiff note to Hester, saying she would never get a cent out of the family, because they all knew that Violet was carrying on with their father when their mother was still alive, but that was her style, and thank God her father hadn't got round to making a will before his escapade in the mountains. They had sent money to bring their father's body back from South America, but nothing for Violet, who'd had him cremated instead, and carried him in her hand luggage on a flight paid for by Hester.

Now there is a small assortment of elderly people who claim to have been clientele of the Violet Café, several of Hester's customers, some staff from the rest home, and Hester and Jessie and Marianne, and Belle with her new husband, Wayne Geraghty. Wayne is a short dark man with a forest of hair poking up above his collar and tie. He's been a real saver, Belle says, when she introduces them at the door of the funeral home. In retirement, he breeds racehorses and, as luck would have it, he was available for marriage when they met. What comes around goes around, Belle says fondly, although quite what she means by this is not apparent. She is dressed in a flowing turquoise and green garment, over a thickening girth.

While Hester is speaking, someone else comes in, but nobody likes to turn round to see who it is. As Hester talks on, extolling Violet's virtues, Jessie finds her thoughts straying back to Bopha's wedding. Her head nods, the days of air travel taking their toll. Bopha has a British passport now, as well as her Cambodian one. She and her husband will come and spend time with Jessie in London, may even decide to work there a while. But she will always go back. As Jessie believes she, too, will keep returning. There is so much rebuilding still to be done.

Marianne shoves her with her elbow. 'Go on,' she says. 'You're not going to let her get away with this. It's open-mike time.'

Time for those who have something to say, to stand up and speak. Jessie shakes her head, but the others are looking at her, as if this is expected of her. She finds herself in front of a small wooden lectern, and places her hands on each side, trying to think what she should say that has not already been said by Hester. In the second row, behind where she has been sitting with Marianne, sits a bald-headed Chinese man dressed in an immaculate suit, with fine gold-rimmed glasses.

John Wing Lee.

Jessie takes a deep breath while seconds pass. She finds herself ambushed with longing. This is the unalterable almost unutterable truth, that Violet Trench is dead, and now they have all been brought together to confront this fact, and each other. John rests one elbow in the palm of the opposite hand, and touches his mouth with one delicate fingertip, as if willing her to speak.

Jessie says, 'Several of us are here because we worked at the Violet Café. I first went there as a diner, late one lovely spring afternoon, when I was a girl. I'd run away from home and I was unhappy and hungry, and I chanced upon the café. The moment I set foot inside the gate, my senses were alerted to the powerful scent of flowers as I walked up the path. At first I could see that I didn't fit the profile of the diner who Mrs Trench, for that is always what we called her, might have expected. Straight away she offered me a job, rather than a meal. But after some negotiation, I was seated and a young man flourished a menu before me, in the empty café. This may sound like a fairy story and in a way it was, because he brought me delicacies I had never experienced. They were the famous truffles of Perigord, and the taste of them placed me in a trance that has never left me.'

Jessie raises her eyes. John sits like an effigy.

'The young man led me to believe they had been grown somewhere around this town. Perhaps, although it would be astonishing if it were so. Soon after I had eaten, I agreed to become a waitress, because I had succumbed to the spell cast by the Violet Café. Very quickly, I learned of the divisions within the society of a restaurant, the differences between those who wait, and those who make. The kitchen, as others have remarked, is the centre of the restaurant universe. All the rest is simply the art of seduction, that which takes you there, and entertains you. After I'd worked there for a while, I went up in the hierarchy, when I moved to the kitchen. Cooking is all about whipping and beating and chopping and heat, in more ways than you could think.'

She pauses to draw breath; still John has not moved, but then neither has anyone else. 'All of us were troubled,' she continues, 'and Mrs Trench knew that. We were too young to know how to hide our feelings. She had experienced loss and pain of her own, and recognised ours. This was part of the power she exerted over us. All the same, I think she wanted to help us solve our problems — and so she might have, except that we were overcome by misfortune. It's easy to think that if none of us had gone there to work, none of it would have happened.

'Hester, I'll always remember you skipping in Owen's arms in the sitting room of your house and the way you looked at each other as if there were no tomorrows, and how truly sorry I am that there would be so few of them.'

She takes another breath, and for a moment she thinks she sees David's white face, and the wingspan of Evelyn's eyebrows, but remembering that David is dead, and Evelyn a mirage, somewhere out there in the world, she sees it for what it is: an illusion, some trick of memory, brought about by distances and sleeplessness. And she has said more or less enough.

'On the whole,' she says, beginning to wrap it up, 'I'd like to remember what it was like before the nightmare. Ever since I left, I've only to smell garlic, or pick up a menu that offers truffles, or even see a girl in an apron leaning against the wall of a café and I catch a whiff of smoke in the air and I think of the café. *Tristesse,* we might have called it in the romantic days when we were young, sorrow that was too much to bear, but also happiness. I think that if we had the chance to choose again, most of us would still have gone to work at the Violet Café. Those of us who survived, learned to live, one way or another.

'Now, that's all,' she says, and bows briefly to the coffin. 'May violets rain on you, Mrs Trench.'

She waits for a moment, not for effect, but because her legs feel as if they might fold under her, or she might simply go to sleep where she stands. John is looking at her, his eyes seemingly veiled by light falling on the gold-rimmed glasses, and the thought flashes before her, that he may not know the true identity of the woman in the casket. He may never know. She takes her seat again.

'So,' says Marianne in her ear, as she sits down, 'not a dry eye in the house. I hope you're satisfied.' She dabs her mascara with a damp handkerchief.

When they have had what Hester calls 'the refreshments' at her house, it is still only two o'clock. John has apologised several times to Hester for his late arrival. His plane from Wellington had been delayed. That's where he is based now, commuting backwards and forwards to business interests in Sydney. He and his wife own a house in Khandallah looking out over the harbour; he shows them pictures of the house, which has a pool and waterfall in the lounge and a roof that they can lift up so that the inside and the outside are all one. His wife, who is called Kittie, although that is not her Chinese name, worries about the grandchildren falling in the pool, and he supposes they will have to think about shifting soon. Perhaps to Sydney. He has given them all hugs, touching his cheek lightly against Jessie's. She thinks she smells a whiff of something like vanilla, but decides it is his aftershave. He feels dry and a little bloodless. They stand around, taking care not to drop their egg and parsley sandwiches on the Persian carpet squares.

'A widow, a spinster and two grandmothers,' Marianne says, in that light way she has.

'And one balding Chinese businessman,' says John. All his gold quivers around his wrists as well as around his eyes, a Rolex and a bracelet.

Belle counts on her fingers. 'We've got eight children between us, two of mine, not counting my stepchildren, three of yours, Marianne, and three of yours, John.'

'Make that nine,' said Jessie.

'And I had Violet,' said Hester, in a more humorous tone than usual.

'I'm hoping my Shantee might come over and meet you all,' Belle says. 'That's my daughter Shantelle, but nobody calls her that any more. I guess we all move with the times.'

'What shall we do next?' says Marianne. Because it is still

early and nobody really wants to leave, but there are just so many things you can say after you've said hello, and what's your job like, and how are the parents these days. (Marianne and Belle are the only ones with any left alive. Belle's mother had been a shorthand typist until she was sixty-five, and her father had gone off to America, where he should be taken into custody, Belle says. As long as he's not around to bother her, they're welcome to him). There is nothing left of Violet's for them to look through, no accumulation of books or scarves or shoes to exclaim over, no old clothes to sort for the Salvation Army, because Hester did it all years before when she first began expecting Violet to die. But she'd just kept going year after year. Not like a vegetable, no not exactly that, just an old woman who sat in a chair and endlessly smiled. As if making up for lost time. No clues to the past, no will, because there was nothing to leave, as Hester reminds them several times, just in case anyone thinks there might be some hidden treasure she has missed. Like the Violet Café, of which all trace has vanished, built over long ago by a hotel chain, Violet has disappeared too.

Wayne has gone outside to smoke.

'Jessie was right,' Marianne says, 'we all smoked like chimneys.'

'No we didn't,' Belle says, 'it was just you and Jessie.'

'No, it was all of us, except for you and Hester,' Marianne retorts. 'You've forgotten Evelyn and David and everybody.' Naming the names at last.

Belle heaves a sigh. 'I could do your colours,' says Belle. 'That's what I'm into, these days. You could use me, you know, Hester, for sorting out your bridesmaids with their proper tones. You know, spring and autumn. You're an autumn tone, Marianne, you'd look lovely in pumpkin and olive green.'

'We could go on a truffle hunt,' says Marianne.

A what? They look at one another and laugh out loud, anything to laugh at.

'Not joking. John, I want to know where she got the truffles.'

'Out of a tin,' he says, laughing harder.

'No, honestly,' Hester says. 'She told me once, they were a present she sent to Hugo and Ming, don't ask me why, but that's what she told me. She sent the truffle culture to them by post. It's what made your family rich.'

'Yes, tell us where, John. Where is the black magic apple of love?'

'Oh steady on,' he says, running round the room, as if they are chasing him, and indeed, Marianne does have him cornered behind Hester's lacquer and brass occasional table. He puts his hands up in front of him fending her off with mock horror. 'Did I ever call them that?'

'Well, if you didn't there was a famous writer who did.'

'Georges Sand,' exclaims Jessie. 'And there was another who warned priests and nuns that if they ate them, they couldn't consider themselves to have truly kept their vows of chastity. It's why I didn't get to be a nun.'

'And did you?' John asks. 'Keep them?'

'Of course not,' she says levelly. 'I never made that vow in the first place.'

Hester says, awkwardly, 'They're supposed to make you fat. Truffles.'

'Well,' says John, 'if you're set on this, how many cars have we got between us?'

'But we might miss Shantee,' Belle says.

'We can see her later,' says Hester, warming to the expedition.

'Well,' Belle responds dubiously, 'I can always give her a tinkle on my cellphone. I think she's going out this evening.'

Wayne says this malarkey isn't for him, but be his guest. What's his is Belle's and if she drops him off at their place, he can use her car if he needs it. Which leaves the five of them to make their way to the lakeside.

It is a windless blue day. In a small bay near the lake they stand among a grove of oak trees, their branches providing a cathedral point of light above them. There is nothing else to be seen, beyond the trees, except a stretch of wasteland, and the remains of a door which had been burnt long ago, on top of a pile of rubble, half covered with creeping ivy. The gardens are long gone.

'Where then?'

'I don't know.'

'You do.'

'No, I don't,' says John. 'You wanted to be taken for the ride.'

'We should have brought some dogs. Or some sows to smell them out.'

'I can see Wayne letting me take a pig in his car,' Belle says. It is a Honda Prelude, painted bright yellow, because, according to Belle, it is a true spring colour, which Wayne has chosen to reflect their joint auras.

'You don't know, do you, John?' Jessie says. The others have gone down to the lakeside, abandoning the search in favour of skipping stones. Marianne is winning.

'No,' he says, stretching himself against the trunk of a tree. She sees that it's an effort to straighten his shoulders, that he has become hunched like all of them, and shorter than when she first knew him. 'I never did. Perhaps they did come out of a can.'

'You'd know the difference. The one you showed me that first day, it was fresh, I'd swear.'

'You've forgotten. I hope you've been happy, Jessie.'

'Happiness? Ah, that. Who knows, until the end?'

'Well, you do know,' he says. 'I've examined the end pretty thoroughly. I thought I'd bought it, just out there on the lake. I'm one of the survivors, as you called it, but I haven't forgotten what it's like to stare death in the face.'

'I do know what you mean.'

'Do you? Really?'

'Oh yes, yes I do. Out East, I learnt all about that.'

'I'd heard you were famous, of course. But I'm afraid I don't follow much in the papers except the business pages.'

'Well, fame is neither here nor there. The things I do that nobody hears about are more important to me these days. Like spending time with my daughter, Bopha. And yes, that is happiness.'

'You know, Jessie,' John says, rubbing his shoulders slightly against the tree, as if that will ease the tension between them, 'I have this strange persistent dream. I dream that I knew Violet long before my father first took me to meet her.'

'Well, that's odd,' says Jessie. 'What else do you see in the dream?'

'I see her rowing a dinghy, which is absurd, because Violet never went near boats. And I'm in the boat with her, looking at her. I'm small and cold and wanting her to stop rowing and just talk to me the way she always does.'

'Well,' she says slowly, 'I guess that's where memory lives, inside our sleep.'

'What are you saying? That this is real?'

'I'm just saying, perhaps you should treat it seriously.'

She thinks that if there is ever a moment to tell him the truth about Violet, this will be it. But even as she is standing there, turning over in her mind whether to tell him or not, and wondering if it will seem like a vulgar piece of gossip she can't resist, the others return.

The five of them eat a meal together in a courtyard café, hanging with vines coming into leaf. Stars are coming out and a chill little wind plays off the lake, causing them to pull their jackets more closely about their shoulders. They are drinking a crisp sauvignon blanc. They touch glasses.

'To us,' they say.

'We survived 9/11,' says Marianne, an edge in her voice, 'we must be indestructible.'

Only Jesse is silent for a moment. She has been to enough wars, doesn't see where it will end.

'We passed the millennium, isn't *that* amazing?' Belle says, and they toast each other again. Belle's cellphone rings at that moment.

'Oh, I am sorry,' she says, pulling it out of her handbag. 'Shantee, darling, where are you?' she says. 'You know I did want you to meet my friends. You're doing what? Shantee, you can't. No seriously, darling. Darling, this is your mother talking — this is a very bad idea. No, I want you to please reconsider this.'

She lays the phone down by her plate. 'Silly girl, she's gone over with her hubby and the kids for a bonfire.' The others had forgotten it was Guy Fawkes night. 'They're burning a boat or something. Round the point, at the old Messenger place.' She says this last part artlessly, as if it doesn't hold great meaning for her. Jessie realises they must have driven past it earlier in the day.

'So what's she up to?' asks Hester.

'Some fool idea about putting their old stuff in the boat and pushing it out in the water. She's put her wedding ring in.'

'She can't do that,' Hester says, looking distressed. 'I did her wedding.'

'I know. But that was a long time ago.'

'Well, I thought she and Geoff were doing all right.'

'They are, she just gets ideas in her head sometimes, I don't know where they come from.' Belle's hand hovers over the phone, her expression distracted.

A choral group of about ten or twelve sits at a long table next to theirs. They are practising a song they are to sing in a competition the following weekend. Jessie calls out and asks them to sing some more, because in this outdoor environment, the old etiquette doesn't seem to apply. Or perhaps it was just a quaint notion that doesn't apply any more. And because they have been asked and they are young and cheerful people, they practise a medieval tune that is a cross between keening and singing. John sits beside her, slightly aloof, as if he is remembering another time when they sat side by side and is afraid that something may be expected of him. Jessie feels him wishing that he hadn't come, perhaps preferring his own company. The tension she sensed beside the lake hasn't gone away. She can tell the music isn't touching him, that he is focused more on his own unresolved discord.

'Can you sing that song about even though it's snowing, violets are still growing?' asks Hester, who knows a couple of the group. One of them is booked in for a dress in February.

'You were a February bride,' says Jessie.

'So I was. Not that I was much of a bride,' Hester says, giving a small girlish hoot of mirth. She reddens and blinks away a sudden tear. 'It's the wine,' she says.

The choral group don't know the song, and, because the meals have been delivered at both tables, the singing ends, and conversation falls away.

As the darkness deepens, rockets start hurtling through the night sky. People emerge from the houses and move towards the lakefront. Out on the water, a trail of fire slinks across the water.

'That looks like a boat burning out there now,' Jessie remarks.

Belle looks as if she's going to cry. Her cellphone rings again. 'Shantee? What are you doing, baby? Are you coming over here? You're what? Oh.' Her face lights up with relief. 'Never mind, another time, I'll tell them you'll see them next time they're in town.' As she switches off, Belle says: 'Silly girl, she's all wet, she's been wading round in the water.'

'Did she get the ring back?'

'Yeah,' says Belle, 'it was all a joke.'

Marianne asks, 'How did Lou get out of the forest, Belle?'

Jessie thinks, so that's why she's come all this way. After all these years. Marianne and Belle had embraced at the door of the chapel as if they were old friends, apparently without any traces of their old rivalry. But she sees it has not been forgotten.

Belle, who is eating scallops cooked in a Drambuie sauce, puts down her fork, and wipes her mouth, smiling in a dreamy sort of way.

'Wallace and I went and got him,' she says. 'Of course.'

'Wallace did that? I thought he beat you,' says Marianne.

'Well, that's not the point, is it?'

'What is the point, then?'

'Wallace really loved me. He'd have done anything for me, you know. Poor guy.'

'I don't get it,' Marianne says. 'Sorry, I just don't.'

'The nature and meaning of love,' says Jessie. 'Well, it's a bit late to be getting deep, isn't it?'

There are general exclamations about the lateness of the hour and the early starts some of them will have to make in the morning. Under the slipstream of words, Jessie says to John, 'I think you should take notice of that dream of yours.'

'You know something about this, don't you?'

'Yes,' she says. 'I do.'

'So if I knew Violet before, who was she?'

'I think that's something you need to find out. I should warn you though, that if you do, you'll also have to find out who Hugo was, and who he wasn't, and the complications will only have just begun.' She fishes in her bag, and finds a business card. 'Here's my email address. Get in touch if you like, though I don't know a fraction of the answers.'

He smiles slightly. 'Long distance.'

'That's close enough,' she says, and it's amazing the way the past slips away, and it is possible suddenly to be free of it.

Between the mains and the desserts the choristers are humming, like an orchestra getting tuned, or a swarm of well-fed bees. A firework explodes near them.

Soon, in half an hour at most, they will give each other a hug for what will surely be the last time. Jessie anticipates the moment when John will hold her just a moment longer than the others, pressing his suit against her jacket and long skirt — or perhaps he will just slip away, the same elusive John. She smells gunpowder, so close that she could be out East again.

'To us,' Marianne says, and their hands touch in a final toast.

A Catherine wheel spins along the pavement. Out on the water, the ship of fire drifts on, collapsing inwards on itself as they watch, causing Belle to exclaim and clasp her hands together.

'Thank you,' says Hester. 'Thank you all for coming.'

Acknowledgements

Lois Daish, sublime cook, food writer, teacher and friend, has been extraordinarily generous with the amount of time and advice she has given me while I wrote this book. I thank her so much for that, and for reading my manuscript.

I owe Ian Kidman thanks, too, for his reading of my manuscript, as well as his love of Cambodia which he shares with me. And, thanks to the Cambodia Trust staff in Phnom Penh who have enabled me to make several safe journeys into the Cambodian countryside.

I am grateful to Emma Hart and Jude Walcott at Radio New Zealand, Jill Nicholas, Nancy and Jack Collins, Colin and Niyaz Wilson, Dame Kate Harcourt, Alice Morris (Pan Jiang Ping) and Zach Kidman for assisting me with research.

The following texts have provided source material: *A Taste of France* by Madeleine Hammond; *The Black Truffle* by Ian Hall and Gordon Brown; *Oh, for a French Wife* by Ted Moloney and Deke Coleman. Tim Page's writing about Indochina has been inspirational.

My editors, Harriet Allan and Anna Rogers, continue to give me the patient support that every writer longs for. I can't thank them enough.

Grateful acknowledgement is made for the following song extract:
'Make Love to Me' Leon Rapollo/Paul Mares/Benny Pollock/ George Brunies/Mel Stitzel/Walter Melrose/Bill Norvas/Allan Copeland (Warner Chappell Music)